# The Light Most Favorable

# By James Jennings

Photograph of the San Rafael Valley by David F. Putnam,
Green Valley, Arizona

Cover art by Legal-Graphics, Inc., Oklahoma City, Oklahoma

.

## <u>DEDICATION</u>

For *VRJ*, quite simply, the finest person I've ever known.

# ACKNOWLEDGEMENTS

A long journey, and God willing, far from over. So many people to thank. Jamie Wolfe, rancher, kindred spirit, veteran of The Midnight Ride. Uncle Pete, a man of tireless good humor and living proof there's nothing as good for the inside of a man as the outside of a horse. Jack McPhaul, a steady hand and giver of sage advice on horsemanship, a true artist. My parents, Jim and Betty, for everything. Dr. Clif Warren for being a visionary, one built for the long haul. Shane Cashion, at Tradeworks, for looking west.

And not by eastern windows only,
When daylight comes, comes in the light;
In front, the sun climbs slow, how slowly,
But westward, look, the land is bright.

*Say Not the Struggle Naught Availeth*
*Arthur Hugh Clough, 1862*

# CHAPTER 1 - GRAVEN IMAGES

The view from the window sent an icy chill through him. The city beyond the frosty pane rose from the frigid ground as lifeless and brittle as a charred matchstick. Touch it, and it would break. Try to hold it, and it would turn to ash.

The man on the nineteenth floor slouched, head low. Fisted hands buried deep in his pockets drew his shoulders down. Dark pinstripe vest lazed against his body, unbuttoned and askew. Crisp white collar gaped like an open wound. In the inconstant light of winter, the man's face had no color, no expression. Eyes stared, empty and unblinking, like marble carvings. He felt so insubstantial he doubted he would cast a shadow or have a reflection, even in a diamond dust mirror.

Jack Breen. At forty-one, an unequivocal success. A big shot, just what he always wanted. He had it all, good looks, social position, influence, money. In record time, he became a prominent lawyer, well known in Boston society. He had connections and a good reputation, though some said his manner tended toward arrogance. His picture often appeared in the society pages of the Sunday paper. He wore designer

1

clothes carefully fitted by fawning haberdashers known only by their first names. He lived in a fine Beacon Hill house, drove an expensive foreign car, aristocratic black, of course. He had a beautiful wife, Carolyn, Carolyn Ford Breen.

Known for being smart and tough, Jack Breen clawed his way to the top of his profession. He worked hard. Time after time, he showed his ability to get the best of his opponents by outworking them, outshining them, simply by being better. With catamount grace and agility, he stalked them, maneuvered into position, then at the right moment pounced on them. Never easy. Not without setbacks. But when he took a fall, he landed catlike on his feet.

Jack Breen had a prosperous bearing. Chestnut hair neatly cropped and well-ordered. The hint of gray at the temples that came in later years added character and maturity to his appearance, he thought. He liked it. Angular features looked chiseled. And, in the kinder light of better days, they gave him a determined aspect. He liked that, too. With his back fence-post straight and his chest out, he stood a shade over six feet. At that, he judged himself a little taller than most men. He liked that even more.

But all of that lay behind him now. Thousands of yesterdays buried in the wreckage of the past. Today, Jack Breen cut a stooped, slovenly figure. Gray in his hair did not make him look mature. It made him look old. Sharply cut features dulled. Eroded by storms, wind might one day erase them altogether. Now, other men towered over him, looked down on him. For better or worse, the former Jack Breen disappeared, extinguished in a momentary hiss of steam like an unsheltered candle in a sudden downpour of bitter rain.

After a relentless pursuit across nearly two decades, reality ran Jack Breen to earth. It dragged him down and gutted him. Put the lie to his very existence. The verdict, loud, screaming, irresistible, pronounced Jack Breen a fraud. It revealed the truth, not only to the world, but to the man himself. He had the air of riches, but he was flat broke, busted. All the gold in California would make no difference.

2

Destruction came over Jack Breen like an insidious disease. A slight error in aim years before caused him to miss his target by miles. Over time and distance, like an errant bullet, his trajectory strayed from its intended course. He caromed through seamless days, month after month, year after year, getting more and more lost, ricocheting off things he never meant to contact. Finally, energy spent, shape altered by unintended collisions, he arrived at a strange and unforeseen place. Disillusioned, disappointed, burned out, and ashamed.

Now, Jack Breen marked time at his office window, swallowed up by a vast, impenetrable silence. The air around him hung thick with remorse. At this late hour, he could not deny the awful fact that everything he took as real for as long as he could remember turned out to be illusion. What he believed to be true, proved false. And not one reward for small victories along the way justified a single moment of the suffering it caused him and others around him, not one ounce of the misery yet to come.

The office door labored open. It arced on its hinges as if an invisible corpse on the floor opposed its motion. In the space between the door's edge and its jamb, the acne-scarred face of Bert Zorn appeared. Heavy black glasses with dusty lenses squatted low on the slightly crooked nose of Jack Breen's loyal partner of seventeen years. In typical fashion, the part in Zorn's hair ran just above his prodigious left ear. From there, a sparse blanket of dark, moist strands stretched tightly across his knotty skull, slicked down in a transparent and unsuccessful attempt to conceal his baldness. As usual, his suit, a thirty-six short, looked like he slept in it. Zorn always had an unkempt appearance. A brand new two thousand dollar Armani suit would make no difference. No matter how much care he took, he could not help looking like a nasty little man who lived his life wadded up in someone's pocket. The effort he made with his hair was both pointless and incongruous.

Zorn took a cautious step into the office and paused.

"Jack," he said in a low voice.

3

Breen did not answer. He did not move. After a moment's hesitation, Zorn spoke again.

"Jack, is it true?"

When Zorn spoke, the corner of his mouth turned up into what some took to be a sneer, a sign of a bad attitude. More than once, an opposing lawyer offered to knock it off his face. But it never happened. It could not happen. It was not a sneer, at least not a voluntary sneer. Nothing intentional about it, though it did seem to reflect the strange little man's view of the world. Just the way he was made, a flaw, one of many, in the architecture of his face.

Both lawyer and CPA, Bert Zorn made an excellent green shade man, good with numbers and details, not slick like Breen, not good with people. Unlike his partner, Zorn lacked the shine to be a front man. He had no style, no personal élan. But he had the ability to provide exactly the kind of behind-the-scenes support Jack Breen needed. Often, Zorn's work made the difference between winning and losing. Breen knew it better than anyone, and he always took great care to give his partner his due. The leading man had many faults, but they did not include slighting Bert Zorn. The two men needed each other. But more than that, they were friends.

Zorn took a second step into the tomblike silence of the office. Breen remained quiet, motionless. He could have been a mannequin in a Brooks Brothers window.

"Jack," Zorn said again, this time slightly louder and bolder but in his familiar shrill, high-pitched voice. "Jack, is it true?"

Breen did not answer.

"Dammit, Jack."

"On the desk," Breen said without emphasis.

He spoke in a languid tone, each word parceled out with an equal measure of breath.

"Read it. Read it yourself."

Zorn stepped to Breen's desk and picked up three white pieces of paper, all neatly ordered and fastened together with a staple in the corner. He shoved his glasses to his

4

forehead, balanced them on his permanently furrowed, slightly simian brow. He raised the paper to within a few inches of his eyes and squinted. In an instant, the bitterness of the words tightened and contorted his face. His nose wrinkled as if beset by a foul odor.

"I don't believe it," he said. "Just don't believe it. The bastards took your license?"

For nearly a year, Jack Breen's life had been coming unraveled. It started when money got tight. A string of bad months. A spate of cases did not go as expected. Fees did not come in. Bills for the house and the car, bills for a lot of things went from due to past due. Slow money got slower. Dominoes began to fall. Every month it got a little worse until the wolf at the door burst in. Breen needed money, needed it fast. Then it happened. Some cash idling in his trust account as part of a large estate he was settling turned his head. Temptation overwhelmed him. He simply could not resist the smell of money. He took a little. Then he took some more. Before long, he "borrowed" more than fifty thousand dollars of his client's money. "Why not?" He told himself. "Just a loan, short term, too. I'll pay it back. Never be missed. No harm, no foul."

But his plan failed. When the money he counted on did not appear, word of his transgression got out. Outraged heirs complained bitterly to the Bar Association. The Ethics Committee conducted an investigation. That led to a disciplinary action. The D.A. considered a criminal charge. Soon, the news hit the papers and all doubt about the outcome of the whole sordid affair departed. Jack Breen climbed the steps to the guillotine, put his head on the block. The blade fell.

"How can this be?" Zorn said. "How can this be?"

He looked up at Breen, then lowered his eyes again to the ominous papers in his hands. When he neared the end of the last page, his mouth fell open and he gasped as if a booted foot planted firmly on his chest emptied him of wind. His glasses slipped from his forehead to his nose. He looked up even before he finished reading.

"So they did it? They really did it?"

Breen did not move. He maintained a stolid silence, seemingly transfixed by the view from the window. After a few moments, Zorn appeared to recover. What had been shock, turned to disgust, then anger.

"You paid the money back. You had a deal. I mean . . . yeah . . . sure, fifty thou is a bunch of money. But you paid it back. Nobody got hurt. No harm, no foul. Right?"

Breen gave no sign he heard a single word Zorn said, or that he even remembered his presence in the room. He did not react at all when Zorn continued talking.

"What about the deal? You had a deal. When we met with those guys last summer, those guys from the Bar, we all agreed. A deal's a deal."

Sure. They had a deal. Breen paid the money back, albeit belatedly. In fact, he paid more than he owed, a little extra to soothe hurt feelings and quiet the storm. He did it after being caught, but only because that's when he had the money. Still, the restitution looked a little less heartfelt than some preferred. But the heirs took it. They did not want justice or revenge. They wanted cash. They spoke the language Jack Breen understood. He expected to buy his peace and sweep the whole ugly business under the rug. That was the deal with the heirs and with the Bar Association, the deal intended to get him on track.

But they made the deal in the season of dog days, a lifetime ago. The Supreme Court did not buy it. They didn't have to and they didn't. The Black Robes wanted Jack Breen's license, at least for a while. They had his number and they were canceling his ticket. The deal evaporated, as Bert Zorn was fond of saying, like piss on a light bulb. Now, King Winter reigned. Outside, limbs of trees stood bare, stripped of leaves by a brutal and persistent wind. Colorless grass beneath them crunched under the feet of shivering pedestrians racing along with upturned collars and stooped shoulders. In low shaded places, patches of snow hard on the surface, stained at the edges, lingered, awaiting the advent of warm sunlight to finish them off.

And a fog of mystery shrouded this day crowded with lies and loss. A night-colored raven perched high among the bare branches of an oak tree in the square beneath the window where Jack Breen lingered without purpose. The bird's wings shone like fractured obsidian, defying the dullness of late afternoon light. With the arrogance of the sole survivor of a holocaust, the raven brazenly and silently surveyed the ruinous world before it. It turned its sleek head from side to side in sharp, avian movements, casting its eyes about for something worthy of a scavenger's attention.

In time, the feathered inheritor of desolation turned toward Jack Breen. With vision undaunted by winter haze and bleary glass, it stared into his eyes. The man answered with his own stare. The raven opened its ebony beak and screamed out a derisive cry, almost human, almost decipherable. Finding nothing to justify a closer look, the somber sentinel leaped from its sleeted perch. Spreading its wings, it grabbed thick, moist air and climbed. It circled once and veered westward, making for a remote sliver of lucid sky that stretched along the horizon. In the partially masked firestorm sunset, the narrow margin of horizontal clarity gleamed like polished copper. It resembled a space left by a door slightly ajar, a door about to close or open.

Breen followed the raven with his eyes, longingly, until it became a tiny black speck in an unsavory stew of dingy clouds and freezing mist. He watched it descend toward the glowing edge of earth, then disappear in the last wink of twilight. That's where he lost it, in the West.

Breen sighed. When he spoke again, his voice had a detached tone. It sounded calm and deliberate, reflective, betraying not a particle of interest in anything Bert Zorn said.

"The raven. Did you know that in some Native American cultures it's honored for bringing light from heaven to a dark world?"

Zorn looked up, joggled his head, incredulous at hearing Breen talk about birds, incredulous that he, having heard the absurd question, responded at all, even with the slightest gesture. He started to speak, to try to steer the conversation in a rational direction, but before he could utter a sound, Breen continued.

"It's true," he said. "I heard it . . ."

His voice trailed off. He became wistful.

"Somewhere . . . heard it somewhere."

When he collected himself and regained his focus, he added, "But some say he's a liar and a thief, can't be trusted. Some say he brings death. I wonder—" Zorn had his fill. He cut him off.

"Jack, what the hell are you talking about? Don't you understand what's happening here? Don't you get it? Don't you care?"

Breen turned, set his gaze on Zorn for the first time.

"Skip to the end," he said without a trace of outrage. "The last paragraph. The best part."

Zorn read aloud.

"The evidence, when viewed in the light most favorable to the respondent—"

"That's me, Bert. I'm the respondent."

Zorn looked up, nodded, then lowered his eyes to the page again.

"When viewed in the light most favorable—"

"That's it. That's the gut. When viewed in the light most favorable to me, I'm just what they say I am, a thief. So they disbarred me."

When Zorn finished reading, he raised a finger in the air. He shook his head.

"Suspended," he said. "Not disbarred."

"Right. You always did have an eye for detail."

"Suspended," Zorn repeated. "Two years and a day."

Breen turned toward his partner and friend.

"Yeah. It's that last day that really hurts. No automatic reinstatement. I'll have to beg on bended knee to get my license back. Just what they want."

"I don't believe it," Zorn said. "The bastards. You hardly did anything. The bastards."

When excited, Bert Zorn sprayed a fine mist from his mouth with every word, especially words starting with a B, words like "bastard." He used the word often.

"Commingling of funds," Breen said, now staring out the window again. "That's what I'm guilty of. Commingling. Commingling."

He spoke his sin in a mocking tone, as if he disrespected the word itself, as much as the truth of it, as much as its application to his own conduct.

"My dad would have been critical of them for using a word like that. It's too . . . obscure . . . too indirect. 'By your language you are known,' he would say."

Time was, Jack Breen, son of a small town high school English teacher and valedictorian of his class, would never do such a thing as commingling, or even consider it. Not even a temptation. A notion as foreign to him as robbing the First National Bank at gunpoint. But what was once loathsome and unthinkable became over time tolerated, then accepted, and finally easy.

Jack Breen started out with the values of his family, a day's work for a day's pay, a penny saved is a penny earned, do unto others, and so on. He saw himself raising a family, being a father to a passel of kids, establishing a law practice, possibly becoming a teacher like his father. He imagined himself living out his days in some small college town, a bearded professor clad in a slightly threadbare tweed jacket, theorizing, pontificating. Professor Breen. Perhaps Doctor Breen. But that was before the serpent charmed him, before he left home and lost his way.

"Commingling."

Breen repeated the word as if to roll it around in his mouth, consider its flavor.

"Commingling. Kind of a fancy name for it, don't you think? They used to call it stealing. That's what it was, you know."

"Not really," Zorn protested. "Not technically. Well, maybe . . . but it was only temporary. The bastards."

Breen turned toward Zorn, smiled a joyless smile. For the first time in a long time, perhaps the first time ever, he saw himself clearly, as if circumstances lifted a veil from his face.

"You remind me of myself," he said. "Looking at you is like looking in a mirror."

"What?"

"Nothing," Breen said, pulling his hands from his pockets. "They were right. Hell. They should have gone all the way. Should have disbarred me. Couldn't blame them. If they'd known the full truth, they would have. They would have locked me up and thrown away the key."

Zorn objected.

"You're too hard on yourself. What did you do that a lot of us haven't done? You got behind. You got desperate. Lied a little. Took a little money. Does it matter that it was fifty-K rather than fifty cents? Just a question of where you put the decimal point."

"More than that, Bert. A lot more."

"Right. A question of getting caught. Who doesn't have a secret? A secret that could ruin him if it got out? A question of degree, a question of luck. That simple."

Unassuaged by Zorn's logic, Breen tightened his tie, buttoned his vest. He lifted his suit coat from the chair where it hung and put it on. He collected his dark top coat from the rack in the corner and draped it over his arm. He paused. Sighed. Stared at the floor as if he could see more than hardwood planks and the geometric pattern of a blood red Persian rug. And then his eyes settled on the wall before him. There, like a frieze of graven images, lifeless objects hung in orderly rows on opulent, mahogany paneling. Photographs,

10

mostly black and white, two dimensional images of smiling men in dark suits, right arms extended, hands firmly clasped. Plaques with brass plates and engraved words proclaiming extraordinary deeds and high esteem. Framed newspaper clippings, headlines in large black letters. Awards. Certificates. Diplomas. A framed check. They formed a legion of unworthy idols and faithless lovers.

"Makes perfect sense," Breen said, sighing again. "About time something did."

Zorn took a step forward.

"What the hell are you gonna do?"

Thoroughly exasperated now, he still held in both hands the papers that sagged at the middle under the weight of unfortunate words.

"You don't know anything else, Jack. This is you. This is what you do. Just like me. Just like all the other hacks out there."

Zorn became agitated, started to pace. He rubbed his forehead, spoke feverishly. He spat out his words with a fine mist, a tone of desperation.

"We can figure this out. We can do it. Listen to me. Think this through. You can stay right here. Keep right on doing what you've been doing. We'll just say you're my assistant. No one will know. Things will be the same. We can get through a couple of years easy. Standing on our heads."

Breen did not respond. For him, the wall replaced the raven as the object of fascination. But in some cranny of his mind lurked the image of the jet-black bird with the demanding stare, its hurried flight toward a thinning crease of light in the western sky.

Zorn stepped toward Breen and raised his hands. His fingers and his voice trembled.

"Hey. This affects me, too. This is not just about you. What do you say?"

A long silence followed. Then Breen turned to his old friend and looked at him with eyes swimming. He shook his head, gave it to him straight.

"I don't think so."

Breen put a hand on Zorn's shoulder.

"I just can't."

For a moment, Breen lowered his eyes and looked away.

"You've been a good friend to me, Bert. I'm sorry, truly sorry."

Breen headed for the door. Zorn stood like a scarecrow, arms frozen in the air. After a few moments, he lowered his inert appendages and turned.

"Jack, what are you gonna do? Where are you gonna go?"

"Home, I guess. Right now I'm going home. After that, I don't know. Looks like I have two years to kill, two years and a day. See ya, Bert."

Zorn stepped toward Breen.

"Have you told Carolyn?"

"Who?"

"Carolyn. Your wife."

"No."

And that was that. Like a snake oil peddler riding a rail out of town, he took his inglorious leave. He stepped out of the office and closed the door.

*****

Hours following, Jack Breen wandered. He roamed the streets of Boston without direction, without purpose. Propelled only by mindless momentum, ignoring the advancing cold that followed the final extinguishment of the sun, he drifted. Following an utterly random course, he lost all sense of time, transformed himself into a nameless face in a crowd of pedestrians.

Unwittingly, he drifted down a dark side street, gave up his anonymity. He took on the look of a wounded creature

12

isolated from the herd. Prey. By the time he had his wits about him again, he found himself in a place he would never choose to be, not alone, not at night, not in the cold.

He looked up. The only mitigation of the heavy darkness of winter night came from the sickly, blue wash of a street lamp a half-block away. He detected a faint scent of rotting garbage and exhaust. Bone-chilling fear set in. *What have I done?* he thought. *I have to get the hell out of here.* But before he could move, a sound with a knife edge cut through him. Footsteps. A scuffle. A woman's scream.

In a burst of panic, he spun on his heels, heart pounding. Strange, unwelcome events began to overtake him. He started to run, but halted after only a couple of steps, when he saw the source of the consternation. Nearby, where an alley met the street, two men pursued a woman on foot and overtook her. Breen froze at the sight of the chase and the row that followed. Laughing, the men slung the woman back and forth between them like gorillas with a medicine ball. The woman squealed, begged for mercy. The men laughed all the more, each taking a turn at groping and taunting, slapping her face.

Breen started to flee again, then stopped himself. He could not simply run away, not from this kind of trouble. By instinct and before caution could set in, he raised an arm and pointed. He called out, first in a weak, tentative voice, "Hey. Hey." Then stronger, "What's going on over there? Leave that woman alone." Not a smart move for a man off his turf and wobbly with knees weakened by cold and fear.

The gorillas halted their game. The larger of the two released the woman and turned his attention to Breen. He would not tolerate an arrogant outsider who would presume to give him orders. He sauntered across the street in Breen's direction. As if his feet had sunk into the concrete, Breen did not move. Too late for flight. There he stood, well dressed, well coifed, looking like the big shot he used to be, looking like he had money. The gorilla now had a dual purpose, revenge and profit.

The second primate released the woman, too, and she clambered away into the darkness of the alley. Now, before Jack Breen hulked two young men, predators, legs planted wide, heads slightly reclined in an attitude of contempt. They clapped their eyes on his. The look on each face seethed with anger, disgust, outright disdain. Breen took their measure in an instant. He could tell the mold set early on these two. Men who placed no value on human life, including their own. Men for whom life consisted of pleasure and pain, nothing more. Men who felt only scorn for the likes of Jack Breen.

In the putrid darkness, the two men, little more than shadows, formed spectral harbingers of annihilation. One of them held a cheap stiletto with a long, thin blade. The other, a tire tool, cold steel, long, black. He gripped the instrument of terror tightly in one hand and tapped its crooked end impatiently against the open palm of the other. From a gaudy chain around his neck, dangled a cheap looking silver pendant of a cougar claw. Ghostly steam rose from each man's mouth. *Death's breath*, Breen thought. He could see the headlines in the morning paper, SOCIALITE SLAIN IN STREET MUGGING, DISBARRED LAWYER FOUND DEAD. *Why didn't I keep my mouth shut and run?*

Jack Breen shuddered. For the first time, he felt the cold. As never before, he felt fear, sheer terror.

"Hey, man," said the larger of the two men, the one with the tire tool and the scabby sore on his lip. "You're a long fuckin' way from Beacon Hill, man."

Breen studied the men without speaking. His body trembled. Eyes darted about in every direction. He saw no one. It flashed through his mind that he'd made one final wrong turn, one that would cost him more than his money, more than his reputation. This one would cost him his life.

The head thug with the tire tool took a half-step forward. He held out a hand, wasted no words.

"Hand over your fuckin' money, asshole. Right now. Let's have it."

14

The smaller man glanced at his partner and blurted out a nervous laugh. Wiped his runny nose with the back of a hand.

A moment of uneasy silence followed. Breen opened his mouth as if he might save himself with glibness.

"You can't just–"

"Shut up," the man with the tire tool grunted. "You heard me. Hand over the cash right now."

Breen reached for his wallet. But his cold, clumsy fingers did not perform as commanded. For the longest time, they failed to navigate the unseen interior of his pocket. Lacking dexterity, they answered for their assigned task no better than elbows.

"Come on," the thief said. "Come on."

And then Breen wrangled his wallet into his hand. The moment he produced it, a police car appeared at the intersection by the street lamp. It slowed, then stopped. The thieves jerked their heads about.

"Shit," they said in almost perfect unison. "Cops."

Salvation arrived unexpectedly. Scuttling away like frightened insects, the hijackers bolted past Breen, leaving him standing with arm extended, wallet in hand. They ignored the money in their haste to flee, but in passing one took time to land a heavy blow to Breen's mid-section.

The impact forced the air from his lungs and put him down. He doubled over, then crumbled to his knees, stomach in a spasm. He hugged himself and gasped for air. When he finally had it, he struggled to his feet. He steadied himself against a parked car and returned his wallet to his pocket. He looked all around, then straightened himself and stumbled down the street toward the blue light. At first, he moved slowly, his gait stiff-legged, but he kept moving. *I have to get home*, he thought. *I have to get out of here.*

He pressed on. Gaining strength and stability, he lengthened his stride. He sharpened his wits and began to appreciate his surroundings, think clearly again. The instinct to survive took hold. He walked faster. Then faster. He had his air now and he ran as fast as he could. Ran and ran and ran.

Soon, Breen rounded a corner. Swinging wide into the intersecting street, his course took him into the path of an oncoming taxi. He tried to stop, but couldn't. His shoes slid on wet pavement and his momentum carried him forward, put him on a collision course with two tons of rolling steel. The taxi headed right for him, bearing down on him, headlights blinding, horn blaring, tires squealing. And then the deadly encounter, man against machine, ended as abruptly as it began. The taxi skidded to a stop. Breen stood dead center of the vehicle's bumper with arms outstretched, tips of splayed fingers not a ruler's length from the hood.

The cabby cried out, gesturing with both hands. He waved his arms in the air and beat his fist against the steering wheel, an explosion of harsh curses rending winter air. He lowered the glass and put his head through the open window to continue his tirade at greater volume.

"Hey, mon. What de hell? You crazy, mon? You crazy or sumting?"

The Haitian-born man with eyes and skin as black as night itself spoke in an ungrammatical immigrant patois, a crude alloy of Boston street talk and French Creole. Breen could hardly understand a word he said, but the man's outrage would be unmistakable in any language.

Breen lowered his arms and stumbled to the passenger side of the car. He opened the door and fell onto the seat, wild-eyed, breathing heavily, sweat pouring from his face. Confused and dazed, he said nothing.

The cabby turned toward him, swung his elbow over the seat. He looked at Breen with anger and disbelief.

"You wan give me a heart attack, mon? What de hell you do down here? Dis no place to be alone. Not at night, mon. You get you throat cut."

Breen still said nothing. He stared ahead. The cabby turned in the seat, studying Breen in the rearview mirror.

16

"So now I gotta haul you ass around? You gon tell me where you wan go? Or do I have to guess, mon?"

"Home," Breen muttered.

"Dat good, mon. Dat real fuckin' good. Now where you home at?"

Breen gave him the address. The cabby shook his head.

"Beacon Hill. What de fuck a Beacon Hill dude be doin' in a place like dis?"

"I guess I'm a little lost."

"More dan little lost, mon. You way lost."

The cabby shook his head. He put the car in gear and sped away into the lonely night. Jack Breen was going home. But when he got there, he'd still be lost. Way lost.

# CHAPTER 2 - NOTHING BUT BLUE

Blue.  Nothing but blue.

Jack Breen sat trancelike in the taxi, staring at the blue vinyl seat back before him.  Only deep pain in his gut tethered him to reality.  Face blank, eyes opaque, glazed by a cloudy mist of regret, all he could see was blue—blue vinyl, blue light of the street lamp, blue of memory.  Blue took him back.

*****

Carolyn.  For Jack Breen, a real prize, his first, his best, the key to his success.  She stood tall and sleek, beautiful and seductive.  He could not resist her.

The first time Jack laid eyes on her he was a third year law student at Harvard on a full ride scholarship.  She was a senior at Wellesley, there on her own hook, at least her family's.  She stepped off the ferry at Martha's Vineyard on Labor Day weekend and caught Jack Breen's eye.  He first glimpsed her legs, those incredible legs.  Golden brown from hours in the

18

sun, they stretched long and lean, like strands of dripping honey, from white shorts that barely covered the curve of her hips. Smitten in an instant, he could not take his eyes off her. As if a fierce squall rolled in off the Atlantic, the man, his plans, his view of the future blew away. Before he knew it, he set a new course, a course that would take him directly into the storm.

Dressed in a white tee shirt, khaki shorts, and boat shoes, twenty-four year old Jack Breen looked the picture of youthful promise. Posture erect, muscles taut, he saw himself and the world with different eyes then. He brimmed with confidence and expectation.

Breen stood slack-jawed on the dock staring at the girl with incredible legs. Eyes hungry for more, he traced every line, every angle, every curve of her body. He started at her ankles, worked his way up along her calves, thighs. He studied her lips, deep red, soft as wilted roses. He studied her azure eyes, blue as the clear daytime sky. And then, without warning, the girl who seized his attention looked in his direction. Her eyes locked onto his. She smiled.

"Hi," she said.

Jack did not answer. He thought she was talking past him, not to him.

She spoke again.

"Hello."

This time her voice had more volume, a playfully insistent tone.

Jack looked over his shoulders, first one then the other, thinking this captivating girl must be speaking to someone behind him. Seeing no one, he pointed to himself and raised his eyebrows.

"Yeah. You," Carolyn said, still smiling, almost laughing.

"Oh. Hi."

"Here for the weekend?" she said.

"Yeah."

"You alone?"

"Well . . . yeah."

A lie, a small one. He was not alone at all. He came to the island with Bert Zorn. But such minutia had no real importance. Why ruffle an otherwise perfect scene unnecessarily?

"Maybe I'll see you on the beach," Carolyn said.

"Sure."

Bert Zorn, Breen's friend and future partner, waited nearby. At twenty-four, Zorn looked forty. Already well on his way to baldness, wearing purple madras shorts, black socks, lace up oxfords, Zorn drew a caricature of himself in casual dress. From where he stood, he witnessed the enchanted moment shared by Jack and Carolyn. When the girl with the sky blue eyes and honey legs took her leave, he moved closer to his bedazzled friend and posted himself at his side.

"Forget about your old friend, did you?"

"Sorry, Bert."

"Well, I suppose you were alone . . . technically . . . at the moment you said it. You were here and I was over there about ten feet."

Jack craned his neck for one more look at Carolyn before she disappeared in the distance. At the last possible moment, just before being lost to sight, she turned and shot a glance in his direction. She sealed it with a smile.

"Careful, boy," Zorn said. "Looks like a rich one. Besides you're spoken for. Could be trouble."

"No sweat. No harm in looking."

Zorn's wise counsel went unheeded.

It happened the second night. The conversation started out innocent enough. And the presence of other weekend revelers gave the encounter a modicum of respectability. Jack even told Carolyn about his engagement. She congratulated him, but showed no interest in the details of his plans.

The night wore on, and wine flowed freely. In time, the look on Carolyn's face turned from friendly to inviting. Her words changed from innocent to seductive. The subject shifted from Jack's engagement to Carolyn's plans for the future. From

20

there, they made the short jump to Jack's potential, to what he expected to accomplish, to how high and how far he knew he would go.

Jack Breen, one smart kid from the Midwest, possessed a fresh masculine appeal that Carolyn could not resist. Not only good looking and sharp witted, he had style. Like Caesar's Cassius, he presented a lean and hungry look that projected danger. Carolyn responded to that. It excited her, made her want him. In no time, he became the prize she simply had to have.

Swept up and carried away in a river of alcohol and infatuation, Jack and Carolyn found themselves alone on the beach. Staring at the cloudless sky spangled with millions of bright stars, soft remnants of waves foamed around their bare ankles and feet. Emboldened by the blood of Bacchus, the dim light of the moon, and a strong sense of entitlement, Carolyn faced the ocean, crossed her arms, and lifted her blouse over her head. Suddenly and without warning her full, supple breasts tumbled free. They bounced with the rising of her arms. Swayed. Filled the night. Boldly, she turned toward Jack. His eyes went directly to her nipples. Summoned to immediate erectness by cool ocean air, they rose from perfect, pale skin. With no sign of uncertainty, the huntress extended her hand, and young Jack Breen, intoxicated by her sweet siren song, took it.

At sunrise, two future stars lay sharing a sleeping bag on the beach, bodies and lives entwined. Promises Jack Breen made to his fiancée and to himself lay in ruins. What he never expected to do, what he never thought himself capable of doing, he did. He took a hard fall.

Within a month, he ended his engagement to an Arizona girl, an unjaded young lady with a good heart and a generous nature, a gifted musician with a scholarship to The Boston Conservatory of Music. Carolyn became the sole object of Jack Breen's attention and ambition. The rancher's daughter named Claire, a girl uncertain about staying in the East after

21

graduation, did not measure up to a rich temptress from Beacon Hill, especially one with legs like honey and eyes as blue as the clear sky.

Jack Breen broke the engagement in a late night phone call. Difficult, but he had to do it. He chose a coward's way, regarded himself with disgust because of it.

"The lowest thing I've ever done," he told Bert Zorn. "My own special place in hell now reserved, I presume. Never hurt anyone like that before. Never thought I would. And I did it over the phone."

Bert Zorn, ever loyal and supportive, came forth quickly to assuage his friend's guilt.

"What else could you do? You don't have any money. You don't have a car to drive over there. You don't even have cab fare. You did what you had to do. Only thing you could do. She'll get over it. Better this way."

"Better for me. Not for her."

"You are not married," Bert said. "Big difference between being married and being engaged. If you were married, that would be an entirely different matter. But you aren't. Big difference. Big difference."

Zorn persisted, spraying every B.

"It could happen to any of us," he went on. "This kind of thing happens all the time. All the time. You have to shake it off, stay on course."

Stay on course. Exactly what Jack Breen did. He put the past behind and looked to the future. He accepted Zorn's logic and pressed on. He subdued his guilt, locked it away. But he did not get rid of it. It stayed with him, festering, throbbing, aching like a splinter slowly rising to the surface.

\*\*\*\*\*

With Carolyn at his side, Jack Breen positioned himself squarely in the fast lane. He needed to pick up the pace. And that's exactly what he did. He never lacked ambition, and now he dedicated himself even more to succeeding. When necessary, he would find the wherewithal to be ruthless. He surprised himself with how far he'd be willing to go.

That spring, months after his Labor Day tryst with Carolyn, Breen neared the end of his last semester of law school. One afternoon, he had a conference with a professor whose class confounded him. Anything less than an A would undermine his grade average just enough to keep him out of the top five per cent of graduates, just enough to defeat his plan for election to the Order of the Coif. Breen had his sights on being a member of the elite group of graduates. Maybe he could schmooze the professor into a generous grading of his upcoming final exam. He might even get a hint of what would be on it.

"Come in. Come in," the professor told him.

"Good afternoon, sir. Thank you for seeing me."

"What can I do for you?"

"Well, I'm a little concerned about my grade in your class. I'm hoping to make Coif."

"Yes. You've done quite well here."

"Until now," Breen said. "I think I've been a little distracted. I'm getting married right after graduation."

"So I understand," the professor said. "I went to school with Carolyn's father."

"I didn't know."

One more small lie. Breen knew well the professor's acquaintance with Carolyn's father. He knew the Ford Family Foundation funded some of the professor's research projects over the years. Why else would he mention his upcoming marriage? Certainly not to solicit sympathy, though he was not above doing that. He simply wanted to make sure the professor knew his connection to the Fords. As it turned out, success on this day did not require such slyness.

A stack of exams sat on the desk between Breen and the professor. In the course of the conversation, the aging pontifical pundit frequently referred to the top page. More than once, he drummed his fingers on it, drawing Breen's attention more acutely to what he wanted desperately but could not have. At first he thought the professor might be taunting him with it, amusing himself the way a child might tease a puppy with a morsel of bacon.

The key to his success, within sight but barely out of reach, called to him. When the professor's eyes fell to the page and the contact of his gaze with Breen's broke off, even for an instant, Breen strained for a glimpse of the forbidden words. He could never quite make them out. The effort served only to whet his appetite for more.

A stolen look at the exam questions would be wrong, of course but not so wrong he could not live with the guilt. It would be in the nature of a hint. Nothing wrong with a hint. He would never go so far as taking a copy of the exam even if he had the chance. That would be going too far. Wrong. Plainly wrong. He would never do that. Never.

But then, a brief interruption of the conference occurred. The professor exited the office to answer the question of a secretary. He left the exams on the desk.

"Excuse me," he said. "Please give me a moment."

He looked Breen in the eyes and rapped his knuckles on the stack of exams before stepping out.

No way to know whether the gesture represented a meaningless sign of preoccupation, or misplaced confidence in Jack Breen, or an open invitation for Breen to help himself to a copy of the exam. It didn't matter. The temptation became irresistible and Breen reacted quickly to the fortuitous opportunity. In an instant, he did precisely what he knew he would never do.

With serpentine facility, he eased himself behind the professor's desk. Hand trembling, he plucked a copy of the exam from the stack. He folded it once and inserted it between the pages of a textbook. By the time the professor returned, Breen once again occupied his assigned chair, legs crossed, manner artificially relaxed. The textbook, now infused with new and ill-gotten treasure, rested on his lap. Another textbook of similar size rested strategically on top of it to conceal the bulge.

In a persuasively sincere but weakened voice and with heart pounding, Jack Breen thanked the professor for his concern. He pledged to do his best.

"Well . . . thank you. I appreciate . . . I appreciate your taking the time."

"I'm sure you'll do just fine, Mr. Breen."

He aced the final. Made the highest grade in the class. He took his place in the pantheon of top graduates. The certificate hung on his wall years later. And no one knew of his perfidious means – no one but Jack Breen himself. A secret. But some secrets possess powers of corrosion. Like acid, in time they consume the vessel that holds them.

*****

That summer, Jack and Carolyn married. A union with a Ford daughter made perfect sense. It offered the kind of opportunities that lured Jack Breen to the East in the first place. He could have stayed in the Midwest, could have attended a top law school there. But he said no to that. Nothing but Harvard would do. Once there, he took it by storm. He worked hard, paid the price. Now, time to cash in. Like all other fundamental choices he made in his life, he calculated this one to serve his own best interests.

Jack prepared himself for assimilation into Boston high society. Carolyn's parents balked at the match a little, but not much and not for long. After all, Carolyn wanted Jack Breen and what Carolyn wanted, she got. Besides, how bad could he be? He was good looking, quick-witted, charming. And a Harvard man, to boot. More importantly, a fellow of the Order of the Coif. Carolyn's father gave his approval.

As a young man, the Ford family patriarch inherited millions. With those millions, he made many more. Developed office buildings, shopping malls, resorts from coast to coast.

Glazed by the purity of self-interest, hardened by the fires of experience, he was not a man to be trifled with. Once, he defended himself against rumors he had an unyielding union boss killed. He laughed off the accusation. "Poppycock," he branded it. "Sheer Poppycock." But rumors persisted. Common folk regarded him as a blackguard of the first order.

Jack Breen's career took off like a shot. With Bert Zorn at his side and a thundering herd of lawyers following close behind, he focused on money, getting it, hanging on to it. For a while, for years, it worked. The pursuit of legal tender kept him from distraction. What remained of the decade of his twenties passed in a fog. His thirties were a blur. And then he hit forty, the Big Four O. And before he knew it, forty-one. By then, Jack Breen had become, by all accounts including his own, an unqualified success.

On the home front, Jack Breen's life followed a less stellar course. But he regarded the imperfections and disappointments he faced there as the price of admission to the big show. That Carolyn did not want children and that she came in time to think of her clubs and fund raisers as her babies, even called them that did not bother Jack. At least, he never fessed up to it. He kept busy. He had a law practice to build from the ground up. With his top academic record, he could have taken a job at one of the big, old line firms. But he eschewed that. No partnership track for him. No billable hours. No boss. No such ordinary existence, not after marrying Carolyn Ford. With the help of her family connections, his practice soared. In a few years, he became the envy of his law school peers. The way Jack Breen saw it, he occupied a position above and beyond the biggest and best firms in New England. Above and beyond, precisely where Jack Breen wanted to be, where he thought he ought to be.

The day Jack Breen received the news about his license, Carolyn was thirty-eight years old. But she did not look her age. People often mistook her for a younger woman. Some said she had not aged a day since her wedding. She kept herself in top shape with daily workouts directed by a personal trainer.

26

Always dressed to the nines, she never allowed a single strand of her chin-length blonde hair to stray from its proper place. So like her. A place for everything, everything in its place. She always knew what she wanted and she always got it. She had no doubt about anything. A confident, purposeful woman. It showed in the way she carried herself. At any party, and there were many, all eyes, male and female, turned toward her when she entered the room. "Striking," her admirers often said. When Carolyn and Jack arrived as a couple, an almost audible gasp rose up. At least, they both liked to think that. Told themselves that.

Carolyn had charm. She had class. Money, but not enough, never enough. She wanted more. Needed it. Unlike her husband, Carolyn came from an old line Boston family. They always had plenty of money. Old money, the best kind.

Over time, the early fire in their relationship cooled. Carolyn and Jack spent less and less time together. Jack worked nights and weekends, stayed late at the office. Carolyn never missed a committee meeting or a charity event. Their shared activities consisted of dedications and ground breakings. Sleeping in separate beds, even when they were both at home, eventually came to seem normal, at least not unusual.

Lovemaking became more infrequent, less passionate, rote. It disappointed Jack, but it did not surprise him. He reasoned that he should expect it after more than seventeen years of marriage. As busy as he and Carolyn were, it had to happen. But indifference reached farther and deeper into his marriage than Jack knew. Like a house built on sand, it had to sink.

*****

The taxi arrived.
"Hey. Hey, mon. You get up. Pay now."

27

The Haitian-born driver angrily demanded compensation from his unresponsive fare. His shrill words struck like a bucket of cold water in Jack Breen's face.

Breen raised himself from the stupor of memory and sat erect. He took a twenty dollar bill from his wallet and handed it to the impatient cabby. It must have been enough, for he eagerly accepted it. It drew no protest or offer of change.

Breen stepped out of the taxi and shuffled toward the house, holding his bruised belly. At the entrance, he reached for the knob, but before he touched it, the door opened. Carolyn stood before him, well-coifed as always, fine features expertly highlighted with just the right amount of makeup. She dressed appropriately for the occasion in a stern, dark business suit. At her side, three Louis Vuitton suitcases waited in stair step formation like dutiful servants with locked heels.

"Oh," Carolyn said, plainly startled.

Jack's dulled senses did not allow a quick response. He remained motionless, right arm extended in thin air, hand empty.

"Jack. Well . . . it's you. You look a mess."

Jack lowered his arm. His eyes settled on the brown leather suitcases.

"You already knew," he said. "About the Supreme Court."

"Yes."

"You probably knew before I did. Maybe before the court did."

"It's over," Carolyn said. "It's time. You'll get the papers next week."

Jack looked at Carolyn, then at the luggage again. No surprise. Hurt, a little. Angry. Nobody likes being left. Nobody likes being kicked out of the party even if he didn't want to go in the first place. But surprised? No. He didn't even know how sorry he was. *Why not make a clean sweep of it?* he thought. *I've gotten rid of my law practice. Might as well get rid of my wife, too.*

"More papers?" he said. "I seem to be getting an abundance of papers these days. Doesn't anybody worry about killing all those trees?"

"It's been coming a long time," Carolyn said.

Melancholy softened her voice.

"We both knew it. Just didn't want to admit it."

Jack lowered his eyes and looked away.

"Where will you go?" he said.

At that moment, a black Jaguar XJ appeared in the street outside the house. A brief tap on the Jag's horn obviated the need for an answer to the question. Jack turned.

"Ahh. Your ride's here. You certainly didn't waste any time."

In the brisk air, the vehicle named for a jungle beast exhaled exhaust from its tailpipe like feral breath. Jack narrowed his eyes, squinted. His gaze settled on the elegantly dressed silver haired man sitting behind the steering wheel, his form dimly lit by dash lights.

"Peter Farrell?" Jack said. "Peter Farrell? I should have known."

"You did know," Carolyn said.

They could tie knots in each other at the drop of a hat. Thrust, parry. Advance and withdraw. The archetypical form of discourse between Mr. and Mrs. Breen these days. But this time, because of his weakened state, Jack had trouble keeping up. Carolyn landed another blow before he could respond.

"Don't feign outrage with me. You haven't exactly been a choir boy yourself, you know."

"No. And I'll bet you can give me names and dates, can't you?"

Carolyn's face reddened. Jaws tightened.

"Damn right I can. My God, who in this city can't give names and dates. Can you imagine the humiliation I've endured?"

She snatched up the smallest of the three bags.

"So can I," Jack said.

"So can I what?"

"Give names and dates. I'm no choir boy. But you're sure as hell no Mother Teresa."

The instant he said it, Jack regretted it. His heart plummeted into an abyss of guilt and shame and sorrow, like a boulder tumbling over a canyon rim. Laid low by the truth Carolyn used to bludgeon him, the fight went out of him. He conceded the round.

But then Jack looked again at the man in the Jag. He slapped an overstated, disingenuous smile on his face and waved vigorously.

"Hey, Pete," he called out. "Hey, Pete."

Carolyn put a hand on his arm.

"Jack, really. Please don't make a scene."

He opened his mouth as if to launch a counter-attack. But then he checked himself. His eyes misted and burned.

Carolyn placed herself in front of him and sighed. She reached for his face and cupped a hand on his cheek, a flag of truce. Jack forced a tattered smile, a sign of acceptance and resignation. Hell. Carolyn was right. This day had been coming for a long time and he did know it. He knew everything.

Tears welled in Carolyn's eyes.

"I really did love you, you know. Still do. God help me."

She picked up the smallest of the bags, pointed to the rest.

"I'll send for the others," she said. "Take care, Jack. Stay in touch."

Jack watched Carolyn move through the open door and stride to the waiting car in quick, definite steps. He watched her toss her bag and her purse into the rear seat. He watched her get in and drive away. The woman for whom he altered the course of his life vanished. And she never looked back. Not once.

Jack Breen stood alone now in a magnificent, hundred-year-old house that would be the envy of any rising star in Boston. For years, it symbolized the success he coveted. And

30

now it meant nothing. On this wintry night, it amounted to no more than a collection of old bricks, aging two-by-fours, and rusty nails. An empty chamber, a cold, lonely place where solitary footsteps echo down empty halls. And cries for help, even if raised, would go unheard and unanswered.

Frigid air rushing in through the open door like a breach in a fortress wall, Jack felt the chill of the world outside. He shivered once and closed the door slowly. He turned. Before him sat his dog, a husky, tow colored Labrador Retriever he called "Ace."

"You still here?" Jack said.

Ace tilted his head. He swept the floor with his wagging tail.

"Don't you have somewhere to go? A life to get on with?"

Ace canted his head again.

"Okay. Stick around then. How about a drink?"

Jack loosened his tie, and with Ace following, he made for the liquor cabinet. He took out a bottle of Glen Turret Scotch and a glass. Still wearing his suit and top coat, he slumped into his favorite chair, a large leather one with burly arms. He studied the glass a moment, then tossed it aside. Opting for a more direct approach, he unstoppered the bottle, put its mouth to his own lips and began the arduous process of downing every last drop of single malt whisky in it. He was no stranger to pulling a cork, but this was a new low.

Ace circled once, then lay at his master's feet. He watched until his eyelids became unbearably heavy, then he lowered his head and descended into sleep. While the dog dreamed and trembled, Jack Breen drank. A long night of determined elbow bending followed. He drank and remembered. His memory carried him away. To a time before Carolyn. To the beginning, the true beginning. To Claire.

Claire Gaynor played the cello like an angel. It came to her naturally. Her mother always said she had a gift. Professors told her that with a little drive, with sufficient ambition, she

31

might earn a living as a cellist. She might make something of herself.

She would sit and play, her instrument resting gently against her slender body. She bowed with a gentle touch, graceful fingers caressing the cello's dark-patined neck, her great mass of earthtone hair cascading over her shoulders, clear umber eyes closed. Seemingly entranced, the rhythm of her heart harmonized with the rhythm of the music. A mournful cry rose from quivering strings. A melancholy sound, sometimes almost unbearably sad. They gave up an instrumental strain best suited to being heard in the evening and in the muted light of the setting sun. In the timbre of the instrument's heavy voice, a suggestion of tears abided. Always a suggestion, but only that. And a hint of sadness, as indefinite as the rumble of distant thunder.

Three years in the East failed to turn Claire bitter and harsh. That time did not fill her with avarice and ambition. What of this notion of making something of herself? She had already made something of herself. When she played, a sweet river of music poured out of her and flowed into the hearts of all who heard it.

Jack Breen first heard Claire play one day when he walked past a practice room at the Conservatory while there for a weekend visit. A friend set him up with a girl from Chicago, a young administrator with a sardonic wit and a sharp tongue, a girl thinking about attending law school. The friend, who thought he knew Breen well, had no doubt he would like her. But before Jack Breen even saw her, Claire's music intervened.

The sonorous air stopped him in his tracks. It spun him in Claire's direction like a magnetized floating needle turned sharply north by forces of nature.

"What is that?" he asked himself in a low voice. "What's that sound?"

He stepped to the half-open door of the room and peered in. There sat Claire, posed with her instrument, sweet music flowing out of her. The sound struck him in the heart, dead center. From that moment on, the woman who was a river of music would never completely leave him. The lives of Jack Breen and Claire Gaynor would be entwined.

Just then, a student bearing an armload of papers passed by. The boy, plump and childlike, round of face, smooth of cheek, managed his considerable bulk with surprising lightness. Breen caught his attention with a jut of his chin. He pointed in the direction of the music's origin.

"What is that?" he said.

The student paused.

"A cello."

"I know it's a cello. What's the piece, the music?"

The student looked at the ceiling a moment, listened.

"Haydn. One of the concertos. C major I think."

"Right. Thanks."

When the music lapsed, Jack entered the room. Claire looked up.

"Haydn?" he said. "Am I right?"

"Yes. Do you like Haydn?"

"My favorite."

"Mine, too. Would you like to hear more?"

"Sure."

"Come in then. I'll play."

And play she did. She played and played. Her music ran through and around her heart and around the heart of Jack Breen. It bound them together like a thorny, flowering vine. For months, they did not stray from each other. The future lay before them, clear and bright. They were in love. But one day the music stopped. On Martha's Vineyard, a Beacon Hill girl lifted her blouse and the trembling strings of Claire's instrument stilled. A season of silence followed.

After the breakup, Claire did her best to consign Jack Breen to the past. She chalked up the whole mess to bitter experience. Though she would spend nearly a full decade in the East after college and after Jack's sudden disappearance, she never really felt at home there. Her marriage to a New Yorker was a charade, a pretense, wrong turn, bad call.

She longed for the mountains of southern Arizona, the faint rumblings of distant storms in summer, the smell of approaching rain. She missed the sullen calls of owls in the evening, silent swooping down of nighthawks at dusk. She always knew she would rather bow the strings of her cello in solitude at the edge of a mountain lake than in Carnegie Hall before a packed house. The applause and money would be nice, but not nice enough. What she really wanted, really needed, was a home, her home, all its quiet, all its serenity, all its history.

Now, years later, Jack Breen sat alone in darkness, whisky bottle in hand, remembering. He cut his wolf loose that night, and he would pay the price in the morning. He already felt like the frazzled end of a misspent life. The insult yet to be added to that injury would be a hell of a hangover.

## CHAPTER 3 - DAY ONE

Death. It must be death. The thieves from the night before actually killed him. They beat him, stabbed him, left him for dead. The rest was some kind of post-mortem dream. Come daybreak, that's what Jack Breen was thinking, to the extent he had the capacity for thinking anything. Still in his suit and top coat, he sprawled in the leather chair with burly arms, sodden with self-loathing and Scotch whisky. The pain that tormented every corner of his anatomy left him no doubt. He was dead, all right, dead and in hell with his back broken. But hell meted out more punishment than mere pain. Sound. An incessantly beating drum in his head. And worse than that, annoyance.

Without letup, Ace nuzzled and licked Breen's limp right hand. The lifeless limb dangled from the arm of the chair. Frozen in the same position for hours, Breen now could not move at all. Something akin to rigor mortis set in during the night.

Senses dulled by drink and unconsciousness, Breen had barely any awareness at first of the wet tongue and cold nose on his skin. After the night he put in, powers of perception would return slowly. Finally, he drew his arm close to his body and turned away. Never opening his eyes, he struggled without success to free himself of the irritant. He searched for a comfortable position in the chair, faced one way, then another, wincing at every turn. His body fell still again. Death, after a brief distraction, returned to make one final attempt to finish him off.

Undeterred and suffering his own torment, the desperate dog persisted. He firmly planted his forepaws on the arm of the chair. Pleading in a pathetic whine, he implored the sleeping man to awaken. With the effects of annoyance piled on annoyance and pain piled on pain mounting, one eye forced itself open to a thin slit. Soon, a second slit appeared. When Breen tried to rise, his limbs grudgingly obeyed. Little by little, inch by painful inch, he ascended along an irregular and uncertain path to consciousness.

Ace complained again.

"Bad dog. Go away."

Ace refused. He chuffed once without separating his jaws. The sound he made did not rise to the level of a full bark. Loose, hairy lips muffled the canine utterance and flapped like curtains over an open window.

"Oh, Ace. Come on. Please."

The first words of the day brought to Jack Breen the harsh realization that his mouth had the dryness of an ancient lake bed. In the night, his breath turned foul as carrion. His spine petrified. Numb feet tingled for lack of motion. Stomach roiled, an ocean of bile and alcohol. A dark shadow of new beard stubble stretched across his face. Hair descended to a wild chaos of disobedient strands. Unemployed. Sick from a night of drinking. Alone. The man had more in common with the lowest skid row bum than he ever had with the highest Boston socialite. Morning of the first day. Only two years to go.

36

Breen finally woke. In the manner of a cadaver rising by degrees from the dead, he righted himself. When he moved, he could almost hear cracks spreading across his face as if it were the surface of a crazed ceramic vase. Dusty sunshafts lanced the dark room through small spaces between drawn drapes. In the light's dim glow and through bloodshot eyes hooded by flickering lids, Breen's gaze fell to the empty whisky bottle on the floor. It's rigid, unyielding neck pointed at him like an accusing finger. He belched. He grimaced, recalling his determined assault on the bottle the night before. In disgust, he kicked the glass inquisitor and sent it spinning.

Ace's voice thundered. No chuff this time. A full bark, a loud one.

"All right. All right."

Breen wrestled himself to his feet. He stood awkwardly, trying to steady himself against the havoc wreaked upon his equilibrium by ardent spirits. With sidelong steps, he zigzagged hunch-shouldered to the front door and opened it. Ace charged through. At last, the dog had the relief he demanded. But at that moment, the bright light of morning sun exploded into the room, and nearly bowled Jack Breen over. In a convulsive jerk, he lowered his head and raised a hand. Eyelids slammed shut, then opened to a squint.

After he recovered from the flash, a more discrete glint of light drew his attention. He flattened a hand against it. On a bare branch of a tall tree stood a husky bird on spindle legs. Black. Shiny. Beak resembling a medieval instrument of war. A raven.

Breen angled his head. He massaged his eyes with thumb and forefinger, tried to blink them clear. When he opened them again, he saw no raven. Only a vacant perch. Had he really seen it? Or had it been a mere artifact of memory from his languorous staring at the office window the day before?

Breen closed the door and dragged himself to the shower. He walked with a clumsy sway, shedding bits of clothing with every step. Like a molting reptile, he peeled away layers of his toughened hide one by one. He dropped his top coat, then his suit jacket. Still without stopping, he jerked his tie from his neck and flung it aside. He unbuttoned his vest and his shirt. When he reached the bedroom, he dropped them where he stood. He deposited his trousers on top of them, left it all in a disordered heap on the floor. He stumbled into the bathroom and turned on the shower. There he stood, completely naked, down to his bare ass and his bare essence.

Eyes closed, head bowed, hands clasping the chrome pipe above, Breen stood beneath the cascading water. What remained of his outer shell melted away. His body began to tremble. Legs grew weak. He collapsed to the shower floor, limp and unformed like the mound of abandoned clothing in the bedroom. The ache in his heart and the burning accusations of his conscience brought forth a torrent of tears. Drawing up his knees, girding them with his arms, he lowered his head and wept like a lost child. He succumbed to the guilt of all the missteps, all the bad calls, all the wrong turns. He sobbed for what he should have been, for what he could have been, for what he became. Like the day of his birth, he was naked. Wet. Crying. He had nothing. But this time he faced the world alone. No loving arms around him, no one to prop him up, no one to feed him and care for him. On his own. At the bottom of a tall hill, looking up.

Later, guided only by familiar tracks laid down in his brain over decades, Breen made his way to the chest of drawers. He took out a pair of faded jeans, a gray tee shirt and slipped them on. Barefoot, he made his way to the kitchen and, continuing to rely on old practiced ways, he made a pot of coffee.

Ace barked. Still moving more like machine than man, Breen's steps carried him to the front door. He opened it and discovered the loyal beast sitting before him.

"Hey, buddy. Feel better? Come on in."

Breen noticed the morning paper on the porch next to the dog. He picked it up. When Ace barked again from inside

38

the house, Breen looked up, half-expecting to see the raven. Nothing. An empty branch. Sounds of traffic in the street. Children at play. Workmen at their labors. The world trundled on, paying him no mind.

Breen closed the door, and with Ace at heel, he returned to the kitchen. After pouring a cup of coffee, he seated himself at the table and opened the paper. Ace reposed at his feet.

As he had so many times, Breen arranged and flattened the newsprint before him and started to read, at least he attempted to read. He tried, but he could not. Each effort to focus on printed words failed. Even with the house empty and quiet as a grave, he could not concentrate. The paper repelled his eyes with the force of identical magnetic poles juxtaposed.

He glanced over his shoulder toward the front door as if the raven were calling him from the other side. In his mind, he could still see the creature's dark eyes, glossy wings. He could feel its pull. *Ridiculous*, he thought. *Ridiculous*. He smiled at himself. He gave up a one-breath chuckle and shook his head, then made a final attempt to take in the morning news. He failed.

Breen thought a moment, then leaped to his feet. With newfound clarity of purpose, he dashed off to the bedroom and disappeared into the closet. Ace stationed himself near the door and watched. Inside, Breen fell to his knees and began searching the obscure recesses of the richly stocked chamber with the excitement of a looter entering a pharaoh's tomb. He came out with the object of his quest, a wooden cigar box with a brass latch. Weathered, somewhat stained, but not a cheap cardboard box with corners frayed down to the gray undersurface. This one was stoutly made of cedar. And the latch worked.

Breen gazed upon the strongbox that held his memories, a time capsule bearing evidence of a former life. Sitting tailorwise on the floor, he thumbed the latch open and lifted the lid. He beheld the treasures within. A key ring with an attached medallion bearing an Indian design. He could remember the rainy afternoon when Claire, the woman he pledged to make his wife, put it in his hand. He thought on that day if he pressed it hard enough into his palm, he'd never stop feeling it there. He searched on, finding a note card inscribed with the words of a favorite song. A cork from a bottle of champagne. A book of matches from a bar. Photograph of a woman—Claire. Rising from it all, a faint fragrance of a woman's perfume he had not scented for nearly two decades. And one more thing; a raven feather.

*****

Breen spent the summer preceding his last year of law school in Cambridge taking classes and working part time in a pizza parlor. Claire went home in June. He did not see her for a couple of months and he ached for her. Finally, when he could not stand the loneliness another day, he borrowed a few bucks from a friend, a local Boston kid in his law class, a kid with more money than potential and caught a plane to Phoenix.

In letters and late night long distance calls there had been talk of marriage. Nothing official, no proposal, no acceptance, no ring. Rings cost money and Jack Breen had none. He did not even know how he'd pay off the loan for the airplane ticket. He just knew he could, somehow. Plenty of time to worry about that later. First things first. Now, he would fly to Arizona, firm up the engagement, win over Claire's parents, and steal their daughter away to New England. He knew he could make it happen. He just knew it. By his last year of law school he'd gotten pretty good at making things happen. He came to believe he had it in him to shape the world to his liking. He knew he could not be stopped.

Claire met Jack's plane at Sky Harbor Airport. They exchanged smiles and waves from a distance at first, then shared a long deep kiss.

"Welcome to the land of sunshine," she said.

"Thanks."

"You know what they say. Once this place gets in your blood, you can never get free of it."

"I know you're in my blood," Jack said. "And I'll never be free of you."

In a few hours, they arrived at the Gaynor ranch in the San Rafael Valley. "Rancho de Cuervos" folks called it, Raven Ranch. Claire explained that her great grandfather established the cattle operation in the last days of the nineteenth century. He said the first time he laid eyes on the spread of some nine thousand acres the stout-chested black birds for which the ranch was named haunted every hogback, buffalo jump, and saw-cut canyon. Each, in turn, answered his arrival with a territorial wingbeat and a discordant call. He could almost make out words. He could swear they said his name.

Indians said that in some time belonging to antiquity a raven brought light to a dark world. That sold the man, who planned to make this valley his home. He figured the birds that preceded him might as well have their name on the place. Like as not, they'd reclaim every mete and bound of it someday anyway, when all the people were dead and gone or some unworthy Gaynor heir lost it in a poker game. But that had not happened yet. The old man held on to the ranch. So did his son and his grandson. The last in the line was Claire's father James.

Jim Gaynor ranched all his life. Like other stockmen, he had land but not much money. He worked daylight to dark every day, some days more, and he hardly ever left the confines of his own property. He saw the world in the 1940's during what he referred to as "that little fracas in Europe," and he did not think much of it. When he came home, he made up his mind to stay put.

Jack Breen had no trouble understanding how someone could find contentment in such a place. Not for him, of course, but he could see how a man whittled down by a world war could want nothing more than to live out his days in the San Rafael Valley. When Claire and her father took him to Bishop's

Dry Goods and outfitted him with a pair of cowboy boots, he suspected an effort to seduce him into staying in the West. Whatever the true intent of the elder Gaynor and his daughter may have been, Jack had no thought of living anywhere but Boston. That was the place for him. There, he would build a life for himself and his new wife. A pair of cowboy boots, even a good fitting pair of rough-outs, made a nice gift, but they did not come close to having the power to change his mind.

Jack's week on the ranch went according to plan. Claire's parents loved him. Why not? Everybody loved him. He was handsome, witty, charming. He had his feet set firmly on the road to success. After a few days, he shook hands with Claire's father, hugged her mother, and promised to take good care of their daughter. Question asked. Answer given. Deal made. Jack and Claire would be married the following spring after graduation.

Jack and Claire enjoyed cool evenings that week, violet hours full of romantic expectations trailed closely by a sweet and irresistible melancholy. After dinner on one such evening, the man and his lady strolled hand-in-hand, taking in the beauty of the setting sun. They paused at the edge of a copse of Palo Verde trees, and looked out over the short grass prairie. Somewhere in the calm still night, an owl called. Jack took Claire in his arms and brought her close. He kissed her.

"I love you," he said. "I never get tired of saying that."

Claire smiled and laid her head on his chest.

The owl called again. Jack turned his head toward the mournful sound.

"What is that?"

"An owl. Indians say its cry is a warning of danger. A bad omen."

"Not for us," Jack said.

Then he noticed a raven perched in the top of a nearby tree, its black form silhouetted against the dimming sky. Jack eased his hand into the air and pointed.

"I know what your dad says about that guy. He brought the light of heaven to a dark world. I think I like him better."

42

"They mate for life," Claire said. "But some say he can't be trusted. Some say he's a liar and a thief."

Jack drew Claire to him and kissed her again. In the sweet afterglow and with the taste of his lips fresh on hers, Claire said, "Is the owl calling to me? Will you break my heart some day, Jack Breen?"

"Never."

"If you do, I'll still love you. I won't be able to stop myself. You're like this place to me."

That week, evening rains fell from a clear sky. Surges of what Indians called *blue wind* brought the moisture. At night, moonbows formed in the firmament. In the mornings, brilliant sunrises. There were kisses and twined hands and long walks. Promises. Commitments that came from the heart, meant when spoken but too fragile to be kept. And the aroma of piñon smoke. It wafted in from near and distant fires. The images and sounds and redolence of the San Rafael Valley marked Jack Breen's memory forever.

But that was in the late summer, barely a month before Labor Day, no more than thirty days before Jack first laid eyes on Carolyn Ford on a dock at Martha's Vineyard. Though no one knew it, not even Jack Breen himself, the change of season that was about to occur would bring a change of plans.

*****

Breen disappeared into the closet again. After casting about through suits and shirts and shoes, he emerged with a black duffle bag. He tossed the bag on the bed, paused a moment, then returned to the closet. He searched it one more time. When he came out, he held a pair of worn rough-out cowboy boots. He studied them with wonder, then sat on the bed. He slipped his feet into the boots and pulled them on.

"Haven't worn these in years," he said. "Haven't even seen them in years."

Breen stood and shifted his weight from side to side until his feet reached a comfortable settlement in the worn leather. He looked down at Ace and smiled.

"They still fit."

He glanced around the room. He felt like a stranger in his own house. That's when he made up his mind. He lowered his eyes to Ace again.

"Let's go. We're leaving."

# CHAPTER 4 - ON THE ROAD

They lit out. Without so much as a parting glance, Jack and Ace piled into the black Mercedes. Man and dog took to the road.

They veered onto I-93 heading south and in no time at all they struck the outskirts of Boston. By then, filthy clouds, stained with smog and other offscourings of city life, started heaping up. They dimmed the bright light of early morning that glinted on the raven's wing, and at the same time, they darkened Jack Breen's spirit. Every mile, he fought a nagging urge to pull over and rethink his abrupt flight. An inclination to be deliberate, to turn around and head home plagued him. In the first hour, he thought no less than a dozen times of going to the office, making a deal with Bert Zorn. He could do it. He could work behind the scenes until his suspension expired. Like Bert said, it would be easy. No one would know.

He thought about calling Carolyn. He could charm her the way he did the day he met her. He'd drunk from the well of forgiveness a thousand times. He could do it again. He could start over.

But no. He had his fill of that life. He fought off the doubt, steeled himself, and kept going. His resolve held until a gust front hit and the wind kicked up. Cloudbound air chilled and a skiff of snow blurred his vision. The car fish-tailed and the momentary loss of control spooked him. *What am I doing?* he thought. *What the hell am I doing?* He turned into a truck stop parking lot to get hold of himself.

Breen sat without moving, staring into the leadened sky through the monotonous sweep of windshield wipers. Then, he broke. *All right, Bert. All right. You win.* He reached for his cell phone. One digit short of making the fateful call, the shrill blare of a horn jarred him. A sound as terrifying as the shriek of an attacking beast. An explosion of enveloping headlights consumed him with the intensity of a strike of ball lightning.

When the fog of confusion lifted, he realized what happened. He had pulled off the interstate onto the access road, then halted before clearing the truck stop entrance. An eighteen wheeler was bearing down on him from the rear. He tossed the phone away and lurched the car forward, heart banging in his chest, ears ringing.

When he cleared the death trap he blundered into, Breen's temper flared. In a conflagration of face reddening, vein bulging anger, he cursed the trucker for nearly killing him, hammered his fist against the steering wheel. Then, he turned his rage on himself. *What a fool I am. What a damn fool I've always been.* In the searing light of self-accusation, he could see justice in the destruction that nearly befell him. Twice in the last twenty-four hours, he came close to being run over. He faulted himself for being the beneficiary of the blind luck that saved him. He branded himself a cheater for it.

By his own lights, Jack Breen owed just about every human being he knew an apology. But now, as an unemployed itinerant, he had only a dog to hear his *mea culpa*. He reached for Ace with trembling hands. He spoke with a quavering voice.

"I'm sorry. So sorry. You deserve better. Everybody deserved better. What else can I say? What else can I do? I'm sorry."

He hung his head. After a few moments, he steadied himself. He took in a deep breath and carried on. Although he had only the dimmest notion of where he was going, he knew he was following the vanished sun. Going west. It worked for men of bygone centuries. Why not for him? At mid-afternoon, Breen crossed into Rhode Island. Then he made his way through Connecticut. New York came next, then New Jersey. By dark he made it all the way to Baltimore. There, he spent his first night on the road. He faced the challenge of it in a place befitting his new station in life—Don's Motel. A green neon sign at the road's edge declared the price of a room, twenty-nine ninety-five per night. Below the price a further declaration, a more important one, "Vacancy."

Breen parked outside the office and, after cautioning Ace to lie down in the seat and keep out of sight, he headed in. The clang of a brass bell on the steel-framed glass door announced his entrance into the motel office.

A slightly-built man with a dusky complexion and slick black hair appeared at the front desk. He wore a crisp, white, short-sleeved shirt with a Michael Corleone collar. The points reached almost to his shoulders. A bushy moustache concealed all but the tip of a toothpick lodged in the corner of his mouth. When he spoke, stained teeth peeked out.

"Welcome to Don's," the man said with a broad smile and what Breen took as some sort of Middle Eastern accent.

"Are you Don?"

"Yes," the swarthy skinned proprietor answered proudly. "I am Don. Would you like a room?"

"Sure."

Breen handed him a credit card.

"Just you?" the innkeeper said, craning his neck for a look into the Mercedes.

Breen did not answer. He didn't know how welcome Ace would be, even in a motel like Don's.

The innkeeper handed Breen a form to sign, then swiped the card through the electronic scanner. A beep sounded. The screen read, "Declined." The innkeeper chuckled nervously and swiped the card again. More bad news.

"This card is no good," the innkeeper said. The chuckle and the smile evaporated. "Do you have another?"

Breen handed him a second card. The man swiped it. It produced the same result as the first. The innkeeper's look turned grave, his manner stern, defensive.

"This one is no good either."

"All right. All right," Breen said. "I'll just pay cash. You do take cash, don't you?"

The man brightened.

"Of course, we take cash. Twenty-nine ninety-five, like the sign says. Plus tax, of course. In advance. Free long distance."

An obsequious smile formed on the innkeeper's face when Breen handed him two crisp twenty dollar bills. Again the man looked around Breen to the car. This time, Ace sat erect in the front seat. His head showed through the window in the light of the neon sign. The innkeeper soured. He took the toothpick from his mouth and commenced a study of the splintered end. He did not look at Breen.

"No dogs allowed," he said.

Breen looked out at the car. The innkeeper wagged a finger in the air and shook his head.

"No dogs allowed. No. No. No. No. No."

Breen laid another twenty on the counter. The innkeeper considered the cash a moment, then arched his eyebrows and gestured with open hands, palms up.

"No dogs allowed."

Breen persisted. He laid yet another twenty on the counter. The innkeeper cocked his head, thought a moment. He returned the toothpick to his mouth.

"Just one dog?"

48

"Just one."

The innkeeper smiled, pushed the key toward Breen. The cash spoke.

In the room, Breen tossed the key on the side table and sat heavily on the bed. Hard as a concrete slab. Save the crinkling of the plastic cover on the mattress beneath the sheets, the bed showed no response to his shifting weight.

Breen turned his eyes to the heavy phone next to the lamp on the table. Free long distance presented an unexpected temptation. He reached for the receiver, but then he hesitated. He rested his hand on the cold colorless plastic, half-expecting it to come to life. When it did not, he lifted his hand with the caution he might use in trying to avoid arousing a sleeping monster. He put his palms together and laced his fingers. He leaned forward, elbows on knees, and hung his head. He gave way to despair.

Jack Breen longed for some kind of absolution, but that would be a long time coming, if it came at all. For now, all he could do was keep moving.

## CHAPTER 5 - DUE WEST

In North Carolina, the travelers turned onto Interstate 40 and the crooked road they'd been following became straight. Their new heading, due west.

In two days time, they made Oklahoma. Old Man Winter may have been standing for a last hurrah in the Northeast, but he had dropped to his knees in the country's heartland. There, the shoulder season amounted to more than a mere promise. It was well underway. The first faint showing of green lightened Jack Breen's heart.

They broke through the weather-edge at the Arkansas River, and the sullen sky cleared. The color of ashes yielded to a vast hemisphere of soft blue. Sun-drenched air warmed the favorable ground below. Incoming light burned off the veil that dulled the West country in the preceding quarter-year and unfurled a quiltwork of rich greens and browns. Spring. The annual ritual of renewal.

Breen switched on the radio. Even tunes coming over the airwaves sounded different. To a New Englander's ear, a little twangy. Voices drawled. The local idiom amused the city boy. He saw more pickups on the road. Folks wore clothing of a different cut. Houses had a different look. He wasn't in Boston any more. No doubt of that.

Along toward twilight, Breen struck the Indian Meridian. He glanced at Ace in the rearview mirror. The pup lay stretched out in the seat fast asleep.

"Hey," he said. "We got sort of a problem, you know. We're broke."

The dog's dark eyes widened.

"Carolyn helped herself to the last of the cash. Credit cards are dead. Gonna need some operating capital."

With less than an hour of daylight remaining, they came in sight of Oklahoma City. When they reached the city limits, they quit the interstate and followed the signs pointing to downtown. Soon they found what they were after, Downtown Auto Sales. The sign at the street confirmed they'd come to the right place— "Buy, Sell, Trade."

The car dealer was a mustachioed fellow in his mid-fifties. Slicked-back gray hair. Barrel chest. Wattled neck. A gob of chewing gum in his mouth. He sat at a metal desk the color of his hair, probably army surplus, booted feet perched on the corner, swivel chair cocked back. He was smoking an unfiltered Camel, and from the look of the overflowing ashtray, he'd been lighting one from the smoldering butt of another since dawn. Tiny brown holes, the work of falling ashes, pocked the polyester of his pale blue pearl snap shirt. Nicotine stains darkened the fingers of his right hand and the midpoint of his bristly upper lip. Further proof of a two-pack-a-day habit.

When Breen walked in, the man at the desk was sitting trancelike, eyes fixed on the pages of the monthly foldout he dangled less than an arm's length from his lusty eyes. At the sight of an intruder, the man shoved the magazine into a drawer and sprang to his feet. When he rose, ashes showered the front of his shirt. Slapping his chest with both hands, he laughed out loud.

"Shit. 'Bout to burn myself up."

The fire extinguished, he turned his attention to Breen again. In character now, he let fly a fusillade of pitchman's greetings and salutations.

"Howdy there. Howdy. You look like a fellow might could use a new ride. Bet you and me could make us a deal. Bet we could make a deal today. What say, amigo? What say? Come on. What say?"

"Well."

Breen started to speak, but the florid faced huckster quickly cut him off. He darted out from behind the desk and charged toward him at a determined pace. He flashed a yellow-toothed grin and held out his right hand.

"Leland Carr's the name. That's Carr. C . . . A . . . R . . . R."

Following the tried and true cheapjack method invented by men of his ilk, he took Breen's right hand in his and pumped it vigorously, grasped his elbow with his left. Two pats and a squeeze, the universal sign of sincerity among salesmen. The verbal hailstorm continued.

"With a name like Carr, reckon I had to be in the car bidness. Yessir. Folks always said I better had. Call me Lee. Now, how about you and me lookin' at some new wheels?"

"Actually, I have a car to sell," Breen said.

He pointed to the street outside.

"That Mercedes out there."

The car hawker, now turned prospective buyer, stepped to the window for a closer look. He folded his arms, held his chin in the crook of a hand. He glanced sidelong at Breen. His manner became serious. Pace of words slowed. The hushed tone of his voice betrayed a fear of being overheard.

"Damn. Fancy rig."

He leaned in as if to share a secret.

"Ain't stolen is it?"

Breen winced, shook his head.

"Not exactly," he answered with a breathy chuckle. "No. Ain't stolen."

The car dealer turned and put a hand on Breen's arm.

"No offense, son. Cain't be too cautious in this bidness, you know. Just didn't take you for the kind of ole boy that oughta be drivin' a car like that."

"I'm not."

The car dealer smoothed his moustache with the edge of a finger. He patted Breen's arm and winked.

"Let's do some bidness. Right now."

In no time, they had a deal. Breen had no doubt he held the short end of the stick, but he could do nothing about it. He sold the car. That's what counted. He had cash in his pocket and a new vehicle, late model Chevy pickup, blue. Less than a hundred thousand miles on it. Engine purred like a kitten. Perfect for a man and a dog on the move and traveling light.

Leland Carr handed Breen a check. Breen traded the keys to the Mercedes for the keys to the truck and Carr accepted them proudly. He stood ramrod straight and ran his thumbs along the waistband of his trousers, taking in air, swelling his chest.

"Gonna keep this one myself," he said. "Darlene's gonna love it. Darlene's my wife, number three. Best yet."

He cupped his hands in front of his chest.

"She's got . . . well, you know. Store-bought but nice. Cost me an arm and a leg."

He rubbed his palms together, widened his eyes. A look of eager expectation spread across his face.

"Gonna treat Daddy right tonight. Hmm. Hmm. Hmm. Gonna get my money's worth. For damn sure."

He laughed a deep, immodest laugh that ended in a coughing fit.

Breen folded the check and tucked it into a shirt pocket. He nodded and turned to go.

"Good luck with Darlene," he said.

The proud Mercedes owner continued coughing and patting his chest. Finally he caught enough breath to speak.

"Thank you now. Thank you."

He reached for another smoke and pointed across the street.

"Bank's over yonder. Don't believe I'd waste any time cashin' that check. Sometimes I fire off a heater, you know. My account can run a little on the lean side, if you know what I mean. First-come, first-served."

Breen took him at his word and headed for the bank.

In the late afternoon, the sun hung low in the west. A heavy mist began to settle in. Breen zipped up his jacket and raised the collar, looked all around, got his bearings. Bank across the street. Down the way, farther to the west, perhaps a block or more, something caught his eye. Looking closer, he saw a small gathering of people in a strange looking place. Some kind of park or memorial, historical marker. He crossed the street and paused a moment on the sidewalk outside the bank. He looked closer, but could not quite make out the curious edifice to the west.

In the bank, Breen endorsed the check and presented it to the teller, a young woman in her twenties with plump, red cheeks. After a short delay for the woman to consult her supervisor and to verify the sufficiency of funds in the account, she counted out the cash and handed it to Breen. More than a touch of an Okie drawl in her voice.

"You're lucky," she said. "This one cleared."

Breen made no expression. He stuffed his grubstake into the pocket of his jacket, then pointed casually with a thumb over his shoulder. He gestured with a slight toss of his head.

"What's that place down the street, where the people are gathered?"

"Bombing memorial," the young woman said, face darkening. "Hundred sixty-eight people died there. Nineteen children."

Breen nodded and sighed.

"I remember."

54

He left the bank and ambled along the sidewalk toward the memorial. The day was much advanced now and a half-face moon appeared in the dampening sky.

He paused at the eastern gate where two towering bronze-plated walls stood ten feet apart, one in front of the other, each with a rectangular opening in the center forming a tall doorway. The gates stood in perfect enfilade with an identical pair of gates at the far end of the memorial, almost a block away.

Lingering at the entrance, Breen lifted his eyes. Inscribed at the top, he read these words:

"WE COME HERE TO REMEMBER THOSE WHO WERE KILLED, THOSE WHO SURVIVED, AND THOSE CHANGED FOREVER. MAY ALL WHO LEAVE HERE KNOW THE IMPACT OF VIOLENCE. MAY THIS MEMORIAL OFFER COMFORT, STRENGTH, PEACE, HOPE, AND SERENITY."

Breen passed through the gate with reverent steps, drawn to a blanket of soft green grass and a field of one hundred sixty-eight bronze chairs arranged in rows. The glass base of each chair bore an engraving of a victim's name. A light from beneath accentuated the letters.

As explicit night approached, Breen wandered among the luminous chairs for a time, then halted. Nearby, a silver-haired woman stood, collar of her woolen coat turned up, hands pocketed, head bowed. She was crying softly. An urge to speak, to offer a word of comfort, rose up in Jack Breen. But he did not make a sound. Caution and doubt, always enemies of the good that might be done, silenced him. He started to leave.

"My husband died here," the woman said, words tiptoeing through tears. "I come here often. At night. So quiet."

Breen stopped and turned. The woman glanced over each shoulder, first one, then the other.

"They call them 'The Gates of Time.' Eastern gate marks the moment before the blast, western gate the moment after. Indians say they're dream catchers. Allow only good spirits to thread themselves through and pass on to sacred ground within. I hope they're right."

"I'm sorry," Breen said. "About your husband, I mean."

A faint smile brushed the woman's face.

"A long time now. But it seems like yesterday. Part of me died that day, too. That's the way we die, you know. Most of us anyway. A little bit at a time."

She took a step forward and extended an arm.

"There's my Jimmy's chair. Sometimes I almost think I'll find him sitting there."

"You must have loved him very much."

The woman nodded.

"Still do."

"I envy him," Breen said.

"Married thirty-five years. After all that time I thought I couldn't live without him. At first I didn't want to. Prayed I would die, too."

Without speaking again, the woman turned and walked away. Instinctively, Breen followed. He kept to her side, moving along a reflecting pool of dark water. Behind them, empty chairs glowed in the gathering darkness.

"I didn't want to live any more," the woman said. "I'd lost everything, I thought. Just didn't care."

They wandered on and for a while no one spoke. When they stopped again, standing side-by-side, the woman lifted her gaze.

"I didn't think I could go on. Then one day I saw that tree. Oh, I'd seen it before, but I never really looked at it, never really saw it."

A lone American Elm stood at the top of a series of grassy terraces. Branches, dressed up with new spring growth, reached liked pleading arms into the dimming sky.

56

"The Survivor Tree," she said. "That's what they call it."

They climbed the terraces and when they reached the tree the woman had new strength in her voice.

"It lived through the bomb. Shaken. Lost all its leaves. Some thought it would die, but it didn't. Finally, one day I knew I had to survive, too. Had to."

The woman turned and looked directly into Breen's eyes.

"I have three grandchildren, you see. I realized I have a purpose."

Tears glistened in the woman's eyes, reflecting the vague glow emanating from each empty chair.

"Do you have a family?" the woman said.

"No. I have no one. And no purpose."

"Yes, you do. Everyone does. You just haven't found it yet. God knows what it is even if you don't."

Breen did not answer.

"Well, I should go now," the woman said. "I've done what I came to do. I'm keeping my grandchildren tonight."

The woman started to leave, then paused. She turned toward Breen.

"I will pray for you. I'll pray you come to know your purpose, that you will fare well. I think you're worth saving."

The woman turned again and walked away. In a moment, she disappeared in the darkness.

Jack Breen set his eyes on the Survivor Tree, then lifted them higher, all the way to where he thought Heaven might be.

"I'm sorry I wasn't more," he whispered. "Sorry for everything."

The sky darkened. Empty chairs waited. The road west beckoned.

# CHAPTER 6 - A STRONG WIND

Next day, the wind came from the East and blew with a wolf's head. Current of air at his back, Jack Breen raced along the interstate in his new pickup like a paper cup whipping down an alley. He made good time.

Morning of the day following, he cleared the west side of Albuquerque and headed on toward Gallup. He figured on making it in a couple of hours, and he'd stop there for gas. He'd need another cup of coffee, too. After a string of restless nights in cheap motels, the last with a Mexican name he didn't understand, he felt anything but rested. Through the dark hours, volley after volley of torturous dreams assaulted him.

The air thinned and cooled when the high country of the West edged into the plains. Smoldering remains of evening fires in homes along the highway daubed the crisp air with the scent of piñon smoke. Breen drove with his window glass partially lowered to take it in. Before sight and sound, a fragrance can find a mere ember of memory and blow it into flame. So it was for the wayfaring Jack Breen on this day. Piñon smoke put him in mind of his first trip west, the summer of his engagement to Claire. His heart ached.

*****

One slow afternoon, with the sun well beyond its meridian transit and waning in the western sky, Claire planted a rapturous kiss on the lips of her intended.

"There's something I want you to see," she said. "Something you'll really love."

"I'm looking at something I really love right now," Jack said.

He pulled her close to savor the warmth of the moment. But Claire had something else in mind.

"Not so fast," she said. "Come on. I'll show you."

"Where are we going?"

"The ruins . . . at Raven Wash."

In the southern reaches of the Gaynor ranch, tucked away in a hidden canyon lost to time, stood the ruins of a cliffside hamlet. The handful of tumbledown structures formed of flat sandstone blocks bound in clay mortar dated back more than a thousand years. It must have been a stronghold for some long-forgotten bronze-skinned clan. A place for a hopeless fight against extinction.

The approach took them through a gunsight pass and across a blind valley carpeted with knee-high native grasses, mostly gramma and bluestem. Clusters of wild flowers bejeweled the valley floor, black-eyed susans with yellow petals and buckeye centers, droopy necked bluebells, whiteflower rabbitbrush. In the twilight glow of zodiacal light, every square inch within the high redrock walls wore a cloak of blue gray haze. Not a breath of wind to stir a stalk.

Near the base of the north facing palisade, Jack and Claire came to a lazy, perennial watercourse cut by episodic runoff. A bone dry arroyo most of the year. But during summer monsoons, chili-colored water surged high within the cutbanks. The day Claire revealed the secret of Raven Wash to Jack Breen, a braided stream ran ankle deep. A few riparian trees towered over the bracken at the water's edge.

59

In the rocky heights beyond the paltry streamlet and above a scattering of hulking, house size boulders on the upslope, stood the small dead city. Higher still, desert varnish streaked the rock face from rim to bulwark. The staining and scouring away of a million years of weather.

At the water's edge, Claire and Jack paused and looked all around. Overhead, a raven drifted. His cry summoned their gaze. The feathered overlord of this hidden corner of earth inscribed the rusty mural wall with his wafting shadow, then joined his mate in their bastion rookery. Claire raised an arm, aimed it in their direction.

"You can see why this place is called Raven Wash. They own it. Let's pay them a visit."

Claire took Jack's hand and led him toward the water. Jack hesitated.

"We're going up there?"

"Sure."

"Never knew you were half-mountain goat."

Claire smiled.

"Come on. It's not that hard."

They crossed the packed sand of the wash bottom and the interlaced filaments of water. On the far side, they ascended a series of benches and intervening inclines. Then they took up a switchback defile that led them through the jumble of boulders. Above, they followed a precarious series of hand and footholds. In time, they gained the platform terrace.

Breathless, they studied the roofless cliff house, jagged walls of a caved-in granary. They turned and gazed out across the wide valley floor, silvering now in the reflected light of the rising moon. This lofty battlement offered a fine prospect of the entrance to the canyon, every corner, and everything within.

"From here, you can see what's coming," Claire said. "Must have been a place for a last stand."

Her eyes lowered and moistened. Voice softened.

"Look. Stains of cookfires. You can smell the piñon. Pot shards everywhere. I can almost hear their voices."

60

"What's this?" Jack said, pointing to a figure on the slab face of a leaning sandstone monolith.

"Petroglyph. Rock art. Looks like a mountain lion. Imagine that. A thousand years ago somebody put his knees on this very ground and carved that image."

"Are there still mountain lions here?" Jack said.

"Sure. They roam these hills and canyons. Never seen one. Thought I did once, but I couldn't be sure. I've heard them."

"They're dangerous. Right?"

Claire nodded.

"The people that lived in this cliff house feared them as much as we do today. The more things change, the more they stay the same, I guess."

Jack sat on his heels before the stone etching.

"So is it some kind of tribute?"

"Maybe. Maybe a warning. A reminder to beware."

Jack rose and turned. He took Claire in his arms.

"I'll never let anything happen to you. You know that."

He held her close.

"I can't tell you how much I love you. I always will. A thousand times longer than these walls have stood."

"Sounds like forever."

"It is. I promise you it is."

That's what the scent of piñon smoke conjured in Jack Breen's memory on a New Mexico highway some twenty years after he first laid eyes on Raven Wash. The memory brought the pain of sorrow. And guilt.

*****

A few miles east of Gallup, westbound traffic slowed. A moment later, Breen topped a rise and found himself running up the backside of a long line of vehicles strung out at a dead stop. He had to stand on the brake to avoid rear-ending the car in front of him. The tire screeching halt sent Ace tumbling from seat to floorboard.

"Sorry, Boy," Jack said. "Sorry."

Ace remounted the seat and shook off his violent displacement. He came to attention at Breen's side.

Ahead, red and blue lights of a squadron of police cars flashed. Near them, sat a fire truck and an ambulance. A string of red highway flares burned on the pavement. Beyond the flashing lights, Breen could see a semi-tractor/trailer jackknifed and overturned on an overpass. The eighteen-wheeler blocked both westbound lanes.

After a good half hour of waiting, a local constable, slope shouldered man, solid, square built, came ambling along the broken white line that divided westbound lanes. He wore brown polyester slacks cut in a western style, black boots and a bone-colored cowboy hat. His pearl snap khaki shirt bore a shoulder patch "McKinley County Sheriff." He had a game leg, hitched when he walked.

The sheriff stopped at every west-facing vehicle along his way. At intervals, he pointed west, mumbled a few words, moved on. When he reached Breen, he leaned against the truck door to take the weight off his bum leg and to catch his breath.

"Hell of a wreck," he said, wheezing. "Hell of a wreck. Truck rolled over. Driver went to sleep, I expect. D.R.T."

He showed a slight smile, before continuing.

"Dead Right There. Road's gonna be blocked a while."

"How long?"

"Hard to say. Lay you even it's a couple of hours. Might could be more."

Breen nodded, rubbed his forehead in frustration. Ace now reposed in the seat at his side, unconcerned about delay.

The sheriff raised an arm and gestured with an open hand, blade or rudderlike.

"Now you could cut off here. Take this little road a ways, catch 371, head west through Standing Rock, pick up 666 south. Devil's Highway. You know. 666. Get it?"

He chuckled at himself, then continued.

"Anyway, you could pick up the interstate thataway. Cain't say if it'll save you any time. Might. Don't nobody else up here seem interested."

Breen looked around at the lengthening line of cars behind him. Standing still and doing nothing did not suit him. Never had.

"Might as well try it," he said. "Thanks."

He turned off the highway and struck out on a two lane blacktop that turned to gravel in a dozen miles. Soon, he was driving across some unmapped wild. A spare land. Immense span of it. Sun bleached. Dull hued. Dusty and dry. Not another vehicle or living thing in sight.

In a while, he came to a gas station and country store, a modest mercantile establishment at the edge of the Navajo reservation. He stopped there. The place appeared to be deserted. At first, Breen could not tell if it was open for business. No sign of life. No sound, save an occasional gasp of wind and the accompanying hiss of swirling sand.

The store was a small rectangular building made of concrete blocks painted turquoise. Paint faded and chipped at the corners. There, underlying gray showed through. The rusty screen of the door in front peeled away from its frame at two corners. A weather-beaten aluminum sign fastened to it bore a picture of a penguin on ice skates smoking a cigarette. The place must have stood in this very spot since the Creation.

Outside, a couple of antique red gasoline pumps, dappled with rust, stood like ancient totems. Glass at the top was wind-scored and cracked. A sign above them said, "*Come on in . . . You'll like our SERVICE.*"

Breen answered the call. Pulling in, he noticed an old Indian standing against a ragged corner of the blue-green building. An earth brown cloth banded his head. Shaggy mane of iron gray hair hung almost to his shoulders. Age and experience showed in the deep wrinkles that furrowed his bronze face. He wore dirty jeans, muslin shirt, moccasins. A stained, moth-eaten blanket cowled his shoulders, enfolded his entire bony frame. An electric blanket, pastel pink. Breen almost laughed out loud when he saw the outline of the wires and the cord dangling from a corner. Motionless as a cigar store fixture, the old man eyed Breen but said nothing.

Breen stopped next to the pumps and stepped out of the truck. Faint smell of piñon. He looked off down country a moment, then pushed the door to with a hip. He glanced at the old man again and nodded. No response. He lifted the nozzle from the pump and inserted it into the gas tank filler neck. He squeezed the handle, but nothing happened. He worked the lever on the pump. Nothing. Numbers that should roll to count gallons and dollars did not move.

He tried the next pump. Still nothing. All the while the old Indian, wrapped in his blanket, studied Breen's every move but remained fixed and silent.

Finally Breen called out, "These pumps work?"

The Indian said nothing. Hard of hearing, perhaps.

"Hey. These pumps work?"

"Not for a couple of years."

A few moments of silence passed. Breen stood blank faced. He could do nothing but shake his head. He studied up on something to say, but all he came up with was a benign, "Thanks. Thanks a lot."

He returned the nozzle to its cradle. It was then he noticed the dangling hose. Not even connected to the pump.

So be it. He didn't really need gas anyway. He had enough to make it to the interstate. Due for coffee, though. Past due. So he headed inside, hoping to find a pot and hoping it worked better than the gasoline pumps.

Breen shooed a snarling, bottle green fly from his face, then swung the screen door open. He stepped in, closing the door behind him to cut down on pesky airborne critters. In the dimly lit interior, he saw no one at first. Then his eyes went to a heavy-set Indian woman wearing pink shorts and an orange sleeveless blouse, standing behind the counter to his right. The quintessence of calmness and patience. She remained still as a statue, mute as a stone, as if she hoped to blend into her

64

surroundings, go unnoticed. She almost succeeded. In contrast to her, the old Indian outside made a fiddle footed, loudmouthed kid.

A toil-burnished counter top separated Breen and the woman. At the end of the wooden planks, stood a roller of ivory-colored butcher paper. Sparse rows of canned goods and stacks of cigarette packs lined the shelves behind the counter. An old lumberyard calendar hung from a thumbtack buried in the edge of one of the shelves. The month, October. The year, 1949. A long ago proprietor must have favored the picture of the mountain lion.

The shopkeeper nodded politely, but said nothing. Except for the squeal of the screen door opening and closing, the quiet and stillness of the place held undisturbed. The woman looked more like a modeled figure in a museum diorama depicting reservation life in the 1940's than a clerk in a thriving business.

"Cup of coffee?" Breen said in a tentative voice. "Maybe?"

"No. No coffee."

The woman offered no alternative.

"Well, uh, do you have something to drink? Anything?"

"Pop."

"Good. Good. Pop's fine. Just fine."

The moment the woman handed Breen the bottle, another Indian woman entered the store. She could have been the mirror image of the first. Twins.

"How's it goin', Margie?" she said in a soft monotone voice.

"Busy. Busy. Busy."

Breen paid for the pop and, with the moist bottle in hand, he headed out the door. When he neared the truck he saw the old Indian, who'd been standing against the wall, now sitting in the front seat on the passenger side with the door closed. Ace sat next to him. Both of them stared ahead. Breen stopped in mid-stride and looked at the Indian. He raised a hand to gesture, but paused when he realized he did not know what gesture to make. He started to speak, but stopped when he realized he did not know what to say. The Indian did nothing. He sat motionless, holding his gaze to the front.

After collecting his thoughts, Breen walked to the truck and opened the passenger-side door. When he finally spoke, his tone had a sharp edge.

"You're sitting in my truck."

The old Indian did not answer.

"You're sitting in my truck," Breen repeated, with greater insistence, this time with the certainty of a man aggrieved.

"Mind giving me a ride? I know the way."

"You don't even know where I'm going."

"Only one way to go from here. Saw where you came from. Not going back that way, are you?"

"Look. I need to get going."

"In a hurry, huh? Got some place to be?"

The question took Breen by surprise. He stared into the wind buffeted distance a moment.

"No. I'm not in a hurry."

Breen sighed. He turned and looked at the turquoise building as if it might hold some answer. The wind whined around the corners. He looked around and thought about his predicament. Then, he surrendered. He closed the door, walked around the front of the truck to the driver's side, and climbed in. In recent days, he'd become more adept at accepting things he could not change. He resigned himself to the fact he had a companion, at least for a while.

Breen started the engine.

"Which way?" he said.

"Like I said, only one way."

"If there's only one way, why do I need you to show me?"

The Indian did not answer. Breen stepped on the gas. He and his new partner were on their way, according to the Indian, the only way.

66

"What's your name?" Breen said.

"Floyd. Pink Floyd."

"Why Pink Floyd?"

"Why not? That is what kids call me. Do not know why. A mystery. Much mystery in this life. I just accept it. What name you go by?"

"What name do I go by? Breen. Jack Breen."

Soon they were traveling across a vast expanse of tableland. In the distance rose the sheer, brown walls of a canyon. The wind surged. Dust augers popped up everywhere.

"A strong wind is coming," Pink Floyd said. "From the East I think. Maybe all four directions at once. It happens sometimes. Do not know for sure. But I know it is strong."

"How do you know?"

"Because I am old. Seen a lot of wind. Ninety-six years old, I figure. The ancestors used to say ninety-six winters. You know, like in movies. Now we just say ninety-six years old like everybody else."

"Don't you talk a lot for an Indian? I thought Indians were supposed to be quiet."

"Not me. Besides, if I am quiet, the wind will be my voice. And it is never still, not for long."

They encountered no other cars on the road that now turned from gravel to dirt. A great eye from above would have seen a single creature, no bigger than a bug racing across the canyon floor, leaving a cloud of sallow dust in its wake.

"Where are we going?" Breen said after a while. "Where am I taking you?"

"Down the road. Like you, I am a traveler."

"Why are you out here?"

Pink Floyd responded with his own question.

"Why are **you** here?"

Breen did not answer. He did not refuse to answer. He simply could not answer. He didn't know for sure. Once again, the Indian's question took him by surprise.

For some little time, no one spoke. And after the two newly acquainted vagabonds drove for what seemed a hundred miles and the road appeared to go nowhere, Breen became restless.

"Hey. I'm getting a little uneasy about this. Where are we going?"

"Up ahead. Almost there."

In the distance, Breen could barely make out sandstone ruins of some kind. They stood silhouetted against the sky of cobalt blue. Vague and speculative.

When they neared the ruins, Breen slowed the truck.

"What is this place?"

"Home of the ancient ones, the ancestors. Where I can hear their voices. Pull over."

Breen pulled over and stopped. The old Indian opened the door and stepped out. He closed the door and stood facing the truck. He leaned, resting forearms on the sill, put his head through the open window. He looked beyond Ace, directly at Breen.

"Come," he said in a firm voice.

The old man walked off and Breen followed him into the ruins. The wind spiked again and dust blew across the trail, erasing the old man's foot prints the instant he made them.

Breen and the Indian wandered through what remained of roofless rooms with high walls and narrow doorways. Each entrance aligned with another in enfilade. Each hallway led to another hallway. Each room opened into another room. The wind raced through and among ancient masonry walls of layered brown stones like breath through reeds of a woodwind instrument. It sang in strange tones like voices from the past.

Breen stayed on the heels of the old man, passing through a maze of long dusty corridors, stepping from narrow door to narrow door, passing from ancient chamber to ancient chamber. Each connected to the next by position and angle. None stood alone.

The old man paused in one of the rooms and looked down at the time-worn floor. He knelt and brushed away the

68

dirt with his hand and picked up a pottery shard no bigger than a half dollar. Ash gray with dark stripes painted across it. He came to his feet, studied the artifact a moment, holding it to the light. He handed it to Breen.

"Here," he said. "This was made by my ancestors, the ancient ones who lived here. Broken, but it is still here, just like them. Just like me. Just like you."

Breen held the fragment in the palm of a hand. He gave it a studious look as if to decipher some ancient riddle. Eyes fixed on the brittle clay, the world around him disappeared. All other sights and sounds retreated from his senses. And then he spoke without looking up.

"What do these markings mean?"

No answer. When he raised his eyes, the old Indian was nowhere in sight. Alone, Breen jerked his head from side to side. He wheeled completely around but saw nothing and for a moment he felt abandoned, lost in a maze of rooms and hallways. A feeling of near panic came over him. He hurried on.

After a few minutes of passing from room to room again and clambering down empty corridors, he came upon the old Indian. He found him perched on the ragged remains of a low stone wall in a corner of a room built more than a thousand years before. He sat with knees bent, drawn up, arms encircling them, fingers laced. He held his head low in the manner of a supplicant.

Breen paused when he saw him, half-startled, but relieved. The wind gasped. The Indian lifted his eyes and spoke.

"All gone now, but I can hear their cries. Their roots withered. Wind blew them away."

"Why?"

"Perhaps they had power but not strength, riches but not wealth. Knowledge but not wisdom."

Breen stood expressionless and silent.

The Indian stepped down from the wall. He squatted stiffly and scooped up a handful of dust. He let it issue from his hand, cascading like a waterfall, thinning as it fell, scattering in the wind. He spoke a few words in an unrecognizable tongue, then rose. He looked into Breen's eyes.

"I told the Creator you were lost. Asked him to bless you and to help you find your way. Asked him to send a strong wind."

"I'm afraid it'll take more than that."

Just then a shrill avian cry penetrated the drone of wind. Breen turned and looked up. High on a ruinous wall above him stood a raven, large, black as night, staring right at him.

The bird cried out again in a loud, alien voice. The jarring sound so startled Breen he lost his balance and fell backward. He sat down hard on the ground and his head snapped rearward, struck the tattered edge of a wall. Looking up, the sky began to spin. Splotchy white clouds rotated with increasing speed, elongating, thinning, finally stretching into lines. The lines lengthened, then evolved into circles. Circles spun faster and faster until they formed a tight cone. Breen felt himself being sucked into it, falling toward the spinning vortex, spiraling, winding through a tunnel, farther and farther away from the sky, away from the clouds, away from the light of day. He saw the Indian's face on his descent. He could make out nothing else as if all light of the sun zeroed in on one spot, the old man's face. He tried to call out, but he had no voice. He tried to raise his arms, but the leaden appendages would not move. He was falling. Falling. Falling. The Indian's face became small. Light faded, grew dim. And then it disappeared altogether. Darkness.

In the course of immeasurable time, Breen felt his body lighten. He felt himself levitate and pull away from the darkness. Only then did he realize the empty void had distinct boundaries. The boundaries formed a great black eye, a Raven's eye. He continued to rise. He drew away from the eye, then saw the raven itself. And finally light, merciful light. A sprawling sky of visible blue. Cottony clouds.

70

Breen awoke. He built himself to his feet and a sharp pain drew his hand to his head. He felt a goose egg swelling. He looked around. No sign of the old Indian. Suddenly, feeling more alone and abandoned than ever, Breen dashed out of the room and into the hall. Still no sign of Pink Floyd, not even a dusty footprint.

He called out, "Floyd. Pink Floyd."

No answer. Only the echo of his own voice. And the wind.

Breen hurried down vacant passageways, retracing his steps as best he could remember them. He searched room after room without success. Alone once again in a strange, unfamiliar place, a haunting place.

He continued on. After a while, he located Pink Floyd seated on the ground leaning against a wall, legs extended, hands resting on his lap, open to the heavens. The old man stared at the sky. When Breen entered the room, the wind stilled. The ruins became strangely quiet.

"Hey," Breen said. "What happened? I must have knocked myself out. Where'd you go?"

The Indian did not answer. Breen rubbed his head again and grimaced.

"Come on. If you're going with me, let's go."

The Indian still said nothing. Did not move. He just looked up, eyes fixed in a skyward stare. Breen stood over him.

"Floyd," he said. "Pink Floyd."

No answer. The Indian remained flawlessly still. Breen squatted at the old man's side. He studied his face. Dull. Listless. No sign of life. Eyes opaque. He put a hand on Pink Floyd's chest. No rise or fall. The man was dead.

Breen lowered himself to his knees. He lifted a hand to Pink Floyd's face and gently sealed the lids of his eyes. He slumped for a while without moving, then scooped up a handful of dirt from the floor. He studied it a moment in his palm. He closed his hand and turned it, letting the dirt stream out.

And then Jack Breen rose and walked away. At the truck, he paused and looked all around. He saw no one, not one living thing. Only ancient ruins, swirling dust. He got into the truck and drove away.

The wind rose. Out of the east, once again. Anything not tied down was going west.

# CHAPTER 7 - THE GREAT DIVIDE

Without knowing it, Jack Breen crossed the Continental Divide. Though it is called the "Great Divide," it showed no trace of greatness in the back country of New Mexico. Not so much as a rusty old highway sign riddled with bullet holes marked its location. But the Divide did have great importance, whether Breen knew it or not. From its high ground, river systems of the entire continent flow in opposite directions, water always seeking water, rivers on a quest for greater rivers, then the ocean. Like one of the lesser tributaries, the forces of nature called Jack Breen west.

As told by the sheriff, in time Breen struck Highway 666. There, he turned south and made his way to the interstate. West of the New Mexico-Arizona line the land took on a different look again. High arid plains became hills, then mountains. Temperatures cooled. Low piñon pines yielded to Ponderosa Pine and other conifers. The predominant color of the landscape turned from brown to green.

Next morning, Breen sat down for breakfast in a booth at a Flagstaff truck stop called "The J Bar J." When he slid onto the red vinyl seat, he noticed a folded newspaper lying at the end of the table, apparently left there by his predecessor. He had not seen a paper for nearly a week and it served as a frank reminder the world marched on despite his absence from it. News of the day was sufficient to fill the pages of the local rag even though he knew nothing of it.

Breen spread the paper on the table. But before he could read even a headline, a pasty-faced waitress with bright red lips and a pink and white uniform appeared. She brandished a coffee pot.

"Gonna have some?" she said.

"Why not?"

"Black?"

"Sure."

The waitress with the ghostly hue poured the coffee into a cream colored crockery mug. Steam rose from the brim.

"What else, Honey?"

Honey. Breen had to smile.

"What are you grinnin' at?"

"Just that it's been a while since anybody called me *Honey*."

"Well, Honey," she said, emphasizing the amusing moniker, "what else you gonna have?"

Breen reached for the menu resting against the wall at the end of the table.

"What's good?"

"It's all good, Honey. Just gotta look at it the right way. How about a short stack and a side of bacon?"

"Why not?"

The heavily powdered waitress spun on her heels, and Breen traded the menu for the newspaper. Before he read a word, his eyes went to a man sitting alone in a booth nearby. He had to be Breen's age, maybe older. Modestly dressed in jeans and an olive drab army field jacket. What appeared to be about a three day growth of beard stubbled his face. Holding a coffee cup like Breen's, the man studied the dregs of the dark

74

drink and the grounds swirling in them as if he were a sorcerer divining the future from the entrails of a slaughtered beast.

The man offered a grave appearance. He must have been possessed of a great sorrow. He cried bitterly. Cheeks glistened with tears. He talked to himself, argued. Mouthed words silently, sometimes angrily, often with great conviction. Between phrases or sentences he buried his face in his hands, elbows resting on the table. With each torrent of tears his body jerked.

The crying man reminded Breen he was not the only person in the world whose life had been shattered. Others faced ruin, too. The sight of the man spoke a fundamental truth. What all men share most with each other is their pain, their sense of loss, their suffering. The common thread that runs through all lives, prominent and obscure, rich and poor, powerful and weak. Breen could not help wondering about the source of this man's sorrow.

The crying man wiped his eyes and tried to catch his breath. His body shuddered. Breen started to speak, to offer a word of comfort, but he hesitated, caught in the grip of a second guess. Kind words he might have spoken died in his throat and, before he made a sound, the crying man took his leave. Breen remained on the outside, a mere observer. He could only wonder about the forlorn stranger's plight. He would share this man's grief anonymously and from a distance.

For this and a surfeit of other sins, Jack Breen judged himself harshly. Once again, a familiar doubt returned. It struck him like a bolt of lightning that he would make a fool of himself with this crazy notion of seeking out Claire. *Good Lord. After all this time, how can I simply show up at her door? What do I say? Hi. Just thought I'd drop by after nearly twenty years. No hard feelings over that broken engagement.*

No. He had done quite enough to make a fool of himself lately. More than a full dose of humiliation. Time for reality to set in. He made up his mind that when he got behind the wheel again he'd be heading east, back to Boston. Time to start reconstructing his life.

Outside, Breen heard a dull crack that struck hard and quickly receded, leaving a slight echo. *The report of a gun*, he thought. He looked up, but seeing nothing, he lowered his eyes to the newspaper again. He had no real interest in the news, but staring at printed words gave him a way to look busy.

From the corner of an eye, he noticed restaurant customers rising by ones and twos, and congregating at the front window. Soon, a small covey of people collected there. A bustle of activity. Breen paid it little mind. He finished his breakfast, and at the cash register, he presented his check to the waitress. Preoccupied, she looked outside above shoulders, strained for a line of sight over the crowd and through the front glass.

"What's going on out there?" Breen said.

"Some guy just shot himself in the parking lot. That guy sitting over there crying. Weird dude. I knew it."

Breen looked outside. A clear but impervious glass pane separated him from events taking place on the far side.

"Here you go, Hon," the waitress said, handing him his change. "Damn shame, ain't it?"

Breen walked outside and waded into the small crowd gathered around a car. He saw in the front seat the man who'd been racked with sorrow. His head lolled against the headrest, turned toward the driver's door. Eyes drooped. Pupilless black disks centered on milky sclera. They stared blankly. A splatter of blood on the headliner and the side window. Revolver in the man's lap. Acrid smell of gunsmoke in the air.

*I should have said something*, Breen thought. *Should have offered to help. A kind look. A word of encouragement. Something.*

Breen turned and made his way to the truck. No choice now but to move on, put some distance between himself and the death scene. But then he paused and looked over his shoulder at the suicide car where people stood, gawking, pointing, covering mouths with hands as if the horror of a self-inflicted death might spread if they put words to it. A chill went

76

through him, a response perhaps to the cool form of a ghost brushing by. In an instant, Jack Breen knew what he had to do. He was not going east, after all. No. He was going south, to Claire.

*****

All day on the road to the San Rafael, doubt haunted Jack Breen's thoughts. Too much time to think. Too much time for cowardice. With the passing of each mile, Breen asked himself again and again what the hell he was doing. He had not been certain of anything since he left Boston. *Going to the San Rafael?* He had a thousand reasons to do it, but they were all entwined and entangled in an intricate cobweb of confusion. He had just as many good reasons not to go. But he had no real answer to the question that dogged him, *What the hell am I doing?*

In the late afternoon, Breen rolled into the town of Victoria, a sleepy berg of no more than three thousand souls at the edge of the Coronado National Forest. A bank and a café. Post office, small hospital, courthouse. Wisp of a town.

At a gas station, Jack filled up and asked the young Mexican man behind the counter for directions to the Gaynor ranch. Not far. In no more than a half hour, he'd be there.

Jack headed east out of town. Right on time, according to the young man's directions, he turned off the main road and onto a winding blacktop with a worn surface and no center line. After a while, the road turned to gravel. He rounded a bend and followed the road into a lush, green valley. After another mile, he passed a rocky promontory with a lone pine tree standing sentinel at its top. The road curved around the rocks, then led to a broad meadow. There, amidst a stand of tall sycamore trees and in the shadow of gathering hills, stood the house. Headquarters of Raven Ranch. It looked exactly as it did more than a decade and a half earlier. Much in the world had changed over those years, but not this place. And now it showed it not only had the power to remain constant, it had the power to bring Jack Breen back.

The house was a two story wood frame structure, green with white trim. A small square window barely large enough to frame a child's face marked the location of the attic just beneath the roof ridge. In front, a broad porch hosted two white rocking chairs. At the end of the house, a gray stone chimney ascended all the way to the highest gable and beyond.

Following the road into the valley, Breen passed a herd of cattle, maybe as many as a hundred head, mostly black, grazing in the pasture before the house. Spring came early this year and green grass stood almost knee-high in places. Just beyond the pasture and at the edge of a grove of pine trees, sprawled a clear water pond. From a distance, the darkness of a raven's wing suffused the water's surface. It appeared to shimmer even in the fading light of late afternoon.

Jack drove up to the house and stopped. For a moment he left the engine running, allowing himself to contemplate the possibility of a quick escape. Ace came to his feet in the seat beside him, alert to new sights and smells. At first, no sign of life. All quiet. Then Jack noticed an old black man sitting on a bench in front and to the side of the house. Looking more like a mere inference of a man than the real thing, he busied himself whittling, carefully forcing the blade of a Barlow knife through a stick, peeling up layer after layer. Thin, curled shavings accumulated in a pile at his feet. A scrawny bird dog with sagging cheeks lay next to him. Neither dog nor man looked up. No one noticed the arrival of a stranger.

Jack stepped out of the truck. Ace quit the seat where he rode shotgun and stood at his side. At the sound of the closing door, the bird dog sprang to his feet and trained curious eyes on the canine intruder. A low growl rumbled deep within him, then within Ace.

"Quiet," Jack said. "Stay."

Ace obeyed. Jack moved with indefinite steps toward the house. The wizened old jasper on the bench suspended his whittling, and spat. He raised himself proudly. He shifted his

78

weight from side to side until he had it evenly distributed for maximum stability. In a strong but grizzled voice, he spoke as if a census taker had come to call.

"My name is Fountain Hughes. One hundred and one years old, I figger. Folks 'round here call me Uncle Fountain."

Uncle Fountain. Now dwindled down to a frayed whipcord of a man. Long, thin body like a shadow of late afternoon. More than a century of living robbed his muscles of tone and mass. Liquid eyes lay deep in their sockets. Skin hung loose on his bony frame like a wet rag. He wore red suspenders and a belt to hold up his britches. On his head, cocked at a rakish angle, rested a brown hat with an open crown and a narrow brim barely the width of three fingers. A turkey feather ornamented the band.

"My granddaddy was a slave," Uncle Fountain said. "Somebody owned him. Don't nobody own me. I work for Miss Claire. In the house yonder, I spect."

Jack offered his hand and the old man took it. Jack could feel every bone covered by leathery hide.

"Not much of me left," Uncle Fountain said. "Gettin' on down to nothin', I reckon. But I don't mind much. Way I see it, every day above ground is a gift from God. By rights, I oughta be on the wrong side of the dirt right now."

"Good to see you, Uncle Fountain. I'm Jack Breen." The old man held Jack's hand firmly. He squinted his tired eyes and leaned into Jack's face. "Do I know you?"

"We met once, long time ago."

"Well, I'll swan. Thought so. Never forget a face, you know."

Jack turned toward the house and took a few steps. He paused in the front yard, hesitating to go forward, uncertain what he should say when Claire appeared. He verged on losing his nerve. He almost made up his mind to turn for the truck, but the screen door whined open and drew his attention. A woman stepped slowly into the open doorway, then onto the porch. Claire.

79

She took another step, then paused. She raised a hand as if to shield her eyes from the sun, though the late afternoon light had already dimmed. She took another step and paused. Utter silence followed. All motion stopped. A distinct but immeasurable interval of time fell between two precise points, the moment before Jack Breen and the moment after. In that interlude, so brief it has no name, hearts did not beat and the earth did not turn on its axis. Within that hairline crack in the everlasting course of events, Claire came to understand she was looking at the face of her long ago beloved. In the bitter sweet aftermath of that understanding, the wind sighed.

Claire's hair fell almost to her shoulders. An unruly strand rustled in the breeze beside her cheek. She swept it away with a graceful but firm movement of a hand. Reading glasses hung around her neck by a braided leather strap. She wore a blue chambray dress and over it a coarsely woven shawl-collared sweater of brown and green wool. On her feet, once adorned with the delicate, black shoes of a cellist, she wore the boots of a ranch woman, a woman with hard work to do. On her face, a touch of make up, at most a little lipstick, something to give her cheeks a hint of color. She was, if she were to be described with a single word, woefully inadequate though it be, beautiful.

Claire quietly studied the man standing in her yard. Without so much as a moment's premeditation, and with the honesty of the involuntary reaction of a muscle to an electrical stimulus, a smile formed on her face. By instinct, Jack's face responded in kind. But Claire's smile faltered. In an instant, the cautious and wary nature acquired through experience swept it away. Jack's smile dissolved in like manner.

For the longest time, no one spoke. For Jack, not a strategic reticence. But an irresistible silence. One of the few times in his life when he did not know what to say. He could not find words to express his feelings. He did not even know for sure what he was feeling. Uncertainty, perhaps mercifully, struck him mute.

Claire moved cautiously across the porch and halted at its edge. She descended each of the five steps without lifting

80

her eyes from Jack, without making a sound. She walked toward him and stopped squarely in front of him. She layered one half of the sweater over the other and wrapped her arms around her body as if to insulate herself against a rising wind. She smiled again, this time only graciously. A guarded expression, not spontaneous like the first. Then, in the benign voice she might use to greet an insurance salesman, she spoke.

"Hello, Jack."

"Hi."

Doubt gave the encounter a hard edge. Masked now with a wary look brought on by the sharpness of the moment, Uncle Fountain eased himself toward the awe-struck former lovers standing barely an arm's length apart. Claire took another step.

"It's all right, Uncle Fountain. I know him."

Claire did not move her eyes from Jack.

"What brings you here?" she said.

The question went deep. It penetrated every layer of the man right down to the heart of him. Strangely, it caught him by surprise. He could not speak, could not make a sound. He had no answer. He drove more than two thousand miles and now he could not say why. He heard what was perhaps the most important question he'd ever been asked. The answer he would give would be perhaps the most important answer he would ever give. And he could offer nothing but silence. Utter silence.

Finally, one word came to Jack Breen, only one word. But when it came, it came with conviction. Not a trace of doubt in it, not the slightest suggestion of ambivalence. The truest word Jack Breen had ever spoken, or ever would speak.

"You," he said. That was the one word. In answer to the question "What brings you here?" he said simply, "You."

# CHAPTER 8 - HIGHER GROUND

Ensconced in white porch rockers, Jack and Claire talked long into the night. At first, they kept the talk small. "Nice to see you. How have you been?" Conversation better suited to a chance encounter between casual acquaintances. But the passing of hours brought greater ease and finally abandon. They lingered only briefly in the penumbra of truth, a place with neither full light nor full dark, a place of half-truths and half-lies but whole regrets. Little by little they worked their way toward honesty, quartering at first, but finally coming at it head-on.

"I have to admit I'm more than a little surprised to see you," Claire said. "Especially here."

Jack said nothing, made no expression.

Claire would not be shy.

"You broke my heart, you know. I was a long time getting over it. But I did get over it. And I swore I'd never let it happen again. It hasn't. It won't."

Like a serrated steel blade, the truth ripped through Jack's heart. He dropped his gaze, looked away. After a few moments, he spoke in a soft, apologetic voice.

"Wouldn't blame you if you ran me off the place at gunpoint. I'd say I'm sorry if I thought it would do any good."

"You could start with that."

"Well, I am sorry. More than I can say. Truly sorry. For a lot of things."

"I won't run you off," Claire said. "But if you're looking for some kind of absolution, better brace yourself for a disappointment."

But in time they blunted the bitterness of the past with candor. Words began to flow smoothly from each of them like waters pouring over the Great Divide.

"So tell me about yourself," Claire said.

"Not much to tell really. Kind of burned out, I guess. Working too hard for too long. Just thought I'd see some of the country."

Claire smiled cautiously, nodded. Jack shifted in his chair, betraying a vague uneasiness.

"Ended up in Arizona," he said. "Then I thought why not go by to see Claire. That's about it."

Before he could stop himself, Jack told Claire the same implausible story he considered earlier and rejected outright. Claire maintained a gracious countenance, but kept her guard up. Less at ease, Jack held his hands in his lap and kneaded his fingers. Suddenly, the movement of his hands stopped. He lowered his head and passed a hand over his hair. He put the same hand to his chin and sighed.

"No. That's not quite right. That's not it at all really. I . . . I got into some trouble. Took some money that wasn't mine. Paid it back. Always intended to. I called it a loan. That's what it was, really. But it was wrong. They suspended my license. Guess I'm lucky I didn't go to prison. So . . . there you have it, the real Jack Breen, warts and all."

Jack's feeble attempt at putting a good spin on recent events failed, sacrificed on the altar of veracity. From that moment on, Claire and Jack enfolded themselves in the surprisingly comfortable darkness of this night as if it were a favorite blanket. They reminisced and caught up. They filled in the blanks of the last seventeen years, tiptoeing, then gliding through an improbable reunion.

Jack told Claire about his law practice, its meteoric rise, precipitous fall. He told her the details of his suspension. Told her about Carolyn, that she was suing him for divorce, that in their childless home solitary footsteps echoed down empty halls. He told the truth, not by calculation, not for sympathy. He had no expectation of forgiveness or acceptance. He told the truth because he simply had no choice. He could not resist its allure. It poured out of him unchecked and uncontrolled, remarkable for a man who built his life on the unsteady ground of artful words, sentences carefully constructed not to lie but to conceal the truth, to shade and obscure it, shape it.

"More than just a run of bad luck," he said. "I blew it big time. No other way to put it. Wish there were. But there isn't. Never would have suspected that of myself."

Jack sat with hands in his lap, fingers laced. He studied his thumbs a while. And then he stared into the darkness sprawling just beyond the reach of living room lights that spilled out onto the porch.

"It all came unraveled," he said. "Guess it had to eventually. But you know, that's the one thing I'm not sorry about. Not anymore."

"Maybe it was meant to be," Claire said.

"Don't know."

"Some things are."

"Yeah. Some things are. At least some things are inevitable."

Jack did not hold back much. But he did hold back some. He never mentioned there was a loose end in Boston, one final transgression that had yet to be discovered. A reckoning yet to come.

84

Claire talked about her family, mostly about her father. Jim Gaynor, the last lion of the ranching clan. For over a hundred years, Gaynors worked the same spread. Like a witness tree used for reference by a surveyor, family tradition stood as the one true thing from which a Gaynor could take his bearings. For each generation, the tree added a ring to its trunk. Roots ran deeper into the ground. Branches rose higher, until they became vulnerable to the torment of gravity. What makes a tree great when winds are calm can topple it in a storm.

"How did you end up back home?" Jack said.

"I was married for a while, about ten years. But he didn't want the same things I wanted. And he didn't understand the part about forsaking all others. It went bad. So, I got up one day and packed my bags, headed west. Decided to cut my losses."

She gave up a low chuckle, shook her head.

"I've had enough of men. I'm well past trusting them."

Jack sat expressionless. Claire continued.

"Mom died not long after I got here. A few months later, Tom. Remember my brother Tom?"

"Sure."

"Horse fell with him. Crushed his chest."

"Sorry," Jack said.

"All that really took it out of Dad. Broke him. He'd be the first to admit he'd pretty well run out his string. Threatened to sell the ranch, burn the house. One day he complained of a bad headache. Raised a hand to his forehead, then he fell to the floor. Just sort of crumbled. Hasn't spoken a word since. Now he just sits in a chair in his room in the Victoria Old Folks Home. Stares. That's all."

"You've had a rough time," Jack said.

Claire shrugged.

"No more than most, really. The only good thing to come out of the last seventeen years is Molly. My daughter."

Jack brightened.

"You have a child?"

"I have her.  And I have this land.  That's all."

"Sounds like a lot."

Claire nodded.

"Otherwise, what I've got is trouble.  Big trouble."

Claire described herself as a woman under siege.  She told Jack about her war with developers and bankers, lawyers.  All of them sniffing at her ankles like predators.  What she had, they wanted.  Land.  Now, she held a century of tradition in her hands.  She was on her own.  God willing, she would not be the final chapter in the family history.

"Like all ranchers we're cash poor but land rich," she said.  "We don't have any money.  When Dad dies, I won't be able to pay the taxes on the place.  Death taxes.  I guess the politicians and the bureaucrats don't want me to have this place.  It's like they want to punish us for being ranchers.  They hate us for trying to preserve a tradition.  And I hate them."

By and by, the ice around Claire's heart melted.  With swimming eyes, she described the small army of dedicated warriors standing with her in the struggle.  Uncle Fountain, the old man who'd been a fixture on the ranch since before Claire was born.  He lived in a camper trailer nestled in a grove of sycamore trees not far from the main house.  These days, he did little more than spit and whittle, worry about Claire.  Jayro Paz, ranch foreman, Claire's strong right arm.  Jayro's wife Maria helped Claire around the house.  The Paz family lived in the pond house, a stone's throw from the main house.  Like Uncle Fountain, they worked for found and a small share of the year's profits when there were any.  Not often.

"Kind of a rag tag bunch," Claire said.  "Not blood kin.  But family.  I love them all."

She explained that developers were wearing out a path to her door with lucrative offers.  Circling like vultures, they could not wait to turn Raven Ranch into a golf course.  They even wanted to use the name for their development.  "Raven Ranch," they liked the sound of it.  They had visions of a club house and a pro shop on the high ground where the house stood.  Beautiful.  They could just see it.

"There's a local guy," Claire said. "A thorn in my father's side for a long time. Mine, too. Says he's in love with me. Wants to marry me."

She looked off into the darkness and sighed.

"Lucien Porter. Maybe I will marry him. Probably should. He may get the place, if I don't. Says Dad gave him a mortgage. It's a lie. Signature's forged."

Claire shook her head in anger and disgust.

"He's tied in with some big shots out of Phoenix. God knows where else. Wants to be a big shot himself. Just waiting for Dad to die. Thinks when he does I'll have to sell. Maybe he's right."

"There ought to be a way out," Jack said.

"Could've been. Dad could have sold the development rights to the Ranchers Association. Could have granted it a conservation easement, prevented development that way. Not now. He's not mentally competent."

"Have yourself appointed guardian."

"I have. Now I have to get court approval to sell the development rights. I'm afraid our local judge won't go along with that."

"Why not?" Jack said. "Why would he care?"

"Crooked. That's why. Crooked as a dog's hind leg."

Claire raised a hand and rubbed the tips of her first two fingers rapidly against her thumb.

"Money. Ruined many a good man."

"No doubt about that," Jack said.

"So you see, I don't need a lawyer. I need an army of lawyers. What I have is Jaime Passamonte."

Jaime Passamonte. A young Mexican kid fresh out of law school. He took night classes at a small college in Phoenix while he worked days at a dude ranch near Gold Canyon. An orphan kid and a would-be revolutionary, he grew up with a chip on his shoulder and a nervous manner. Mad at the world. Genuine bad attitude. Hothead. But short on nerve. Sort of a fraidy cat.

Passamonte had long black hair that he gathered in a ponytail with a rubber band, usually green. He wore jeans with a tan corduroy jacket on the rare occasions he went to court. He had good intentions, but he couldn't help being green as his rubber band. According to some of his most vocal critics, he couldn't find his ass with both hands. No Harvard man, but cheap and eager. That's what drew Claire to him. He gladly took her on as a client. Didn't really have much choice. He needed the work and he agreed to wait for better times to be paid. Nothing unusual for him. He only had a handful of clients, all of them dead broke.

About the time Claire finished her description of Jaime Passamonte, the screen door leading from porch to living room squeaked open. A little girl with long honey-colored hair and wearing a blue flannel nightgown appeared in the doorway. Barefoot, she tiptoed toward her mother.

Feigning outrage, the little girl spoke with elongated pronunciation.

"Mama, where have you been? I've been waiting."

Claire leaned forward in her chair, opening her arms to the child. Her face brightened, tone softened.

"Come here, baby. Come on."

The child raced to her mother, smiling, and leaped into her lap. Claire encircled her with her arms, held her close. She kissed her on the cheek, rubbed her bare feet to warm them.

"This is Molly," Claire said. "She'll have a birthday soon. Coming six years old. Molly, this is an old friend of Mama's. His name is Jack."

Jack smiled. He leaned forward, halting the movement of his rocker.

"Hi, Molly."

The child frowned, looked away. She buried her face in her mother's shoulder, peeking out with suspicion from the corner of an eye.

Maria Paz, a full-bosomed Mexican woman with gray-streaked hair bound in a bun, apron tied around her waist, appeared. She held the screen door open. Claire stood Molly on the porch before her and put her hands to her shoulders.

"I'll be in soon," she said. "Go on with Maria. Say good night now."

Molly hurried to Maria, but ignored the stranger on the porch. The matronly Mexican took the child by the hand and led her inside. Claire rose. Jack came to his feet in courteous response.

"I don't think she cares much for me," Jack said.

"She's just shy. I need to put her down. Be right back."

The end of a long day neared. Jack put hands on hips and arched his back. He yawned and stepped to the edge of the porch, folding his arms, resting his chin in the crook of a hand. He gazed up at the moon, rising above the outline of a near peak. Full and round, bright enough to read the fine print of a newspaper. Nothing like the moon in Boston when he took time to notice it.

Jack stared off into the wide circling dark. Ahead and to his right, he sensed movement. He turned his head sharply toward it. In the blank night, he could make out a vague figure, featureless, indistinct. He smelled the aroma of pipe smoke, saw a red glow. Like a city kid on alert for muggers, he lowered his arms and stood silently. Details built and the imprecise shape became a silhouette, the silhouette became a man, and the man came closer.

"Who is it?" Jack said. "Who's there?"

"Oh, just me. Just old Uncle Fountain."

Jack chuckled.

"You startled me."

"Well now, don't mean to be spookin' nobody."

Uncle Fountain moved toward Jack, a well worn pipe in the corner of his mouth, crooked ribbon of smoke rising lazily from the pipe's smoldering bowl. He wore his trademark brown hat bejeweled with a turkey feather, brim swept low in front. The man also wore a knowing smile, tight-lipped, circumspect.

Uncle Fountain rested a booted foot on the lowest of the series of steps rising to the porch. He leaned. Steadied his pipe in his mouth with a hand.

"Gonna get a little chilly," he said.

Jack nodded, folded his arms. Held them tight against his chest.

"Been studyin' on it," Uncle Fountain said. "Member you pretty good now. Strutter. Yessir. You was in tall cotton in them days. Proud as a peacock. 'Member them days after you was here that time, too. Years ago they was. Dark days, sho nuff. 'Member 'em like they was yesterday."

The expression faded from Jack's face. He lowered his hands and buried them in his pockets. He wilted. Suddenly impassive, he had a strong sensation of a yoke of chain mail bearing down on his shoulders. A cloud moved in front of the moon.

"Whatchoo you want?" Uncle Fountain said, voice hardening. "Whatchoo doin' here?"

The directness of the question and the accusatory tone stunned Jack Breen. Left him feeling small and weak. He tried to fashion an answer.

"I . . . I'm not here for anything. I mean . . . I don't know why I'm here. I mean –"

The old man didn't let him finish.

"Not here for nothin'. Well, I declare."

Uncle Fountain leveled a stern gaze at him. Nodded to himself.

"I be watchin' you. I be watchin' you."

The old man turned to walk away. When his blackness disappeared in the darkness of night, Jack heard him say, "Um huh. I declare. I declare."

Seconds later, Claire returned to the porch. Jack hardly noticed her, still transfixed by the brief but powerful encounter with Uncle Fountain.

"Molly's down," she said.

90

Jack did not speak. He didn't acknowledge Claire at all. He just stared, unseeing, into the lightless distance. He did not move.

Claire put a hand to his arm. In the night sky, clouds shifted and unveiled the moon. It shone bright again.

"Jack," Claire said. "Jack."

"Sorry. I was just mesmerized by that moon."

Claire kept her hand on Jack's arm and gave it a gentle tug. She lowered herself to the topmost step, and Jack sat at her side.

"Molly's beautiful," he said. "She looks like you."

Claire smiled. For a few moments, no one spoke.

"You love her very much," Jack said. "I can tell. I mean, of course, you love her. But more than that. You really love her."

"She's everything to me. She makes the struggle worthwhile. I wouldn't change a thing about the past. If I did, I wouldn't have her."

Jack could see in Claire's face and hear in her voice a purity of unselfish purpose he never experienced. This woman was where she was meant to be. Doing what she was meant to do. He saw in her a toughness that equaled her gentleness. She had not lost the tenderness that drew him to her the first time he saw her. She refined it. She had not become less of the woman he fell in love with years before. She had become more.

"It's late," Claire said.

Jack nodded.

"Right. I should be going."

Jack and Claire rose in an almost perfectly synchronous movement. They took a few steps and stopped. Claire spoke.

"Tomorrow night there's a meeting of the Ranchers Association. You can come if you're still here. We can always use a lawyer, especially one willing to work cheap."

"Suspended lawyer," Jack said.

"That, too. They're very cheap."

Jack turned and looked into the shadows where Uncle Fountain stood moments before.

"I don't know," he said. "I don't know. I'm not sure."

"Well, anyway. If nothing else, we had a nice visit."

Claire extended a hand. Jack accepted it and a sort of handshake followed, a long, lingering union of flesh. Even in the dim light of the moon Jack's eyes went to Claire's and the long lost soulmates looked deeply, penetratingly, into each other. For Jack, the feel of Claire's hand in the hollow of his own struck a familiar chord. Gentle. Comfortable. He held it even after he began to pull away.

Claire inclined her head, raised her eyebrows.

"You going to take that with you?"

"Oh, sorry."

Jack released her hand like an awkward, adolescent suitor.

The separation of Claire's flesh from his left Jack with a sudden hunger and an imprecise longing, a vague desire that would not soon leave him.

"So maybe I'll see you tomorrow," Claire said.

"Maybe tomorrow then."

"Tomorrow."

"Tomorrow."

Jack nodded and moved toward the truck with uncertain steps. He halted and turned, squaring himself to Claire. What he saw took his breath away. Standing in front of the door, the backlight from the living room darkened her features, but illuminated her edges so individual strands of hair could be seen.

After studying her in silence for a moment, Jack turned to go. He took one step, but stopped again. He wheeled about slowly.

"Claire," he said.

He spoke her name as if he were about to make an important announcement, as if he'd left something essential unsaid. But then he pulled up short and thought better of it. Caution set in.

"Thank you," he said in a low voice.

"Thank you for what?"

"Thank you for . . ."

He stumbled, uncertain of his next word.  Tried to lighten the moment.

"Thank you for the hospitality of your rocking chair."

Claire smiled.

"You're welcome."

Later, driving into town to find a place to spend the night, Jack studied his hand, the place where Claire's skin touched his.  He searched it as if he might see an imprint like the one left in a mattress after a night's sleep.  He raised it to his face, hoping he might catch her scent.  He pressed his palm to his cheek.  He lowered his hand and closed his fingers, gripped them as if the feel of Claire's hand might still reside there.  For the first time in a long time, he allowed himself to dream.

## CHAPTER 9 – A RUMOR OF RANGE WAR

Jack passed a tolerable night at the Starlite Motel in Victoria. Despite a lumpy mattress that reached only to his ankles, he had his first good night's sleep in weeks. He spent most of the day following on his back. The rest helped him work up the courage to accept Claire's invitation to join her at the meeting of the Ranchers Association the next evening. Finally, the appointed hour came.

Beneath the twilight arch, a remuda of pickups stood picketed in a row against the curb outside the Victoria High School auditorium. To Jack, they called to mind horses drowsing at a hitching post. No late model vehicles, nothing fancy, except one. A shiny new Suburban belonging to Lucien Porter, the would-be tycoon bent on marrying Claire Gaynor and making a name for himself in real estate. This night, the meeting of the Association drew an especially large crowd. Emotions ran high. Everyone in the room had his blood up.

Claire helped form the Association a year earlier. Its purpose was to acquire development rights from property

94

owners in danger of going under and selling out after generations of a ranching heritage. A land trust would acquire a conservation easement on the land by sale or donation and protect it from development forever. The encumbrance would lower the value of the property, make taxes affordable, help the family stay on the home place.

The crowd, some thirty odd people, was already gathering when Jack Breen entered the auditorium. A dull roar rose from a chorus of discordant voices engaged in disconnected conversations. Mostly in their sixties and beyond, the men wore jeans and boots. Hair generally thin and gray. The head of every man bore the subtle imprint of the sweatband of a broad-brimmed hat that now rested in his lap. To a man, ruddy cheeked, faces harrowed by weather and wind. Across each forehead lay a distinct horizontal line distinguishing shaded pale skin above from red sear of sun below. Women wore plain cotton dresses and practical hairdos. Working people, all. Salt of the earth. Like the Gaynors, families of most of them had been ranchers for generations. Claire stood at the front of the crowd. Engaged in a conversation with a handful of brethren, she held a sheaf of papers. Off and on, she pointed to important words, knitted her brow. Members of her small but attentive audience nodded from time to time.

Jack took a seat in the last row, well away from the people and the action. Slouching low, he hoped to be a fly on the wall. Several rows to his front, sat a man duded up in a polyester suit. In this crowd, he looked as out of place as a vicar at a cock fight. Now and then, he whispered something to himself. He shook his head and his body jerked with suppressed laughter or annoyance.

Claire ended her conversation with the small group in front and turned toward the crowd. She scanned the faces, then consulted her watch and stepped forward. She raised a hand and held it toward the crowd open-palmed, pushed against the air to call for quiet.

"All right, everybody. Let's go ahead and get started."

Sitting cheek by jowl, besieged ranchers fell still and attentive.

"I think you know why we're here," Claire said. "I want to tell you what's going on with the Ranchers Association. I want to tell you what it does and why we need it."

A man on the front row stood.

"We need it 'cause we're all gonna lose our land if we don't have it."

Unmistakable anger in his voice.

"That's right," Claire said. "Like many of you, my family has been ranching in this valley for four generations. That's all we ever wanted to do. Couldn't imagine being anything but ranchers. We never expected to get rich. Ranchers don't want to be rich. They want to be ranchers."

Heads nodded. A low rumble of affirming voices swept across the assemblage like an incoming tide. People shifted in their seats, leaned forward.

"We're in a war," Claire continued. "There are people out there that don't want us to be ranchers. They seem to think we're bad for the world, bad for the land. But ranching keeps the land in balance. Keeps it productive, actively engaged. Ranching is good for the land. God created the land for us to use. We're not outside the environment. We're part of it."

Bud Taylor, a man skinny as a fence rail, with caved-in cheeks, put up a hand and stood. Claire nodded in his direction.

"We're sellin' out or dyin' off," he said. "Y'all know Nyle Kent. He sold out. Chic Coleman, too. Both gone. Families been ranchin' for damn near a hundred years. Just gone. Sold out to a sumbitch from Phoenix. Probably gonna build a damn golf course. Put up a hotel."

At his side, the old man's wife grimaced at her husband's indelicate language. Raised a hand to stay the flow of it. She tugged at his sleeve and hauled him to his seat. Claire followed up.

"In normal times no rancher would think about cutting his land up into small pieces and selling it to developers. But these aren't normal times. Cattle prices down. Expenses high

96

as a cat's back. A lot of us going broke. We're in the middle of a serious drought. BLM pulling grazing permits every day. Developers out there offering more money than we could make in a lifetime."

A woman with large gray-framed glasses and salt and pepper hair cropped close to her head jumped to her feet.

"Ranchers don't want money," she said. "If we wanted to get rich we never would have been ranchers in the first place. We love the land the way it is, wide open and beautiful. This is our way of life."

A groan of agreement rose up. Claire spoke again. Her voice trembled with emotion.

"Like Bud said, we're dying off. Not just here but all across the West. Did you know the average rancher today is about sixty years old? Turn around. Look at yourselves."

Heads turned. The small army of besieged stockmen surveyed its own ranks.

"Chub Davis, what are you?" Claire said, pointing. "Sixty-five, sixty-six?"

The man nodded.

"Clint Fowler, you gotta be close to seventy."

"No kid. That's for sure."

Claire smiled, but did not slow down. She continued as if she were taking roll.

"Frank Dobie, how old are you?"

"Seventy-seven. When I make ninety, I'm gonna retire."

The old man set the group to chuckling, but it did not last long. And it didn't alter the collective mood.

"You're not gonna retire," Claire said. "Not if you're broke. Not if you've lost everything. Did you know that over the last five years nearly ten per cent of the ranchers in this whole country have gone broke or sold out?"

Giving time for the question to sink in, Claire looked out over the sea of faces. That's when she saw Jack. A hint of a smile brushed her face. For a moment, the sight of him distracted her. When she collected her thoughts, she continued.

"It's true. It's called 'attrition.' Kids are selling out. They get dollar signs in their eyes when they hear the big money these developers will pay. The temptation is too great."

D.C. Grubbs rose. A heavy boned, barrel-built fellow.

"I guess maybe I'm a voice in the wilderness here. But I ain't sure about all this. I'm a pretty tough old boy, but I'm practical, too."

A few heads nodded.

"I got a stack of bills a mile high. And they're the real thing. Gotta be paid. I don't much like the idea of goin' broke and livin' out the rest of my days suckin' on the government tit."

A few scattered voices sounded approval. Grubbs continued.

"So this ain't no lead pipe cinch, Claire. Here the other day, I got a offer I'm gonna have to give a hard look. Maybe we oughta hear from Mr. Porter."

Grubbs turned toward the rear of the auditorium. Eyes followed.

The polyester-suited man rose. Long, rangy fellow. He cleared his throat loudly.

"Y'all know me," he said. "I grew up down here."

He hiked up his britches and cleared his nostrils with a crude, forceful snort like some barnyard critter. Swallowed hard.

"I'm Lucien Porter. One of them evil developers from up to Phoenix, I guess."

He chuckled and ducked his head, trying to play to the crowd's favor with self-deprecation. The attempt failed. No one reacted at all. He side-stepped into the aisle, sauntered forward a bit. Glaring eyes stayed on him.

Porter was one member of a retinue of errand runners, manipulators, and enforcers. He did the dirty work so his out-of-town principals didn't have to soil their hands with the details of their schemes. Sometimes, he had a piece of the action.

Gangly and pencil-necked, Porter displayed a maladroit manner. Looked uncomfortable in a suit, western cut or no. With sleeves and trouser legs a little too short, he suggested a

98

gawky juvenile delinquent in hand-me-down clothes more than a real estate mogul. His Adam's apple bobbed beneath his bolo tie when he talked.

"You know what your problem is?" Porter said. "Yourall's land is worth too much. That's a problem most folks would love to have. Progress ain't evil, you know. Ain't bad to use the land the way people want to use it. Think about it. The kind of development we could do in this valley would bring in a whole buttload of money. Pardon my French, ladies. Create jobs, I mean. Now what's wrong with that?"

Claire glowered.

"We don't want your money," she said. "We don't want your jobs. This is ranch country."

The crowd applauded. Porter shook his head in frustration.

"It's gonna happen. Y'all know it. I know it. Everybody knows it. Eventually, this valley's gonna be developed. That don't mean there won't be ranchers. Always be ranchers. Ranchers just won't be broke all the time."

Porter's words fell on deaf ears.

"We appreciate your looking out for us," Claire said. "But we don't need less land. We need more. And with all the city people coming in and paying big money we can't get it. Can't afford it. So don't tell me you're not going to put us out of business. We know better."

"Look," Porter said in almost a pleading voice, "I know y'all been ranchers forever. That's good. Porters never could afford it. You know us. My people was just short pay day workers. Work for a dollar to make a dime. Every day. But that's okay. This is my chance. And your chance. What I'm talkin' about is progress, for all of us."

"We don't believe that swill," someone said. "And we don't want your damn progress."

"Not so fast," another man said. "Let's hear him out."

The turncoat raised the ire of the others.

"You oughta be ashamed of yourself, Cletus," someone said.

Porter grimaced, shook his head. He started to say more, but checked himself. He returned to his seat, folded his arms, crossed his legs.

"You better hear me good," he said as a parting shot. "Like it or not, it's comin'. You best get that on your minds."

Claire subdued her anger and frustration, despite the apparent rift in her own ranks. She got back to business.

"We need money to buy development rights. The land trust will take an easement and protect the land from development forever. We'll keep this valley the way it's always been. The answer is conservation easements. Here's how it works. You donate or sell your development rights. It reduces the value of your land, lowers inheritance taxes. Your kids won't have to sell it just to pay the taxes. The Association needs money."

"I don't know," Jesse Bennet said. "Money's scarce as hens' teeth these days. What you say sounds right, but it ain't that simple."

"I know," Claire said. "I know some of you feel cornered. I do, too, maybe even more than you. But that's the time to fight. We need your help. We need each other."

Claire took a bundle of papers from a satchel. She ordered them in her hands and held them aloft.

"I want everybody to have one of these. It'll tell you more about what we're trying to do. Please read it. Please think about it. We're just getting started and we have a long way to go."

People in the crowd rose to their feet. Dozens of small conversations broke out. Claire surrendered the stack of papers to a woman in the front row and began making her way through the crowd toward Jack.

Porter intercepted her. He popped a piece of chewing gum into his mouth and began working it vigorously. He dropped the wrapper on the floor, cracked his knuckles.

"I wish you'd back off a little," he said. "You're gettin' these people riled up for nothin'."

Claire did not answer.

"Claire," Porter said in a sincere voice, a near whisper. "I don't want you and me to be crossways. You know how I feel about you. Have for as long as I can remember. We need to be on the same side. I can help you and these other people."

Exasperated, Claire put a hand to her forehead and looked away.

"Oh, Lucien."

"And you know I've got that mortgage on the place. Comin' due pretty quick."

Claire bowed her neck.

"It's a forgery. Not worth the paper it's written on."

Porter shook his head.

"Claire, you know better. You know how hard up your daddy was for money, how desperate he was. He took a chance. Just didn't work out. That's all. But it still can."

Porter put a hand on Claire's arm.

"I swear you are pretty as a picture. Can we go somewhere? Talk? Just you and me? I got a present for Molly."

Claire sighed and shook her head.

"Not now. I . . . not now."

She tried to go around Porter. He blocked her way.

"Please. All I want to do is talk. That's all."

Claire gave no answer.

"Listen. We can do business. It'll be good for everybody."

Claire declined. She flanked Porter again. When he turned quickly to press his suit, he came face to face with Jack Breen.

"I don't think the lady wants to talk to you," Jack said. "Why don't you just go on."

"Who are you?"

Jack did not answer. He stood motionless, staring cold-eyed at Porter.

Toe to toe, the two men did everything but paw the ground.

"You better tend to your own knittin', boy," Porter said.

Breen's stare held uninterrupted.

After a few moments, Porter blinked. He turned to leave and, as he did, he looked over Breen's shoulder at Claire. The wind went out of him in a long sigh.

"Claire, Claire, Claire. Can I come by tomorrow?"

Claire did not answer. Crestfallen, Porter's shoulders sagged. When he looked at Breen again, he stiffened.

"Well, I guess I best be gettin' along."

He turned and took his leave.

Brief as it was, the encounter with Lucien Porter raised in Jack Breen a familiar surge of ardor. He liked it. It pleased him to discover he could still summon it on command. Squared off with an adversary, knowing the right words to say with the right tone and inflection, he felt oddly at home. For better or worse, some parts of the old Jack Breen remained intact.

"Who is that guy?" Jack said.

"Lucien Porter. The man that wants to marry me."

Jack winced. He eased up when Claire spoke again.

"Wasn't sure I'd see you here," she said.

"Wasn't sure myself. Want to go get a drink or a cup of coffee or something?"

"No place to get a drink, or even coffee. This isn't Boston. Besides I get up about five. And I need to get home to Molly."

"I understand."

"But if you want to come by tomorrow I'll fix you a cup of coffee. Might even give you the fifty cent tour of the ranch."

"I'd like that," Jack said. "What time?"

"About six."

Jack's eyes widened.

"A.m. or p.m.?"

"Too early for you?"

"No. No. It's perfect. I'll be there."

102

## CHAPTER 10 – FIRST LIGHT

Jack Breen stepped out of his room at the Starlite Motel and into the purple dawn. Miles away, Claire busied herself with daily chores. They began this morning, as they did every morning, in the last hour before sunup.

Mile by mile, Jack wondered what effect the new day might have on Claire. Would second thoughts cause her to regret her invitation? Did Uncle Fountain persuade her to steer clear of him? Perhaps her manner would be cool, her response to him perfunctory. The practice of law and bitter experience trained Jack Breen to maintain low expectations. Cynical perhaps, but strong armor for a fallen, secretly hopeful dreamer.

At first light, Jack reached the ranch. The rising sun burned the dark away and its incandescence glinted on heavy dew clinging to grass tops. The wind lay quiet in draws and shallow swales. Not a soul in sight. Still as a photograph. For a few nervous moments, he sat motionless in the truck, hardly breathing. Making a run for it might be the better part of valor here.

Ace rose to his feet and looked out sharply. He and Jack exchanged restive glances, each appearing to seek guidance from the other.

"What?" Jack said. "What are you looking at?"

Ace canted his head.

"She did invite us, you know. Me, anyway."

Jack stepped out of the truck with the same quickness he might use in removing a band-aid from a scabbed-over wound, fearing a slower separation might overwhelm his courage. Ace followed him out, stood leaning against his leg.

Keeping a hand on the door, Jack scoured the area within view for some sign that last night's invitation still stood. Ace's eyes fell on the bird dog he encountered the first day at the ranch, the one Uncle Fountain called "Gus." Mutual growls rumbled deep within both animals. They showed their teeth. But this time the bird dog lacked sufficient interest to come to his feet. After an intense stare, he lowered his head to the ground. He took in a deep breath, exhaled slowly. Ace heaved a muffled bark.

"Quiet," Jack whispered gruffly.

Then a noise drew his eyes to the barely open barn door no more than an underhanded stone's throw from where he stood. He homed in on the sound. A skinny sliver of light lay on the barn floor, pointing inward. Pushing the heavy door open, the sliver of brightness widened to a wedge. He stepped into the light.

"Good morning," called a distant voice.

"Claire?"

Jack looked squint-eyed into the barn's dim interior.

"Come on in."

Answering the invitation, Jack ambled down the barn bay. Strong scent of Alfalfa hay and grain, horse. He found Claire in a stall at the far end. Wearing a red, down-filled jacket, collar drawn tightly to her neck, she stood brushing the stout haunches of a sorrel mare. Standing a good fifteen hands, the mare accepted Claire's singular attention with a regal air, head held high. Unmistakable pride in the arch of neck.

104

"Morning," Jack said. "Make that, howdy."

"Hi. This is Sugar."

A thin fog rose from Claire's warm words in the crisp air.

"Her real name's a mile long. Sugar's just what I call her. She's a grand old dame and well bred."

The old mare swiveled an ear in Jack's direction. Jack layered his forearms on the top rail of the stall's gate, leaned forward, resting his chin on them. Claire continued brushing the mare's sleek hide, face flushed with exertion.

"Twenty-two years old," she said. "And she's going to have a baby. Her last. Getting a little old for that sort of thing. We've always had trouble getting her in foal. This time, she settled."

"She's beautiful."

"She stays in the pasture mostly. I'll bring her in here at the right time so she'll have a good, clean place to foal. Her time's coming. A few months yet."

"Who's the father?"

"The sire?"

"Right. The sire."

"A grandson of Doc Bar. Doc Bar was a top of the line cutting horse. In the Quarter Horse world that means something."

Jack nodded as if he knew what Claire was talking about.

"Massive stud fee," Claire said. "More than we could afford. Took every dollar Dad could scrape up. A lot riding on this mare. A good foal will be worth a lot of money, especially now. The old stud colicked and died a couple of months ago."

Claire finished brushing. She slipped the bright green halter off the mare's head, coiled the white lead shank. Outside the stall, she hung the rig on a high peg. The mare eased her head over the gate and Claire rubbed her bristly, gray muzzle.

"This horse is my ace in the hole. She's going to help me hang on to the ranch. Not sure what I'd do without her."

Claire gazed wistfully into the old mare's dark eyes. A warm smile graced her face, but in its margins lurked a shadow. Although it was spring, the look on her face, tinged with melancholy as it was, seemed more a thing of autumn.

Claire turned to Jack, put her hands together.

"Now, how about that cup of coffee?"

"Why not?"

In the kitchen, Claire handed Jack a white enamel cup with a contrasting black rim. Steam rose from the dark liquid when she poured it.

"I wondered if you would have changed your mind," Jack said.

"About what?"

"About your invitation. I thought–"

"Nope. Didn't change my mind."

"Just thought you might have."

"Well, I didn't."

Jack sipped the coffee and watched Claire through steam rising from the cup's dark rim. He studied her hands, as she took another cup from the cabinet and filled it. Small, delicate, once a cellist's hands. Now the hands of a mother, a rancher. Made wise and wary by life, her hands bore the inscription of their experience, innumerable run-ins with all manner of obstacles, barbed wire, cold wind, foreheads aflame with fever. Busy hands, sometimes tired, but always determined. And always loving. Through it all, beautiful. Like the heart within the woman, bruised but strong.

"Would you like to see the ranch?" Claire said. "It's changed since you were here. A lot."

Jack drained his cup.

"Sure. Love to see it."

*****

Claire and Jack climbed into an old red pickup, the one built about the time Richard Nixon was resigning the presidency.

106

"I think you had this truck the last time I was here," Jack said. "It was old then."

"Hoping to get one more year out of it. That's the thing about ranching. Always trying to get one more year out of something. Need to tune her up."

"You do your own tune-ups?"

"Tune her up. Bust the tires. Everything. On a ranch you do it all. I can change oil and I can change points and plugs. That's in the morning. In the afternoon I might do an emergency C-section on a mother cow."

Claire amused herself with the rapid-fire litany of her talents. She wrinkled her brow and cast a wry smile in Jack's direction. She invited a response with a coy tilting of her head. Jack obliged, showing his approval with a deferential nod.

Claire continued. Proud and wary, she explained the ranching operation.

"We run about three hundred seventy-five head, mother cows and calves included. Mostly cross-bred Angus, Hereford, Charolais. Little bit of everything."

At pains to prove her independent mind and to show nothing intimidated her, she pointed out the calving barn, where heifers, young cows bred for the first time, deliver their calves. The squeeze chute where cows are vaccinated against disease and all manner of doctoring occurs. Corrals and pens, barns stacked high with bales of hay.

After a while, they ascended a low rise and dropped into a valley. The narrow road turned from blacktop to dirt and soon resolved into a grassed-over trail. The house and barns and all things man-made disappeared. Claire stopped the truck and killed the engine. She gestured with a graceful sweep of her hand toward the vast expanse of Raven Ranch.

"Indians call it *The Blue Vision*," she said.

Wide meadows of green grass sprinkled with scarlet flowers. Low rolling country. Outcroppings of mottled gray rocks. Timber in the distance. Overhead, a hawk circled effortlessly in the sky. Except for the low sighing of wind, quiet prevailed, the kind of quiet known only in places such as this, an insouciant stillness Jack Breen seldom experienced. Not merely an interruption in the noise or a time of waiting for the next sound. True quiet.

On a near hill, stood a small chapel built of gray stone. A simple structure, crudely made and large enough for no more than a handful of worshipers. Weathered rafters ribbed the roof, left it open to the sky. From the ridge line, directly above the chapel's entrance, rose a small cross formed of two branches of an Arizona sycamore. The longer vertical piece about the length of a man's arm. Shorter crosspiece lashed to it with a rawhide thong.

Claire pointed to the chapel. She looked at Jack, then at the chapel again.

"Jayro built it," she said. "We call it 'Clouds Hill.' In the summer, we cover the roof with thatch. Family cemetery up there."

Hilltop grasses stirred in the breeze.

"Sometimes," Claire said, "especially in the early morning, clouds hang low and cover the high ground. Completely envelope that little chapel until you can barely see it. Sometimes you can't see it at all. Jayro says he talks to God up there."

"Does God listen?"

"Jayro says He does."

Jack studied Claire's face in profile, faint lines left by sun and wind and the passage of time, soft brown of her eye, crimson hue of her cheek. First hint of gray at her temple. Angle of her jaw. He contemplated the precise outline of her lips and the cautious upturn of the corner of her mouth. A smile, a fraction of one, that could never quite gain full purchase on her face.

"I like to think Molly might be married in that little chapel some day."

"I'd bet on it," Jack said.

Claire turned toward Jack. In an instant, he remembered everything he ever knew of her, what made him

108

love her. At once, all of it came to him in a torrential confluence of memories and expectations, filling him to overflowing. Warmth of her cheeks when they pressed against his. Sweet woman's scent. Everything. He remembered too well and too much.

"Come on," Claire said. "I want to show you something."

She stepped out of the truck and onto a narrow trail overgrown with grass. She looked through the truck's open window at Jack. She put out a hand, entreating him to join her.

Jack stepped out of the truck and followed Claire across a chromatic meadow sprinkled with poppies and other wild flowers, distinctly edged on one side by a stand of trees. At the timber, they dropped off into a creek bed and followed the silty watercourse at the breaks, leaving a footprint with every step. Down the center of the channel, meandered a filament of water, no more than three long strides wide.

Soon, they came upon two cathedral cottonwoods, standing opposite each other, arching over the narrow waterway, each almost touching the ground on the far side. Massive trunks and their smaller offshoots muted and fractured the brilliance of the sun, filling the space beneath the rooflike tangle of branches with soft ambient light. In places, it bent the light, dispersing it prismatically in unbroken shafts.

Claire and Jack paused and eyed the murmuring flow of spring runoff. They raised their eyes and fixed them on the arching trees. The mighty arboreal monoliths implied reaching, straining, seeking.

"Beautiful," Jack said in a low voice. "Like being in church. How long have they been here would you say?"

"Since long before either of us. And they'll be here long after we're gone."

"Why are they bent like that? Is their own weight too heavy for them? Are they after something?"

"Maybe they got too big and too heavy," Claire said. "Too many regrets. Maybe they're just trying not to break."

"Not here. Surely this is a place of no regrets."

"Oh, there are always regrets. Even here. When I hear someone say, 'I have no regrets.' I don't believe it. Everyone has them. Every choice you make, even the wise ones, means you didn't make another. Every decision cancels out other possibilities."

Claire and Jack gazed up at the branches, let a few quiet moments pass. Around them, the world fell still and calm except for the low trickle of water.

"Do you play the cello any more?" Jack said.

"No."

"Never?"

"Never."

"You should."

"No time."

"There's a regret," Jack said. "At least for me. You should play."

"Maybe someday."

Just then a great swarm of Monarch butterflies filled the air around Jack and Claire. They perched on tree branches above them, blanketed the ground. World aflutter with orange and black wings. The delicate insects silently flew and glided, wafting on gentle updrafts and down. They rose and fell effortlessly with incredible lightness. Some joined as mating pairs. Others lowered themselves to the water and drifted on floating leaves.

Claire raised her hands and stood amazed at the quiet storm of dusty wings.

"Look," she said. "They're beautiful."

Jack lifted his arms in a spontaneous gesture of wonder and welcome. He turned in a circle, marveling at the swarming creatures.

"Amazing. Truly amazing."

"They move north out of Mexico every year about this time," Claire said. "They go all the way to Canada. I've never seen so many at once."

110

A butterfly lit on Claire's hair. On Jack's shoulder, a mating pair rested.

"I guess they have no regrets," Claire said.

Jack admired the slender united bodies.

"I know this guy doesn't."

Claire moved toward Jack and the winged lovers lifted off. She raised a hand, and they alighted on a finger for a moment before rising again in tandem flight. She held her hand still in the air as if she expected their return. But a butterfly did not take Claire's hand. Jack did. He took it in his and caressed it. He pressed it gently against his cheek, looked longingly into Claire's eyes. He turned toward her hand, buried his face in it.

For a moment Claire did not resist or object. But then she lowered her hand and took a step back.

"Come on," she said. "Better be going."

When they turned to go, their eyes dropped to a mosaic of footprints in the soft moist alluvium. Intermingled, overlain. Indistinguishable as to source, all save one.

After a few steps, Claire halted and froze. What her eyes beheld, fretted the morning calm.

"Wait," she said.

She lowered herself to a crouch and studied the welter of tracks. One among many leaped out at her.

"What's the matter? What is it?"

"Animal sign," she said. "A track. Big cat. Look at that. Wide as a man's hand."

Jack sat on his heels beside Claire and studied the imprint. He held out a hand and splayed his fingers.

"Mountain lion," Claire said. "No doubt about it."

And then she rose and stared with silent circumspection into the trees. A sense of foreboding bayoneted her. She raised her collar to her chin.

"We've been losing stock to something. Now I know what."

Jack felt the contagion of her fear. Like Claire, he stared into the trees, but saw nothing.

"He's out there somewhere," Claire said, looking into the tangled branches above the creek as if she could see beyond them but could make out nothing in them.

"Watching and waiting," she said. "Mexicans call him *El Fantasma de las Montañas*, Ghost of the Mountains."

"Never seen one," Jack said.

"You can be standing right next to one and never see him, not until he strikes. Suddenly he's just there and then like a ghost he's gone. *La muerte quieta*, quiet death."

"Sounds pretty mean."

"Not mean. Just who he is."

Jack and Claire turned and looked down the creek along their backtrail. No sign of butterflies that abounded moments before. Air still and wingless.

"Better get back," Claire said.

Claire kept her own counsel on the drive home. The spontaneous and uncomplicated lightheartedness that accompanied the swarm of butterflies did not last. The mountain lion track and the joining of her hand with Jack's hand and his face made short work of that. All the way to the house Claire kept her heart tightly fenced. She restricted the conversation to the price of beef, landmarks they passed, aspects of the ranching operation she had not already explained.

Jack saw his indiscretion clearly. He went too far. He now knew with certainty he would soon be on his own again and on the road, bound for some unknown, pointless destination. Away. Simply away. But at the house, when he verged on conjuring up some forgotten obligation that would explain a quick departure, Claire took him by the arm.

"Tonight . . ."

Her voiced trailed off. She struggled with the words, then spat them out.

"There's a party tonight. At the VFW hall. A birthday party, for my banker. I wouldn't miss it. You could come."

At first Jack did not answer. The invitation caught him off guard.

"I want you to come," Claire said.

Jack regarded her in silence for a short time, then made up his mind. He shrugged.

"All right."

"About seven?"

"Shall I pick you up?"

"I'll meet you there."

Jack Breen would stay in the San Rafael for at least one more night. After that? Time would tell.

## CHAPTER 11 - VIVA LA REVOLUCIÓN

In town, a short block from the Starlite Motel, Jack stood looking at a pigeonhole office next to a barber shop. On the window, painted in gold block letters: "J. Passamonte, Attorney and Counselor at Law." Through smudged glass, he could make out a small reception area, vacant. In the back, a dim light burned.

Finding the door unlocked, he opened it and stepped in. He breathed in stale air. On the reception desk's weathered surface, a ceramic ashtray brimmed with crushed cigarette butts. A scattering of weeks old newspapers. A Styrofoam cup bore a red lipstick stain. A dollop of gray mold floated on the oily surface of the cup's dark dregs. For Jaime Passamonte, this rat's nest stood for a law office.

Jack peered into the interior chamber. There, in the sallow light, a young man with a great wealth of shoulder-length blueblack hair reposed. Installed in a swivel chair, he reclined with feet propped on the corner of the desk, legs crossed at the ankles, hands folded in his lap, eyes closed. He wore jeans faded to pale blue. At one knee, white threads spider webbed a gaping hole. On the bottom of one boot an oblong crater penetrated all the way through the leather to a white sock. A pair of stereo headphones callipered the man's skull. Like the sign said, "J. Passamonte, Attorney and Counselor at Law."

The young lawyer's lair had barely enough room for a desk and one client chair, green vinyl, empty. In the corner on the floor, stood a lopsided, disordered stack of manila file folders. Random papers everywhere. A few law books. On one wall, a framed law license hung askew. On another, a poster of Che Guevara hung perfectly level. Beside the desk, a small table held the dusty components of an obsolete stereo system. On the turntable, a warped twelve inch LP turned methodically at thirty-three revolutions per minute. The office matched the man. Defiant, rebellious, but unfocused. Everything at least slightly out of true, if not down right off kilter.

Jack eased closer. He studied the young man at the desk. Detected only one sign of life, the slight movement of a thumb tapping out a rhythm.

Jack lowered himself into the chair opposite the desk. He made no sound. After a while, a slit appeared in one of Jaime Passamonte's eyes, within it a hint of white. An identical slit soon appeared in the other eye. And then, at the sight of another human being in his office, Jaime Passamonte, attorney and counselor at law, came completely unglued.

He jerked upright, lost his balance, fell backward. The chair squirted out from under him. He ripped off the headphones in mid-air and crashed hard to the floor. He flailed around a few moments, almost completely out of sight, then struggled clumsily to his feet. Frantic, breathless. Pissed. He dusted himself off.

"Dammit. You scared the shit out of me, man."

Jack remained seated and calm. Passamonte tried to recover his wits and catch his breath. "Son of a bitch. What the . . . son of a bitch."

"A little jumpy aren't you?"

115

Heart pounding, face flushed, Passamonte righted the chair and threw his butt in it. He swung toward the stereo, touched the power button with the tip of a forefinger. He swiveled toward Jack, then widened his eyes to the size of a handheld funeral home fan. He took in a deep breath and let it out, fluttering his lips like a grade school pup. Ready now. He conjured a professional air.

"What can I do you for? Need a lawyer?"

"I am a lawyer," Jack said. And then in a low voice, almost under his breath, "Was a lawyer, actually. Past tense."

The truth slipped out of him again before he knew it. For a moment he regretted it.

"Claire Gaynor is a friend of mine. You're representing her."

Passamonte smiled, nodded.

"Ahh. Claire. Great lady. Yeah. I'm her lawyer. What—"

The young man interrupted himself. He became suspicious, leaned forward.

"Wait a minute. She got a beef with me? She think I can't handle it? 'Cause I can."

"No. No. No," Jack said. "Not that at all."

Passamonte eased back in his chair. Jack continued.

"She says you've got some trouble with the judge on her father's guardianship. Tell me about him."

Passamonte remained suspicious, became sullen.

"Just who the hell are you, anyway?"

"Like I said, a friend of Claire's. What's up with this judge?"

"You think I'm just gonna sit here and start spillin' my guts to you? Ever hear of attorney-client privilege? You used to be a lawyer. You know what that means. For all I know, you're wearin' a fuckin' wire. I'm not stupid, you know. Not one bit. Who you workin' for?"

"I'm a friend of Claire's. Call her. Check me out."

That's exactly what he did. Claire gave him a brief rundown on Jack Breen, Harvard, big shot Boston practice. She

116

even told him about the suspension. She gave Passamonte the green light to proceed. When he confirmed this to Breen, he left out what Claire said about the good help Breen would be and that it wouldn't cost her a dime. Nor did he mention Claire's assurance she would watch her back.

"Now, tell me about this judge," Jack said.

The kid's face remained a study in resentment and suspicion, but he loosened up enough to give Jack the lowdown on The Honorable William D. McGrew.

"Ugly as galvanized sin," Passamonte said. "Inside and out. At least nine tenths crooked. On the take. Gotta be. There's a local wheeler dealer type—"

"Lucien Porter."

"Know him?"

"We've had some words. Probably have some more. Tell me about him."

"Simple. He wants Raven Ranch. Nothin' but an old fashioned land grabber. Small time all the way, though. Mean as a snake, but dumb. Just a goon suckin' up to some dudes out of Phoenix. Says he's got a mortgage."

"You seen it?"

"Yep. Claire says it's a forgery."

"Should be able to prove that."

"Sure, except her old man don't know come here from sic 'em. Brain's mush. Can't say a word."

"Still should be a way. And, you might get some dirt on this judge. Nail his ass. Break him."

"Great idea, man. Really great idea. I'll get right on that."

"Might work."

"Might be a good way to get killed, too."

"Bet we could do it," Jack said.

"We? So, we're partners now? We gonna sit around the campfire singin' Kumbaya?"

Breen shrugged.

"I got a better idea," Passamonte said. "If you really want to help, why don't you just kill the son of a bitch, be done with him?"

"Clever. Really smart. As an alternative, why don't you use your head. I know this judge's type. Corner him and he'll show yellow. All we gotta do is corner him."

"Not exactly easy, you know."

"Maybe not, but I'll bet it can be done. You know what you need?"

"No, but I got a feelin' you're about to tell me."

Jack crooked a finger in Jaime Passamonte's direction. The young lawyer looked around the minuscule office as if he feared being seen or overheard. He leaned in. Jack could tell the kid wanted to know what he had to say, but he didn't want to show it. And, he'd have to overcome his cynical and suspicious inclinations.

"Let's talk turkey," Jack said.

Jaime Passamonte listened a while, then leaned back in his chair and pushed away from the desk.

"Who the hell are you, man?"

"Like I said."

"Yeah. Like you said, a friend of Claire's. But I mean, really. Who are you?"

In the hour that followed, the young lawyer and the jaded elder marked with a scarlet letter formed an unsteady alliance. Jack owned up to enough of his personal back story to convince Passamonte he had the required *bona fides* and the required *cojones*. By late afternoon, Jack Breen was back in business. And he had a new partner. This kid was no Bert Zorn, but he'd do.

Jack rose to leave and when he reached the reception desk, Jaime Passamonte called to him. He raised a hand and made a V with two fingers. He flashed a wry smile and tossed his head.

"*Viva la revolución, amigo.*"

Jack hesitated. He felt circumstances pulling him back onto the trail he'd been on for years, the one he quit after doing

118

what he swore never to do, after being caught with his hand in the till and shaming himself. *No thanks,* he thought. *I've had enough of that. I don't want to judge anyone. I don't want to be judged. I don't want to be smarter or faster or better than anyone else. I'm through with that.* But it was like a drunk vowing to give up the bottle when he had a belly full of whiskey and a drink in his hand. Cheap talk. Easy. A promise made to be broken. Old ways die hard.

And now, Jack Breen had more baggage than ever. He sensed Jaime Passamonte admired him. In spite of himself, the kid looked up to him. He had expectations. And Jack Breen could not help feeling the allure of a possible success. But, at the same time, he felt a familiar tightness in the chest. Pressure. Just what he did not want. But what he craved.

Jack glanced around the room, then back at the young turk. He felt the weight of the ill-fitting skin of a mentor. Despite that, he gestured with an officious sweep of a hand.

"Get this place cleaned up. I'm not working in a dump."

*****

Outside, Lucien Porter waited. In an insolent slouch, he leaned against a front fender of Jack's truck, toothpick in the corner of his mouth. He was cleaning his fingernails with a pocket knife. A man on the prod.

Jack caught his first glimpse of Porter when he stepped out of Passamonte's office. He paused a moment at the door, then strode directly toward him, stopped no more than an arm's length away. Porter looked up, but continued his public display of personal grooming. He spoke through a yellow-toothed grin.

"Well, looky here. The mysterious stranger. You know, I never did catch your name."

Breen made no reply. Porter's grin held.

"Don't have a name, I guess. My. My."

Jack held his tongue.

119

With an air of nonchalance, Porter folded the blade into its handle and tucked the knife away in a jeans pocket. He methodically cracked the knuckles of each hand, then took the toothpick from his mouth and flicked it away. The smile went with it. He rose slowly from the fender and set his feet wide apart.

"You and that shirt tail greaser kid got big doins goin' on?"

Jack still said nothing. With his identity and his association with Jaime Passamonte now in play, an economy of words made sense to him. He chose silence, for now. That did not sit well with his antagonist.

"You a regular hard case, ain't you? Kinda feedin' off your range, too."

Porter glanced toward Jaime Passamonte's office, and screwed up his face.

"You know what really bothers the hell out of me is when somebody sticks his nose in my bidness."

Jack tensed, narrowed his gaze. His silence ended.

"Is that a fact?"

"Yeah. That is a fact. Here's another little fact for you. Stickin' your nose in my bidness can get down right unhealthy."

Jack said no more. After a long uneasy silence, he stepped to the door of the pickup and opened it. Before he got in, Porter's smile reformed.

"And, by the way, that good lookin' little split-tail at the meetin' the other night. Woman and a half, ain't she. Her and me's gettin' married. She ain't quite come around yet, but she will. You figure on beatin' my time?"

Jack did not answer. His breath caught in his throat.

"Funny," Porter said. "But I don't see her takin' up with you."

Porter looked away, spat on the sidewalk. He looked at Jack again.

"Weren't for me, they'da already lost the home place. That old man needed money. A right smart of it. He had his hand out and I filled it. Straight up deal. Now, don't seem like nobody likes the idy of payin' me back."

Again, Jack said nothing.

"Well, no need to pull a long face. I'm the only chance Claire's got of hangin' on to her daddy's ranch. Like I told her, if she sides with me, she'll do just fine. I'll have her fartin' through silk."

The crude remark galled Jack Breen to the bone, but he managed to let it pass with no response except the rippling of jaw muscles.

"That it?" he said, cold, deliberate.

"That's the short of it."

Porter glowered and took a half step toward Jack.

"One more thing. Don't get in my way. I don't take kindly to nobody runnin' my stock. So, don't be gettin' no big idies."

After Porter gave the stern admonition time to sink in, his expression brightened.

"Well, I best be gettin' on. Sure has been a nice little chat. See you again. You can count on it."

Porter's ripe language made Jack Breen's blood boil, but all he did was stare, rigid-faced. Showing nothing of his hand, he got into the truck and drove away. Porter stood watching him until he disappeared from sight. He took note of the number on the license plate, wrote it in the palm of his hand.

Jack Breen studied Porter in his rearview mirror. The man's image appeared above the words OBJECTS IN MIRROR ARE CLOSER THAN THEY APPEAR. Jack knew the gangly minion of Phoenix dudes had one thing right. They would meet again. No doubt about it.

# CHAPTER 12 – HEARTS AT A PRECIPICE

Jack arrived at the VFW hall at the shank of the evening. From where he stood at the side of his truck, he could hear within the brown stone walls the low murmur of friendly conversations and, laced through it, the whimsical strains of a violin. In these parts, a fiddle. Claire once told him, "A violin sings, a fiddle dances." Both were in store for this night, singing and dancing. A genuine romping, stomping affair. What folks in the San Rafael might call, "shakin' a good hoof."

As always, Ace rode shotgun. At Jack's direction, the dog leaped out of the cab and into the bed. Jack fastened a chain to his collar at one end and to the side rail at the other. He poured a bowl of water from a plastic half-gallon jug retired from an earlier life as a milk container. He patted the dog on the head, then looked with a sort of exhilarating trepidation toward the amber-toned rectangles of light framed by the building's windows.

Uncertainty and crisp evening air gave him a momentary shiver. He breathed into his hands to warm them.

"I don't know about this," he muttered to himself. "I do not know."

But he did know. He was going in. He had enough courage for that. What would come next, he could not say.

Earlier, after his meeting with Jaime Passamonte and his run-in with Lucien Porter, Jack blew in some cash at Bishop's Dry Goods. There, he outfitted himself with a pair of stiff, new jeans and a couple of pearl snap shirts. He was wearing the white one with blue pinstripes. He couldn't quite talk himself into a hat, not yet. But, at the Jesus Is Lord Pawn Shop next door to Bishop's, he did buy a belt with an Indian buckle, a silver oval with a green turquoise stone in the center. Despite the tone implied by the store's name, the pawnbroker showed him no mercy on the price. The new getup set him back plenty.

Dark thirty neared. In the smidgin of remaining light, Jack glanced at the rearview mirror. He slicked up one last time and pronounced himself presentable. Like a moth to a flame, he headed in.

From the open door, he peered in at the small gathering of friends visiting in a genial fashion. Many of them held clear plastic cups sloshing with a red liquid. He recognized some of the faces from the high school auditorium the night before. But now, in this place on this night, their animated manner betrayed lighter hearts, brighter spirits. An occasional peal of laughter enlivened the room. Folks were decked out for the occasion. Men had their hair neatly cropped. Shirts and jeans freshly pressed. Boots greased. Women wore bright dresses. Faces powdered and rouged. Hair deliberately coifed.

Jack lingered outside the door, for now, a mere spectator. Nary a sign of Claire. For a moment, he felt a tremor of doubt.

And then, mercifully, he heard a voice behind him.

"Hey, cowboy."

Jack turned.

There stood Claire. Beautiful, as always. But more than that. Her hair descended to her shoulders in a natural fall. A touch of makeup enriched her cheeks. Lips full and supple, deep carmine. Eyes clear and sharp, whites of them almost lavender. Irises a deep, earth brown with remarkable crispness. A warm, welcoming smile. She wore jeans, tucked into knee-high boots. White cotton blouse, high choke-neck collar. Over it a three quarter length tan-colored suede jacket, Indian beadwork on the collar and sleeves. Nothing short of stunning.

"You lost?" Claire said.

Jack regained enough bravado to make a wisecrack.

"I was about to go in. Thought I might scare up somebody to do-si-do with."

"Too bad. I was thinking more of tripping the light fantastic."

"I'm game for that, too."

Claire put a hand on his arm.

"New duds, huh?" And with mock amazement, "You clean up pretty good."

The remark left Jack slightly self-conscious.

"Not like you," he said. "You are downright beautiful."

He spoke before caution could bind his tongue. Claire accepted the compliment with grace, but she could not help lowering her eyes and turning her head slightly.

"Ready to go in?" she said.

"I don't know. To tell you the truth, it looks kinda scary."

"Stick with me. You'll be all right."

Claire took Jack's arm. Together, they stepped into the warm light. Handshakes, hugs, warm greetings followed. Claire introduced Jack as an old friend from back East. Over time, the crowd formed and reformed, configured and reconfigured. It changed shape as conversations started and stopped, paused and resumed. Little by little, Jack's natural charm kicked in. People could not help liking him.

It did not take long for Jack to hear the question he should have anticipated. It came from Pig Campbell, the charge nurse at the local hospital. A woman of considerable mass, she'd dress out at better than two hundred pounds. Her real name was "Peggy." Her folks called her "Peg." That's what the chubby little girl's name tag said when school started in the first

124

grade. But a six year old bully named "Butch" changed it to "Pig." The cognomen stuck.

Pig grew into her name. It came to fit her more and more, the older she got. After a while, everybody called her "Pig" and that's what she called herself. She even emblazoned it on the brass name tag she wore over her nurse's uniform. Everything about the woman was big, bosoms, belly, haunches, even her hair. Sprayed hard as a rock, it rose a good six inches above her head. Even without it, she'd still stand a head taller than most men in the room, and outweigh all but a few. Her thighs rubbed together when she walked, and when she wore hose, they made a sound like a carpenter sanding a two-by-four.

Pig had big hands, too, fingers like sausages. She could barely force off her rings, even with butter. Her watchband had barely enough length to encircle her wrist. She was a porker all right. But the biggest part of Pig Campbell was her heart, pure gold, through and through. She did not have a mean bone in her sizable body, despite the laughter at her expense and the abuse she took all her life. As a nurse, she found her calling like few people do.

"Hidy," Pig Campbell said, when Claire introduced Jack. "What do you do back there in the East?"

"I'm a lawyer," he answered without hesitation. But added quickly, "I'm retired."

Before he knew it, he gave an unthinking, mechanical response. If he'd been more cautious, he might have hesitated. Given time to think, he might have lied. But he did not. And, of course, even if given by rote, his answer was correct, technically. He was still a lawyer, at least he had a diploma. That he had no license to practice did not alter that essential fact. A fine distinction, the kind Bert Zorn would be quick to make.

"I took you for a lawyer right off," Pig said. "I can spot one a mile away. What brings you to the San Rafael?"

That's where Jack's words became more artful.  His explanation of his presence in Arizona involved a narrative of his decision to take some time off work and see the West.

While Jack gave account of himself on what must have been at least the third go-round and before anything could be done to prevent it, Claire was spirited away by women who inquired about Molly and Claire's father and pressed for details about the handsome man escorting her to the party.  Men, who excoriated the government and railed against the evil of inheritance taxes, sequestered Jack. They demanded justification as if he bore some responsibility for tax laws simply by being a lawyer.

Pig accepted the good looking stranger right off.

"I like your cut," she said.  "Even if you are a lawyer. And any friend of Claire's is a friend of mine."

Others welcomed Jack with equal warmth. "Come on in and eat a bean," one fellow said.  Pig Campbell seconded the motion.  "I'm with you, Emmett.  My tapeworm's hollerin' for fodder."

Beyond the small crowd in the corner of the room, stood a tall thin fiddler, front man of a four-piece band.  The fiddler wore jeans so tight they plainly outlined the essential aspects of his private parts.  On his head, sat a black cowboy hat with the brim turned up sharply on the sides like a taco shell. At his feet, lay a blue-eyed cow dog with a speckled hide, black and white and every imaginable shade of gray in between, a smattering of brown.  A tooled leather collar at the dog's neck bore his name, "Radar."  The fiddler explained later the pup earned his moniker by barking at airplanes when they passed overhead.

The young man in front struck up the band again.  He put the fiddle to his shoulder and secured it with his chin, began plucking strings and tuning up.  Then he played.

The tight-jeaned minstrel bowed sweet music, a distant cousin to the music Claire once made with her cello.  From the beginning, with melodious sounds in his ears and Claire's scent in his nostrils, Jack Breen knew his heart would not come

126

through this night untouched. Already, without warning and without leave, it quickened deep within him.

Soon, the tempo changed. The fiddler became a caller, summoned dancers to their feet:

> *Choose yo' partner, form a ring.*
> *Figure eight, an' double L swing*
>
> *First swing six, then swing eight,*
> *Swing 'em like swingin' on the old gate.*
>
> *Ducks in the river, goin' to the ford,*
> *Coffee in a little rag, sugar in a gourd.*
>
> *Swing 'em once an' let 'em go,*
> *All hands left an' do-si-do.*

The caller's picturesque lingo and carefree delivery left folks spellbound. Soon, they answered the call and took to the floor. The fiddler kept time with his head, his feet, his entire body. Partners dipped and twirled, stomped their high-heeled boots. Pig Campbell whispered in Jack's ear that some folks were going to dance themselves right out of the church. They'd have to be saved at the next revival.

After a while, the music paused and the fiddler spoke in a voice raised above the low rumble of applause and conversation.

"Y'all gather round," he said. "Come on in. Everybody take a seat. We're gonna sing Happy Birthday. Gonna be a special version of it."

Feet shuffled. The hum of conversation wound down and quiet set in. People disengaged from one another and began to seat themselves in metal folding chairs placed around the room's perimeter. Jack searched the dimly lit sea of faces for Claire. And then he spotted her. She was smiling, light-hearted, burdens seemingly lifted, at least for a while. He followed her with his eyes and she followed him. He started to move toward her. But before he took a step, Pig Campbell laid a meaty hand on his shoulder.

"Come on, darlin'. You can sit by me. Claire won't mind."

"But."

"Right here," she said and virtually forced him onto the chair beside her.

Jack was not about to stand up to Pig. So, he and Claire ended up on opposite sides of the room. And then the fiddler spoke again.

"Most of y'all know Radar here. But I wonder if you know he can play the fiddle."

The curious comment prompted a swell of laughter.

"No. Really," the fiddler said. "He is quite possibly the only canine musician in the entire state of Arizona. Watch this."

With that, the fiddler leaned down. He patted Radar on the head, stroked his shoulders. The dog sat erect and his human maestro placed the handle of the bow between the dog's teeth so it extended horizontally. He clamped down the critter's jaws with his hand, tightening the pup's grip on the bow handle. Another wave of low laughter swept across the room.

Now, with the dog holding the bow in his teeth and with the man moving the fiddle up and down, thin strands of cat gut gave up the familiar strains of "Happy Birthday. Happy Birthday to You."

The crowd loved it. At the conclusion of the tune, it erupted in applause and laughter. And then the appreciative spectators began to sing, rendering a more conventional vocal version of the same ditty. A portly, silver haired gentleman, the birthday boy, blushed and smiled. He waved graciously.

When the applause and laughter abated, the fiddler returned to his playing and Radar lay down to sleep. At once, the music of the violin infused the air again. Jack and Claire gazed at each other longingly. Eyes remained tightly fixed, unblinking and intense, each demanding the gaze of the other in return, insisting upon undistracted focus.

128

Next, the sinewy fiddler played a mournful tune, bitter sweet in its tenor and effect. A melody to mark an end of something and a beginning of something else. As a time of day, evening. As a month, October. And at any time of day or year the spell it cast would be wistful, filled with the ardor of new discovery and the melancholy of old hurts. It awakened feelings long dormant and stirred the hearts of Jack Breen and Claire Gaynor.

The fiddler played on. The music did not relent. The kind of music that lingers in the air and in your soul long after quivering strings are still and the players have cased and packed away their instruments. A forlorn tune, the kind that leaves your heart craving, desires unsated, spirit aching. The cry of terrible lostness, of loneliness and need. As desperate as the plea of a handful of dust in a strong wind.

Music playing, Claire rose and crossed over to the door. Jack held her with the warm embrace of his eyes, refusing to let her go. He studied every move of her body, fluid graceful steps, sway of hair. She paused at the door and looked at him. She made no sound, showed no expression. Spoke only with her eyes. "Come. Come to me." And then she disappeared into the night.

Jack rose and followed her. Her scent lingered in the air among razor-edged shards of violin music. Passing through, they lashed and lacerated him, urged him on.

He stepped outside, but at first he did not see Claire. Turning, he saw a dim outline just beyond the reach of inner lights. At a distance, an undefined mystery. But when he came closer, he saw Claire. He went to her and without speaking, without making a sound of any kind, he took her in his arms and firmly brought her body to his. He kissed her gently but with conviction, a long, deep, rapturous kiss. He kissed her and she returned his kiss.

But then her heart clouded.

"Don't love me," she said. "I'm not the woman I once was. You don't know me."

But Jack refused. He held her close and kissed her again.

"No," she said. "I meant it when I said I'd had enough of men."

But Jack could not stop himself. He could feel the contours of Claire's body against his. Beneath her jacket he could feel the firmness of her breasts. With his hands he could feel the taut muscles of her back, beneath them the stacked vertebrae of her spine, angular relief of shoulder blades.

He kissed her once then he kissed her again, still not speaking, not allowing her to speak. And when their lips parted, the woman sighed.

"It's the wine," she said.

"No. It's not the wine. It's much more."

"Jack."

But before she could speak another word, before any question could be asked or caution urged, he kissed her again. He extinguished words and doubts with kisses. Within his embrace and with his lips pressed against hers, her wary heart opened.

On this night, a night like no other, all doubt left Jack Breen. He loved Claire Gaynor as he never loved anyone. He always had. Now that he had her, he would never let her go.

# CHAPTER 13 - ABOVE ALL, MUSIC

Having nothing, Jack Breen had nothing to lose. He became a free man. Thus liberated, he made a new beginning.

The day after the banker's birthday party Jack decided to throw in his lot with Claire and her small band of immortals. He moved his possibles into the twelve by forty double-wide known as the "Bunk House." Spare as living quarters, but just right for him. Seasonal hands slept there during the spring roundup and the fall gather, a time for branding and castrating, vaccinating everything on the hoof. Transient cowboys that hired out for day wages stayed there when they needed a place to bed down for a night. Army surplus cots outfitted with clean bedclothes thanks to Maria Paz served well.

After a while, Jack came to think of the bunk house as home. It offered no luxuries, no television, not even a radio. The morning paper did not arrive at the door every morning. A maid didn't turn down the bed and lay a chocolate on the pillow every night. But it was comfortable enough. Perfect for Jack Breen, defrocked big shot. Exactly what he needed a quarter of the way through a two year suspension. Besides, he didn't have energy for more. Days began before sunrise and ended after dark. Hard physical labor purified the man, body and soul. He had only what he needed, a place to sleep the phantomless sleep of a man at peace with himself and the world.

Ace adapted well to his new life, too. With ease, he grew accustomed to having full run of the ranch. And, after an initial tussle or two with Uncle Fountain's growling bird dog, the canines made peace. Now, in the warm days and cool nights of summer the two dogs often slept side by side, sometimes back to back, now and then, overlapping.

Jack Breen took on the look and feel of the San Rafael. Under the tutelage of Jayro Paz and the watchful and suspicious eyes of Uncle Fountain, he became a rancher. These days, Jack carried a Buck knife in a leather scabbard on his belt. He often had a pair of wire cutters in his hip pocket. Sun coppered his face. He no longer had soft city hands, lawyer hands. He had a rancher's hands, a man's hands. They could build fence, work a horse in a round pen or at the end of a lunge line. They could level a horse's hoof with a steel rasp.

Spanish words crept into his lexicon. He said "*listo*" when he was ready. He said "*buenos días*" in the morning and "*buenas noches*" at night. "Thank you" became "*gracias*" and "you're welcome" evolved into "*de nada.*"

Jack Breen made a quick study. New skills came easily to him, as everything did. But not so with Molly. She was a tough nut to crack. She had a father and Jack Breen would not take his place. She knew nothing of her daddy's betrayal of her mother. She knew only that she missed him. For Jack Breen, winning the little girl over would not be easy.

\*\*\*\*\*

Above all, there was music. One late afternoon, following years of silence and the unmelodious racket of daily living, Claire lifted her cello from its case. She ran her fingers along slender strings, remembering their feel, their sympathetic vibration. She plucked and tightened them into tune. The sweetness of the sound stirred memories and feelings long

132

dormant inside her. For the first time in years, she could see herself as a rancher, a mother, an heir and an artist all at once. And, she could see herself as a woman.

Claire loaded the cello into her truck and set out alone for Lago Esperanza. Though known as a lake, it amounted to no more than a pond, what ranchers call a "tank." A man with a good arm could skip a rock across it in three jumps, if he had the right angle. Claire's grandfather gave it the name "Esperanza." Hope. That's what he said its beauty and stillness brought him. And now, it held true for Claire.

Esperanza lay in a high meadow of the north range, in the place where the Sierra Madre from the south and the Rockies from the north overlap. Its water, icy run-off from upper elevations, collected in a still bedrock pool, fresh, clear, dark as India ink. The water flowed into the lake from Loon Creek, a meltwater trace that descended from above and coursed through pines and junipers. Up high, it started out sluggish, but then muscled up with declining elevation, from time to time ramping over rocks in low falls. Below, it roiled and surged, at times producing a convulsive roar. Near Esperanza, the water moderated to a narrow riffle with a soothing voice. By the time it reached the catch basin, it calmed to a trickle.

The lake's water stretched still and taut from bank to bank. A needle would float on the tension. At morning, a low mist often suffused the surface until the risen sun burned it off. On a clear summer day, blue sky showed in the lake. Mountains, trees, clouds. Late in the year, the water's blackness turned golden with the reflection of autumn leaves. In any season, a face would show in it as clearly as in any looking glass.

Claire carried her instrument to the water's edge. She seated herself on a granite rock the height of a concert chair and steadied the cello with her knees. Watching her mirrored image in the water, she raised the bow and held it in playing position. She bowed with grace and purpose. Strings began to quiver and sing.

Music. In this place where there had been only stillness, save the occasional surface strike of a trout or the flap and cry of a caw bird overhead, the air swelled with the sweet strains of a concerto. The pleasing sound drew Claire in. It caressed and enveloped her, refreshed and restored her like a sonorous poultice applied to the heart.

After a while, Jack appeared. He heard the music as he heard it the moment he first laid eyes on Claire – that day in the long ago. It summoned him the way it did then. He followed it like a child of Hamelin following the piper, until he stood behind the cellist, within an arm's length of her.

When his reflection appeared in the water, Claire paused in mid-stroke. She froze, bow against strings, eyes fixed on the shimmering reflection of the face before her.

"Don't stop," Jack said. "Play."

"How did you know I was here?"

Claire spoke without turning, addressing not the man, but the water's rendering of him.

"Maria," he answered. "She saw you leave. The rest was a guess."

A moment of silence followed. Claire held her gaze on the man in the lake.

"Play," Jack said again. "Please."

And play she did. Claire purged herself of silence with music. Hills and swales of Raven Ranch resounded with it.

Claire finished the piece with a flourish as if she were sitting on the stage at Carnegie Hall. When she lifted her bow, Jack applauded.

"Bravo," he said. "Bravissimo."

Claire lowered her head in a gracious bow. She rested her instrument against the rock and rose, turning, offering a hand to Jack.

"Come on," she said. "I want to show you something."

"Where are we going?"

"The springs."

"Aren't you afraid of mountain lions out here?"

134

Claire made no reply. She only smiled and took Jack's hand. Together, they crossed the meadow of lush, ankle-high grass and disappeared in the trees beyond. With Claire in the lead, they followed Loon Creek up a gentle rise. A thick crosshatch of interwoven branches above darkened the trail. The adjacent crease cut in the earth by the sharp edge of flowing water grew deeper along the ascent. Walls became steeper, more obscure.

And then the trail flattened and played out. They reached their mysterious destination.

Here, the run-off poured over a rocky rim and collected in a shallow pool. Beside it, only a few feet away, a natural hot spring formed a smaller thermal basin. Within a few seconds a man or woman of stout heart could jump from one to the other for a seventy degree temperature swing, cold to hot, hot to cold.

Fallen logs and large rocks carefully set in place by Claire's father years before formed the boundaries of the smaller body of water. Steam rose and hung low in the cool, shady air above. Somewhere deep within the earth, rocks warmed by smoldering primal fires heated the water of an underground spring and sent it to the surface. Like a small, fiery tributary of a sunken river of flame, it worked its way above ground over centuries. The water possessed legendary healing powers, Claire explained. According to myth, it issued from the great fire that created the world, an inferno that still burns deep within the earth. A symbol of new life.

"Indians say this water will cure what ails you," Claire said.

She knelt and tested it with a hand.

"Perfect. So hot you can barely stand it."

Claire looked around a moment. She removed her jacket and hung it on a low branch. She turned to Jack and gazed into his eyes. She drew a circle in the air with a finger.

"Turn around," she said.

Jack smiled, hesitated.

135

"Turn around," she repeated, emphasizing each syllable individually.

This time, he complied. Behind him he could hear the sound of Claire slipping off her clothes, rustle of cotton fabric, dull buzz of a zipper, snap of elastic. He girded himself with his arms, locked them down tight, resisting the temptation of flesh.

"This takes enormous will power," he said. "I want you to know that."

"It's good for you."

"Right. Oh, yeah. Right."

And then Jack heard the sound of Claire lowering her naked body through the thermal fog inch-by-inch into steaming water. Warily, she sank to her neck.

"All right," she said, breathless. "You can turn around."

Jack turned. Only her head cleared the dark water. She was smiling, so fair and fresh and beautiful he could hardly believe it or bear it.

"Well, are you going to get in?" Claire said.

Mimicking her, Jack made a circle in the air, gestured with his hand.

"Now you."

Claire smiled, dropped her chin to a mischievous angle. She sank lower into the water, shook her head.

"Huh uh."

"Come on."

"Huh uh."

"Okay," Jack said, nodding, accepting his fate. "If that's the way you want it."

He started skinning off his clothes, first his shirt, then his boots. The disrobement went on and Claire's eyes widened. When it neared its dramatic conclusion, her mouth fell open. Then, in a sudden splash and with a girlish squeal she turned and looked away. Creamy shoulders rose from dark water like twin peaks of an Atlantic iceberg in moonlight.

After Jack eased into the water, gasping all the way, he and Claire sat, sighing. They lolled in the steaming liquid to

136

their necks, Jack at one end of the pool, Claire at the other, toes touching.

"What made you decide to play?" Jack said. "The cello, I mean."

"I don't know. Time was right, I guess. Felt right anyway."

"I'm glad."

Claire smiled.

"I'm still pretty good, aren't I?"

"The best," Jack answered. "The very best."

# CHAPTER 14 - BURDEN OF PROOF

Jack Breen took up the cause of Claire's injustice with a vengeance. Lack of law license be damned. No need to hang out a shingle to take Jaime Passamonte in hand, train him, prop him up in court. Though Breen would have to stay behind the bar, he could still whisper instructions in the young lawyer's ear and pass him notes. Breen knew Jaime Passamonte would play his part awkwardly. And he knew his work as offstage impresario would have the subtlety of a two-by-four to the head. Dangerous for a man with a checkered past and unreckoned sins back East. So be it. He had no choice.

*****

The appointed day and hour of a pretrial conference with the judge arrived. The judge would set the schedule for the case, disclose the likely date of a trial on the merits. On such occasions, he enjoyed pontificating and berating lawyers. Never passed up a chance to take a shot at one.

A few minutes before nine, teacher and student climbed the courthouse steps. A depression era structure built as a WPA project, the building had gray granite walls and heavy double doors of steel and glass.

Half way up the steps, Passamonte halted. Breen turned.

"What? What is it?"

"I don't know if I can do this. I . . ."

"Sure you can. Just don't let these guys run over you."

"What if I screw up? I don't want to let Claire down. I . . . don't want to let you down. I'm not you, you know."

Jack put a hand on the kid's arm.

"It's a scheduling conference. You'll do fine. Let's go."

"Wait. Wait. I've been poor all my life. Never considered it much of pleasure. Family didn't amount to much. All dead now. I don't know how I got through law school. Some kind of miracle, I guess. Then, you came along. Now . . . now . . ."

Jaime Passamonte started to choke on his words.

"You'll do fine. Come on. I'll be right behind you."

Jack Breen took to the role of teacher. And Passamonte could not help admiring his mentor. He looked past the failure of character that led to Breen's fall from grace. He appreciated the old warhorse's skill and wit, his creativity, his nerve. Jaime Passamonte wanted Jack Breen's approval, more than anything. He would pay any price to win his favor.

Inside the courthouse, Jaime Passamonte pointed to a bronze plaque hanging on a wall near the entrance. The inscription read, "Dedicated to Judge Harold Malloy who died during erection 1932." Passamonte rolled his eyes. "Stupid bastards." He explained that the inartful language rendered the building a subject of ridicule from day one. A photograph of the plaque made it all the way to the pages of Playboy Magazine in the sixties. A dubious honor.

Over the course of seven decades, cigar and cigarette smoke and sweat permeated the water-stained interior walls. Floor sweep the janitor used at night gave the odor a pungent edge. Breen called it the stench of corruption, said it aroused his sense of competition. Passamonte agreed. Always ready to please. Always ready to be just like Jack Breen.

On the ground floor, local folk hero Dan Shumate ran a small snack bar. "Blind Dan" wore glasses with dark lenses and hefty frames. He moved with the tentative gait of a man condemned by fate to live his life in darkness.

Dan lost his sight and his right arm in Vietnam. A man in his squad dropped a grenade when he reared back to throw it. Dan picked it up and let it fly a split second before it exploded. He saved a half-dozen men, but his heroics cost him an appendage and his sight. The Army awarded him a Purple Heart for his wounds and a Silver Star for his bravery. These years later, every day without fail, Blind Dan wore a green jungle fatigue shirt with the right sleeve turned up and pinned. Hair, now thinning on top, streaked with gray, hung to his shoulders.

Despite having only one arm Dan could make coffee, sell candy bars and cigarettes, operate a cash register, make change. He claimed to know the denomination of a bill by the weight and feel of it. And he could smell a skunk a mile off.

Blind Dan figured Judge William D. McGrew for a crook long before he had any proof of it. He hated the man's guts, too. McGrew signed the foreclosure order on the Shumate home place when the small produce business his family operated went under. Dan had a long memory, and he held a grudge. He was the only man in town to tell the judge to fuck off, to his face. His disability gave him cover no one else had. He didn't work for the county or the state, anyway. He worked for a private organization that contracted with the state to provide snack bars in courthouses. Under the Americans with Disabilities Act, he could claim all the accommodations he needed. Besides, he had an army pension and he didn't need the money. To Jaime Passamonte, Blind Dan Shumate made a regular Che Guevara. A true hero. *Viva la revolución.*

"Hey, Dan," Jaime Passamonte called out when he passed the snack bar with Jack Breen.

Dan recognized the voice right off. The loss of sight sharpened his sense of hearing.

140

"Hey, Jaime my man. How about some coffee?"

"No time, Dan. Thanks."

"Make time. You need it. Trust me."

Jaime stopped. He glanced at Jack, then stepped to the snack bar. Jack sided his friend.

"Who's that with you?" Blind Dan said.

Jack looked at Passamonte as if to question whether Dan really lacked sight. For a moment, no one spoke. Dan Shumate sensed the unspoken question.

"I'm blind, not deaf. Heard two sets of footsteps. It ain't magic."

"This is Jack Breen," Passamonte said. "A friend. One of the good guys."

"Damn few of those around here."

Dan reached across the counter and offered his hand. Jack took it, gave it a firm shake.

"What's up?" Passamonte said. "You get wind of something?"

Dan turned his head from side to side as if to check the hall for eavesdroppers.

"We're alone," Passamonte assured him. "Go ahead."

Dan set his elbow on the counter and leaned forward. He spoke in a low voice.

"You may not know it, but you're fixin' to get fucked."

He shook his head in disgust.

"Billy McGrew. Like to wring his scrawny neck."

Jack and Passamonte exchanged glances.

"You're probably asking yourselves how I came by this information," Dan said. "X-ray ears. I can hear through walls, man. Hear through noise. Hear through anything."

"So what have you heard?"

"Vinegar Bill McGrew. That boy was raised on dill pickles and sour milk. But he'll show yellow in the end. Know the type."

Dan aimed his sightless eyes up and down the hall again.

"Anybody around?"

Jaime Passamonte looked, shook his head.

"I heard McGrew talking to Lucien Porter. If that ain't a pair to draw to. Gag a maggot."

"Dan, I'm runnin' out of time. What did you hear?"

"Anybody around?"

"Nobody's around, man. Come on, what'd you hear?"

"Never ceases to amaze me. Just because you're blind, people think you're deaf and simpleminded, too. Them two guys was standin' over there. Right down the hall yonder. Talkin'. Talkin' 'bout how they're gonna nail your ass. Must be something big."

"Why? Why do you say that?"

"Cause McGrew told Porter he was really gonna have to come through big time. If he was gonna come through for Porter, Porter was gonna have to come through for him."

"When's it going down?"

"Don't know. Soon, I figure. Got an idea where."

"Where?"

"Heard 'em say something about the old drive-in. What do they call it? The Rio. Closed up now, you know. But I don't mind. Don't go to the movies much anymore."

Dan smiled.

"Thanks, man," Jaime Passamonte said.

"*De nada.*"

Jaime Passamonte backed away from the counter.

"Keep your ears peeled," he said.

"All the time, brother. All the time."

*****

The courtroom loomed larger than Jack Breen expected the first time he saw it. Dark oak paneling. Faded green industrial carpet. Overhead, art deco light fixtures of stainless steel with opaque glass panels hung like stalactites from the ceiling by long, silver rods. A row of six foot casement windows with rusty, metal hand cranks ran along the wall. Between the bench and the rail stood two dark wood counsel

142

tables with ornately carved legs and glass tops. Beneath each table, lurked a brass spittoon.

When Passamonte and Breen walked in, their opponents waited. Two grim-faced city lawyers, looking like pallbearers in pinstripe suits, sat at one of the counsel tables. The older man with thin, gray hair wore a pair of tortoise shell glasses with round lenses. His young associate had dark hair, moist, slicked down. At the sight of them, Jack Breen's jaws tightened. He had to suppress a gag.

Behind the city lawyers, in the first row of pews, sat Lucien Porter. He eyed Breen and Passamonte warily, but said nothing. The two city lawyers nodded with mock sincerity, but did not rise. They maintained an air of smug assurance.

Dressed in jeans, looking more like a ranch hand than a lawyer, Jack Breen stood outside the bar issuing last minute instructions to Jaime Passamonte. He rested a hand on his shoulder.

"Look," he said, low voiced, confidential. "All we're here for is to talk about scheduling. Just get us as much time as you can. We need to work up our case. Tell the judge about Claire and her dad. Tell him we need as much time as we can get. Don't let these guys run over you."

Jaime Passamonte nodded. Face slick with sweat, he breathed through his mouth.

Soon, a door opened and a coarse-skinned old man walked in. Bailiff and sometimes bag man Sid Cantrell.

"All rise," he called out in a stern voice.

A man in his mid-seventies, Cantrell always had a soggy cigar stub in the corner of his mouth, even in court. Backs of his hands resembled alligator hide. Deep furrows lined his face and neck. Wiry gray hairs bristled from the top of his nose and the lobes of his ears.

Cantrell never wore anything but black and white, black trousers, black tie, white shirt. Sleeves rolled up to his elbows. Around one of his thick, liver-spotted wrists he always had at least half a dozen rubber bands. They left a permanent mark.

At Cantrell's command, everyone in the courtroom stood. Jaime Passamonte moved to one of the counsel tables and laid a file folder on the glass-covered top. He was wearing his tan corduroy jacket, jeans, white shirt, red tie, dressed up for him. His trademark green rubber band secured his pony tail.

"Court is now in session," Sid Cantrell said. "The Honorable William D. McGrew presiding."

McGrew, rail thin, long nose, high cheekbones, entered the courtroom through a small door behind and to the right of the dark wood bench. With his black robe unzipped, the two sides flared like bat wings. In his hand the wiry judge held a lighted cigarette, unfiltered. The first time Jack Breen, former big shot lawyer, saw a judge smoke in court.

The judge ascended the one step to the law-giver's throne and seated himself in a high-backed leather chair. He reclined and struck a recumbent pose, one foot hooked on the corner of the desk. Without a word to anyone, he spread a file folder out in his lap and started leafing through its contents. After a long, uncomfortable silence, Jaime Passamonte looked at Jack and shrugged. The city lawyers remained on their feet, hands at their sides, humorless in manner.

Marlene Slemp, the court reporter, another courthouse burnout with flaming red hair and an excess of makeup, sat at her post near the judge. She waited, amusing herself with a mouthful of chewing gum and a study of her fingernails. When she glanced at Passamonte through gaudy-framed glasses, she rolled her eyes.

At last, the judge spoke and the court reporter raised the steno mask to her face. It was her job to take down every word spoken. She usually got most of it, maybe eighty percent. For a moment, Jaime Passamonte wondered what would happen to the gum.

"So what's on the docket today?" the judge said without raising his head. In a moment, he answered his own question. "In Re the Matter of the Guardianship of James Gaynor, an Incompetent. What's this about?"

Jaime Passamonte cleared his throat.

144

"It's our motion, Judge," he said, voice quivering. He could not bring himself to say, "Your Honor." "Our motion to approve donation of the development rights for the Gaynor ranch to the Ranchers Association."

The judge peered down at Jaime Passamonte through the tops of unblinking eyes. Palpable hostility and arrogance in his expression.

"Donation? You're gonna give away the assets of the estate? Now how does that work? Why is that a good idea?"

The judge leaned forward. His fingers walked across the surface of the bench like tarantula legs to the ashtray. He dragged the tray toward him and stubbed out his smoke.

"Well, Judge, it's a way to keep the ranch in the family. You donate the development rights and the value of the property goes down. That way–"

The judge raised a hand and cut him off.

"Whoa. Whoa. Hold your horses. Stop right there. You want to lower the value of the property? Now that just sounds hunky dory, don't it. I kindly wonder if maybe you ain't a little wet behind the ears for this. How on God's green earth can that be a good idea?"

"Well."

Before Jaime Passamonte could get another word out, the elder city lawyer interrupted him.

"It's not a good idea, Your Honor. It's a bad idea."

The judge looked at him and softened his expression.

"Sounds bad to me right off the bat. Most folks aren't too eager to see the value of their property go down."

Passamonte showed a pained expression.

"Well, don't look so down in the mouth, son. These boys here might be tryin' to save you from yourself. Could be you're 'bout to make a terrible mistake."

The judge hacked a smoker's cough and raised a fisted hand to his mouth. He looked at the city lawyer again.

"Who are you, anyway?"

The bespectacled lawyer rose, spoke with an air of pompous reserve.

"Your Honor, we represent the San Rafael Development Company, a joint venture with Mr. Porter. My client has a mortgage on the property. Donating the development rights would render that worthless. We offered a sizable sum to the estate through the guardian Claire Gaynor. We want to buy the property, at least a big part of it. We have plans for a development."

"Well," the judge said. "Now you're talkin'. Be good for the whole county, wouldn't it?"

"Yes, sir. We anticipate creating at least five hundred jobs, maybe more. Millions of tourist and recreation dollars will be pumped into this area every year."

"Well now, that sounds pretty good to me. What about this mortgage, Mr. . . . What's your name again?"

"Passamonte. Jaime Passamonte."

"Well, what about this mortgage, Mr. Passamont?"

By dropping the last syllable, the judge did his best to make a mockery of the name.

Jaime Passamonte tensed. He opened his mouth, but no words came out. He swallowed hard, caught some air.

"It's a forgery," he blurted out.

The judge looked up, sat back.

"Well now, that is quite a claim."

Lucien Porter squirmed in his seat, grimaced. He shook his head.

"Are you prepared to prove that, Mr. Passamont?"

"Well . . ."

"Your Honor," the city lawyer interrupted. "The mortgage is genuine. My client has intervened in this matter to oppose the depletion of the incompetent's estate by donation of the so-called development rights. The loan is in default. The mortgage is subject to foreclosure. If the development rights are given away . . . well, we can't have that."

Jaime Passamonte swallowed hard again.

"It's a forgery," he repeated.

146

"I know, son. You already said that. What says the intervenor?"

"Well, I have to admit being more than a little flabbergasted. And, a little outraged. I think they know the mortgage is genuine. Mr. Porter, who's sitting right there, can testify to its authenticity. We could probably go ahead and take care of that little issue today."

Jaime Passamonte knew he was losing ground. His eyes darted toward Jack Breen. Jack leaned forward. He scowled and mouthed the words, "Stop him."

The city lawyer continued.

"We would argue that it's not in the best interests of the estate to diminish the value of the property. We would urge that the guardian be directed to enter into good faith negotiations for sale of the property. In fact, we are prepared to put on evidence to show—"

Jaime Passamonte cut him off. Anger scorched his face. Despite the firm grip of terror, outrage gave him courage.

"Judge, we need more time. We . . . we . . . we demand time to get ready for trial."

Poor choice of words.

"Demand?" the judge said.

"Yes, sir," Passamonte said, leaning forward, planting both hands firmly on the counsel table. "We need time to prepare."

The judge glared at him.

"I'd be real careful about demanding anything in my court, Mr. Passamont. That's generally not a good idea. But, under the circumstances I don't suppose it'll hurt to delay this just a little while."

Passamonte straightened himself. He dried the palms of his hands on his jacket, but he did not waver. He didn't lose his nerve despite the judge's severe injunction.

"We'll set the trial on the merits over to . . . let's say ninety days from today. Judgment day. Same time. And if I were you, young man, I'd get busy and see what kind of deal I could make with these boys with the deep pockets."

It was clear what the judge was thinking. A little delay might be good for everybody, even for him. It would allow him to avoid an error in the record that might lead to an appeal and a reversal of his ruling in favor of the developers. And a little suspense might make them up the ante, sweeten the pot a bit.

The judge rose. He aimed his gavel at Jaime Passamonte.

"Don't be making demands in my court. You hear?"

Like a lot of judges, McGrew favored use of the phrase, "my court." He liked to think of the court as his. Of course, it was not. Even in a place like southern Arizona and despite what William D. McGrew might think, it was not his court at all. He was merely the temporary custodian of it. Still, in this place, at this time, McGrew's reference to the court as his probably held truer than in most venues.

McGrew took a parting shot.

"I don't take too kindly to lawyers making demands."

Jaime Passamonte nodded.

"Court will be in recess," McGrew said. He turned to leave. In the next instant, he stepped through the side door and disappeared.

The city lawyers packed their brief cases and headed for the Mercedes Benz parked outside. Jaime Passamonte bored holes right through them with his eyes.

Lucien Porter stood and followed the city lawyers out, smiling. When he passed Jack Breen, he widened his smile. He paused right in front of him. The smile vanished.

"You ain't gonna screw me outa what's mine. I give good money for that mortgage. Every dime I could scrape up. That old man wanted it. Couldn't take it fast enough. You and your lap dog here ain't nothin' short of liars. Be damned to you."

Porter headed for the door. Passamonte headed for Jack.

"Man. That was close. How'd I do?"

148

"Uh . . . great. You were . . . great."

Jack punched him gently on the shoulder and smiled. Passamonte took in a deep breath and swelled his chest. He exhaled and puffed out his cheeks.

"Man. We were about to get screwed. Damn kangaroo court."

"Are you kidding?" Jack said. "This place isn't fit for kangaroos. No self-respecting marsupial would be caught dead in here. More like a prairie dog court. Let's go."

\*\*\*\*\*

An hour later, Jack arrived at the ranch. At the house, he encountered Uncle Fountain sitting on the front porch steps, whittling. He was putting a fine point on the end of a cottonwood stave as long as his arm and as big around as his bony wrist. Jack got out of the truck, walked toward the old man, and stood before him. Uncle Fountain lifted his gaze.

"You gonna be able to help Miss Claire hang on to this place? You gonna be able to whup them sons-a-bitches?"

"I don't know," Jack said. "I hope so. Think we can take a pretty strong position."

"Po-sition? That what you gon' do? Take a po-sition?"

Uncle Fountain shook his head. He spat.

"Um huh. Reckon that's what lawyers do, ain't it? Take a po-sition."

Jack started to nod, but refrained. Uncle Fountain continued whittling, sharpening the point of the stave. Jack watched him in silence. The old man looked up.

"This ain't no triflin' lawyer spat you in. And this ain't no common barn rat you up against. Don't need to take a po-sition, boy. Let the other feller do that. You take a stand. Ever take a stand? Really take a stand?"

Jack thought a minute before speaking.

"No," he said.

"Figgered."

The old man rose. He raised the white, finely tapered point of the whittled stick to his face. Blew the dust and shavings away, admired the perfection of his work. And then with a quick, violent movement that defied the age of muscles and brittleness of bones, he drove the stake into the ground. He planted it there as if he were running it into the heart of the devil himself.

"Now's the time," he said. "You best take a stand."

Uncle Fountain folded the knife blade into its case and slipped it into a pocket. He underlined his stern admonition to Jack with a curt nod, then shuffled away.

The old man was right on the money. Jack Breen never took a stand in his entire life. Always took a position. But in this fight, fancy words and wily lawyer ways would not suffice.

Jack put a hand on the stake. It stood strong, firm, deep in the ground, not easily withdrawn. At that moment, Jack Breen took a blood oath. He would take a stand. Even if it meant putting his life on the line. God willing, he would not fail.

# <u>CHAPTER 15 - PLAYING DIRTY</u>

Despite his failure of loyalty to it, Jack Breen still believed in the law, and in his own ability to use it to advantage. He intended to beat Porter and his confederates fair and square. But he was not naive. He knew what could happen to the best laid plans. He needed a fallback position. If all else failed, he could play dirty. As Bert Zorn liked to say, "When you're in a piss fight with a skunk, you don't use distilled water."

*****

At the appointed time, Jack Breen met Jaime Passamonte in his office and the night's real work began.

"You know where McGrew lives?" Jack said.

"Sure. Little acreage south of town. Why?"

"Maybe we ought to drift out there and nose around a little."

"You lookin' to get shot?"

"Come on."

Jack turned to leave.  Passamonte hesitated.

"I don't know, man.  I . . . I . . . I don't know."

"Come on," Jack said.  "Sometimes you get lucky."

Jack walked out the door.  Jaime Passamonte rolled his eyes and shook his head.  Then he smiled.

"I'm with you, *jefe*.  Where you lead, I follow."

They parked a quarter of a mile from McGrew's place and stashed the truck in a stand of trees.  They hopped a three strand barbed wire fence and made their way cross country in the darkness.  They stopped suddenly about the length of a football field from the house.  Jack crouched behind a row of low bushes at the edge of a long driveway.  He grabbed Passamonte's arm and forced him into a similar posture.

Jack put a finger to his lips.

"Quiet," he whispered.

McGrew stood in the yard with another man.  The second man's size and shape struck a familiar chord with Jack Breen.  When he turned and the porch light caught his face, he recognized him.  Lucien Porter.

"I knew we could get some dirt on this guy."

"Man.  I don't believe it," Jaime Passamonte said.  "I don't believe it."

"Shh."

Jack listened for a while, then withdrew from inside his jacket a camera fitted with a telephoto lens.  Passamonte flinched when he saw it as if he were rolling out a cannon.  Jack raised the camera to his eye.  He trained the lens on Porter and McGrew.  Zoomed in.  Focused.  Shot.

Through the lens and in the dim light of the porch he studied the face of Judge Billy McGrew.  Hairline receding on the sides.  Sharp corners and a peak in the middle of his head.  That, with his small eyes and pointed nose, gave him a reptilian quality that often earned jokes and unkind comments among lawyers.

McGrew's descent into corruption did not happen overnight.  He started out honest, even self-righteous.  But thirty years on the bench changed him.  Took all his worst

152

qualities and magnified them. He turned surly and unpleasant. Over time, just plain mean. He became a bitter little man who considered himself better than everyone, especially lawyers. He resented the money made by lawyers in private practice and complained openly about the low pay of judges. He came to see himself as a victim.

Many judges Jack Breen knew over the years convinced themselves of their own unique insight and wisdom. They would often presume to instruct and chastise lawyers. Not all crooked like McGrew. Just arrogant and naive. Such a judge once lambasted Jack during a trial for failing to be complete in his investigation, for failing to locate a witness and develop a key piece of evidence. Jack accepted the criticism and acknowledged his lack of preparation with contrition. The judge gloated at his superior grasp of jurisprudence and the legal process, his more highly developed work ethic. Of course, in truth, Jack had contacted the witness and he had the key piece of evidence in a drawer in his office. Both would have torpedoed his case. So, he deep-sixed them.

That kind of thing happened to judges like McGrew a lot. Of course, they never knew it. Feeding at the public trough, they remained blissful in their ignorance and smug in their self-assurance, however baseless it might be.

McGrew ruled his tiny fiefdom like a stern overlord. In time, his self-righteousness turned to bitterness, then meanness, then dishonesty. Though he lacked the courage to take the risk of self-employment, the strength to bear its burdens, and the resilience to weather its uncertainties, he wanted to be paid and paid well. What he could not do honestly, he would do dishonestly. He ended up on the take. Over time, he became brazen about it. Taking bribes became so routine he almost forgot it was illegal.

On this night, Porter stood facing McGrew, speaking in an animated fashion with dramatic gestures. He extended an index finger like an ice pick. Planted it firmly in the center of

McGrew's chest, and held it there.  Breen's camera shutter clicked.  A powerful image captured on film.

"Man.  I don't believe it," Passamonte said.

"Quiet."

McGrew did not move.  He suffered the abuse in silence.  In a strange reversal of roles, he found himself on the receiving end of someone else's wrath.  Porter tapped the little man's chest with his finger twice more.  Then, the gawky would-be real estate tycoon turned and sauntered to his car.  He drove away and the moment he passed the mailbox emblazoned with the name "McGrew" Breen snapped another picture.

*****

On the drive to town, Passamonte could hardly contain his excitement and outrage.

"Man.  I don't believe it.  Do not fucking believe it."

He repeated that statement over and over.

"We nailed him.  Nailed his ass.  Just like you said.  You are amazing.  Truly amazing."

"Not quite," Jack said.  "We didn't get them doing anything but talking."

"I don't know, man.  Nobody talks to McGrew like that.  Around here that would mean something."

"We need more," Jack insisted.  "We need some real dirt.  We need cash.  You know McGrew's getting paid.  We need to get some evidence of that."

"How?  That could be a little tough."

"Tough maybe.  Not impossible.  We've just got to keep looking.  We have time.  Ninety days before the hearing on the development rights issue."

Jaime Passamonte nodded.

"*Viva la revolución*, man," he said.  "Viva la fuckin' *revolución*."

*****

154

But Lucien Porter knew how to play dirty, too. While Breen was surveiling him and McGrew, Porter was investigating Breen. In no time, he and his joint venturers traced him to Boston, learned about his suspension. They knew about his pending divorce. They knew about Carolyn. Knew all they needed to know, and they had no qualms about using it. Jack Breen was a marked man. Might as well have pinned a bull's eye to his chest.

Later that night, Jack stood filling the tank of his pickup at the self-serve station in Victoria. Pump whirring, rubber hose throbbing. Odor of gasoline vapors. Ace stood on the seat, wagging his tail, head protruding through the driver's window. Jack stroked his ears. A wooden wedge propped the gas station door open and allowed the muted strains of a Mexican song sent north of the Rio Grande over the air waves to waft through and hang in summer air. Overhead, a frantic swarm of gnats swirled in the spray of yellow florescent light.

A silver Suburban pulled into the station and stopped opposite Jack's truck. Running boards. Windows darkened to what cops call "felony tint." At first, the driver wasn't visible through the darkened windows. Then the door opened. A skinny, blue-jeaned leg leading to a snakeskin-booted foot appeared beneath the door. Driver stepped out. Lucien Porter. He stretched and snorted. Hawked and spat on the pavement. Then, he noticed Jack. A gloating look formed on Porter's face.

"Well," he said. "Lookee who we got here."

Jack said nothing. Porter sniffed, popped his knuckles.

"You know, never did catch your name."

Jack ignored the remark. Porter hawked and spat again.

"Don't have a name, I guess. Maybe that's why you always slinkin' around and such."

Jack held his tongue. Porter did not relent.

"We know who you are. Mr. Jack Breen, big shot Boston Lawyer."

Porter smiled, raised a finger.

"Make that ex-lawyer. Little run-in with the law, I understand."

Breen still said nothing. Porter took a step toward him, glowered.

"You ain't foolin' with Ned and the First Reader here. We got ways of knowin' things. We got ways of makin' things happen."

Breen tensed. He opened his mouth, but made no sound.

"We know all about your little problem. And we know you got more comin' down the pike. Your troubles ain't nowhere near over. Long arm of the law fixin' to slap the shit out of you."

Breen listened. Porter took a step back and smiled.

"But no need to get our panties in a wad. We don't want trouble. Not for you, not for me, not for nobody. Live and let live, that's what I say. Believe we could make it worth your while to stay out of our way, just hit the road. You done it before. Probably scrape up enough for you to cure whatever's ailin' you back East. Nothin' like a greenback poultice."

Breen remained silent, but he listened.

"Think about it," Porter said. "You got time. But not all the time in the world."

He started to leave, then stopped.

"One more thing. That mortgage ain't no forgery. It's good as gold. Claire knows it."

Jack refused to acknowledge Porter's words. He finished filling his tank and returned the nozzle to the pump. He walked inside and paid the kid behind the counter. When he came out, Porter was standing beside the pickup petting Ace through the open window on the passenger side. Jack stepped to the front of the truck and looked Porter squarely in the eye.

"Leave the dog alone."

"Oh, he don't seem to mind a little pettin'."

"I do. Stay away from him."

Jack got into the truck and drove away. In his rearview mirror he could see Porter standing in the jaundiced light beneath the cloud of swarming insects. The grin had disappeared.

Jack rubbed Ace's ears. He looked at the dog and shook his head. Ace studied him, as if he were about to receive instructions.

"What's the matter with you?" Jack said. "Stay away from that guy."

# CHAPTER 16 - IN THE CLEAR

By mid-year Jack Breen could sit a horse with the sureness of a man born to it. In no time at all, the tenderfoot from the East made a top hand. At ease in the saddle, not one for choking the horn, he had a gift, Jayro told him, a talent few men have.

In the dark eyes of a horse, Jack Breen saw his own reflection. The inscrutable mystery of the bond between man and *Equus Caballus* enchanted him. In the confluence of species, he recognized a new creation, the completion of something started by God but not finished until a man climbed onto the animal's back and subdued its wildness. He saw strength in the alliance, beauty. Horseback, Jack Breen became more than a mere human being. Better. Nobler. More significant. So, too, the quadruped. Not broken in his domestication. Not vanquished. Fulfilled.

*****

158

Beneath a paling sky, Jayro Paz and Jack Breen made ready to ride. Each man smoothed a long-sweated Navajo blanket onto the wide back of a horse, one the color of night, called "Dodger." The other, a bay called "Rabbit." Each man hoisted a saddle and worked it into place, spicing the air with the rich odor of horse and leather, dank earth.

Morning held still, save the sounds of saddling and the doleful cry of a dove rising from some unseen roost. No one spoke. Horses stood without moving. Lead ropes dangled from halters, draped loosely over heavy muscled necks. When Jack ran the tag end of the latigo through the buckle and hauled on the front cinch, Dodger angled his head in his direction.

"Hooo . . ." Jack said. "Easy."

When they had the horses saddled, Jayro and Jack shared looks of satisfaction.

"*Listo?*" Jayro said in a low voice.

"*Sí.* Ready."

Jayro nodded.

"*Vámanos.*"

They jumped the horses into a slant load trailer hitched to the pickup, and struck out for the southernmost reaches of Raven Ranch. They would ride out the entire spread, searching for renegade cows that wandered off, wild from isolation. They would check fence, downed sometimes by the struggle of bulls, old and young, in a clash of generations. Investigate water levels in stock tanks, take an overall inventory of the ranch. Jayro took on the task in segments several times a year. No more than half-work for him, especially now that he had an *amigo* to share both the burden and the joy of it.

Jack and Jayro drove until they ran out of road. Each maintained a reverent silence in deference to the newness of day. No place for talk. Too much to see and consider on the drive. Losing themselves in *la frontera* had a calming effect. Both men studied the region Mexicans called "The Far Quarter," but said nothing.

They followed the blacktop ranch road until it became gravel. Followed the gravel until it became dirt. Followed the dirt until the dimming trace played out altogether, yielded to grass. At the last semblance of civilization, Jayro stopped the truck and killed the engine, set the brake. He turned to Jack.

"Time to mount up."

Jack nodded. Riders stepped out of the truck and stood, stretching the stiffness from their limbs, hands on hips, gazing into the distance. Before them lay a wide sweep of low, rolling country, golden Arizona grassland, *el llano*. New light glinted on dewy blades. Above, loomed an immense dome of clear sky.

Jack raised his eyes to the welcoming blue, looked all around. He could hardly believe what he saw. *Incredible*, he thought. *Just incredible*. So much trouble and loss in the East. Here, he broke into the clear. Like men of centuries past, he came west to find a new life, make a new beginning. And, by God, he did just that.

In the trailer, restless horses shifted their weight. Metal framework and welded joints groaned under the load. Horses stamped their hooves, scented the air for danger. They nickered and blew. Time for work, and they sensed it. Ready and eager.

Jayro threw the iron bolt on the trailer's tailgate and swung it wide. Horses clambered out, heavy steps echoing on floorboards. Dull thud of hooves striking earth. Each man caught a lead rope when a horse came to ground.

Outside, the horses held heads high, tails upright and rigid. They looked around wide-eyed, nostrils quivering. Animal spirits flushed. Ears pointed forward, they cried out in powerful equine voices, the legacy of their ancestors, and calmed themselves when they heard no reply.

Men snugged cinches, filled saddle bags with sandwiches prepared by Maria Paz, hung canteens on saddle horns. They traded halters for bridles and slipped bits into horses' mouths, routed split reins. Acting upon the evolution they claimed as their just inheritance, each man put a foot in a stirrup and swung up on a horse. Saddle leather creaked. Spurs jingled. Horses steadied themselves. In the transformation of walkers to

160

riders, the men became taller, faster, stronger. Became what their progenitors longed to be, horsemen.

The two friends rode south across vast meadows of grama grass, dense tufts at the tops of tall stalks swaying in the wind, brushing stirrup bottoms. They rode all morning, studying the condition of pastures, surveying fences, occasionally dismounting to make repairs. For long stretches, no one made a sound. They used their voices more to communicate with horses than with each other.

They rode up low, grassy hills, down shallow swales. Followed *arroyos* that wound through the tall and uncut like dusty, brown arteries. They watered their mounts in stock tanks, and Jayro made cryptic notes on a scrap of paper with a stub of pencil, then tucked both away in a shirt pocket. The two men carried on the affairs of ranchers in the way stockmen did it in this valley over a hundred years before, from the back of a horse.

When they laid eyes upon an especially long, flat reach of open ground, they reined up. They looked out from beneath broad hat brims through eyes squinted against sunglare. Jayro twisted toward Jack and smiled, gave him an inquiring look.

"Want to stretch 'em out?"

"Why not?"

Each man squared his hat, lowered it on his head, gathered up reins. Horses danced with anticipation.

"Keep a short rein and a deep seat," Jayro said. "Leg on each side, mind in the middle."

Jack nodded.

Jayro brought his heels to the sides of the spirited bay. He leaned forward, shouted, "*Vámanos.*" The horse collected himself and leaped forward, raising a cloud of dust. He extended his long, delicate legs and accelerated.

Jack followed on the dark horse. At first, the horses held to an easy lope. Then they lengthened their gait, lined out. The two riders exchanged furtive glances and fixed their hats firmly in place again. They pressed their mounts, spurs to sides.

Horses put out their heads, laid back ears, flared nostrils. Riders gave them rein. Long tails went whipping and streaming in the wind. In an instant, fleet-footed animals stepped up to a hard gallop. Staccato hoof beats filled the air. Hearts of men and horses pounded. Lungs labored. A rush of excitement surged.

At the end of it, the men pulled their mounts up to a trot, then a walk. They laid reins to lathered hide and ambled to the shade of a sentinel pine at the edge of a stock tank. Horses blew and snorted. Chests heaved with exertion, glistened with sweat. Riders stood in stirrups, broke into joyous whoops and laughter. They patted their horses firmly on their stout necks. They complimented them and praised each other. Heaped upon themselves flattering assessments of their horsemanship, marveled at their deeds.

"Fantastic," Jack exclaimed. "Amazing."

"Sí," Jayro said, smiling. "*Increíble*."

"Pretty good, amigo"

Jayro agreed. "Pretty damn good."

When the horses calmed and cooled themselves, the riders eased them forward to the water and let them drink. Reins fell slack. Dusky muzzles dropped to *agua pura*, sucking in the life-giving liquid with quiet draws. After a while, the horses raised their heads and gazed about, clear rimfall strands descending from whiskery chins. They drank again.

While the horses refreshed themselves, Jayro fished from his shirt pocket a plug of chewing tobacco. He dug a Barlow knife from his jeans pocket and trimmed off a chew. Holding it between thumb and blade, he stretched out his arm toward Jack. Jack studied the offered delicacy with skepticism. Jayro lengthened his reach. Jack accepted. He touched the wad to his nose. Pungent. Cloying, sharp-edged sweetness. He put it in his mouth, and chewed it into a toxic cud. Jayro smiled approval.

Jack sensed trouble right off. He began to salivate profusely. His lips and tongue burned. Fighting off a case of the heaves, he looked at Jayro and smiled, close-mouthed, tight-lipped. He feigned pleasure. He spat, trying but failing to miss

162

his knee. His belly roiled and rumbled. Nausea began to tell on him. He thought he might lose his breakfast.

"*Bueno*," Jayro said. But Jack did not hear him for the ringing in his ears.

"*Bueno*," Jayro said again. "*Bueno. No?*"

No answer. Jayro gestured toward his mouth.

"Tobacco."

Horrorstruck, Jack nodded, tried not to swoon.

"Hmm," he said, keeping his lips tightly sealed. "Hmm." Not a word. Just a sound. All he could manage for a sign of appreciation.

When the horses had their fill, Jayro reined the bay and motioned for Jack to follow. They rode out of the shade and into the open. Before going far, Jayro halted the horse and Jack stopped at his side. Jayro stood in the stirrups and pointed into the distance.

"*Mira*," he said. "*Qué es?*"

Jack blasted the chew from his mouth. He shook his head and grimaced, spat. He wiped his mouth with the back of a gloved hand, and spat again. He stood in the stirrups and looked where Jayro pointed. Something on the ground in a heap. Horses saw it, too, and peaked their ears.

"Come on," Jayro said. "We take a look."

They put the horses forward and cautiously searched the range ahead. When they got where they were going, they ran onto a mauled, suffering calf, a long yearling, crossbred Hereford. A blend of gray and brown, red of blood. Ground fetid with spilled guts and cow shit.

Jayro stepped down and handed the reins to Jack. Skittish horses stepped nervously, scent of a killer and his prey in the air. Heavy reek of death. Instinct told them to be on guard. Muscles tensed for flight.

"Easy," Jack said. "Easy."

Jayro went to the fallen critter, and stood over it. Not quite dead, the mangled body trembled, legs worked without purpose. A bloody mess. Ripped across the shoulder blades by what must have been razor sharp claws. Neck deeply slashed. Belly torn open. Eyes milky white. Breathing labored and shallow. Blowflies and other feasting insects hummed. This animal, like many in wild places, would live out its last moments in agony.

Jayro returned to the bay and shucked his rifle from the leather scabbard. Lever action Winchester, 30 - 30. Standing over the gutted calf, he jacked a round into the chamber. He paused a moment and looked around, searching distant trees and rocks for movement, some sign of the killer. He saw nothing.

Jack tightened his grip on the reins. Jayro brought the rifle up and fired. A bullet put an end to the animal's suffering. Horses jerked and backed away. Jack steadied them. Powder smoke soured the air, singed his nostrils.

Jayro squatted on his hunkers at the dead calf's side, resting the rifle across his knees. He thumbed his hat back on his head.

"Something pretty big done this," he said. "Keep the horses back."

"What? What do you think?"

"*Un gato.* Mountain lion."

Jack pointed toward the calf.

"What do we do with it?"

"*Nada.* Coyotes and crows get rid of it. Maybe *el gato* come back."

Jayro stood and studied the overcast rolling in from the Southwest, dulling the noonday sun. He sniffed the air, then looked at Jack.

"Rain. Sky says a storm coming. Need to get home."

Jayro cleared the empty from the rifle, lowered the hammer and slipped the gun back into the scabbard. He mounted. Jack followed. The men rode on. Together. Friends. Horsemen.

\*\*\*\*\*

164

In the high country, heavy weather set in. Brooding clouds bunched up, clung to far peaks. A rain column formed. Offshooting tendrils tracked the distant blue, now gone dark.

The lowering sky grew angry. Gave up a peppering of hail. In remote places, cloudbursts filled dry washes with chili brown water. Old streams awoke and cleaved the land with keen edges. *Arroyos*, normally dry as the dust of ancient bones, ran high. When the riders' trail cut the leading edge of the storm front, slanting rain began quirting their faces. Shivering, jaws clamped, Jayro and Jack took up yellow rain slickers tied behind saddle cantles and slipped them on. They turned up collars, tugged on their hats. Lowered chins.

"*Gran tormenta*," Jayro said over the roar of the sudden tempest.

"What?"

"Blue screamer. Bad storm."

Lightning struck nearby. A fire ball took down a leafless scrag, splitting it from arthritic crown to shriveled taproot. An ear shattering boom followed an instant later. Horses reeled. Riders flinched. The smell of burning wood saturated humid air. Jayro pointed, the bay spinning beneath him.

"*Relampago*," he called out. "Lightning."

The riders advanced into the thick of the storm. In some little time, they halted the horses beside the wild, chaotic flow of a newly formed rainwash rapid. With astonishing quickness, the deluge unleashed a flash flood.

At the margin of the riled water, the men sat their horses, trying to judge the strength of the current and whether they could cross without being swept away. Rain pelted their hats and slickers like machine gun fire.

"I don't think we can make it," Jack said, straining to raise his voice above the racket of the whooping downpour and the fierce rumble of hydraulic fury.

"Too deep. Too fast."

"I try it," Jayro said.

"No. Don't. Don't do it."

*"Tengo cuidado."*

Jayro smiled nervously and eased the grudging bay forward. He touched spurs, but the frightened animal wanted no part of the adventure. Answering instinct, he opposed the command. He balked, danced, wheeled and stutter-stepped, humped up. Jayro talked to the horse and urged him forward again. With great misgiving, the tentative beast stepped into the surging brown water. When it rose to his hocks, he reared and Jayro leaned onto his neck, seized a handful of mane to stay in the saddle. When he had the horse under control, he reined him about.

"No good. Too strong. Too wide."

"What do we do?"

Jayro pointed with a yellow-slickered arm running and dripping with rain.

"Head west. Go around. I know an old iron bridge we can cross. Work our way back to the truck."

"Iron bridge?" Jack said. "In this lightning?"

Jayro smiled.

"The long way. But it will get us there."

They decided to pull for the bridge. Horses game. Riders game. And they had no choice. Beneath a lightning riven sky, thunder booming, they took to the muddy trail. With every flash and every explosive report, Jayro's words echoed in Jack's memory "iron bridge, *relampago*, lightning."

*****

The rain did not let up. Clinging wet clothes bound the riders. All afternoon, they kept their heads low before the lash of water, scream of wind. Hat brims drooping, they withdrew into their rain gear, seldom spoke. They followed the dim trace with dogged determination. Where Jayro led, Jack Breen simply followed. When they could, they steered clear of hilltops and ridge lines. At times, they had no choice but to take their chances on higher ground.

The horses carried on, undaunted, their gait seldom rising from a walk. They worked. They served. Followed commands. The men on their backs fell into the rhythm set by the animals' steps, bobbing of their heads. They moved as one, horse and rider, through the storm.

By the time they reached the iron bridge, unforgiving dark enveloped them. Moon and stars obscured by clouds, the only light came from occasional flashes of branched lightning overhead. And now, as if the storm sensed the nearness of iron, it slammed to earth with new power. Crooked fingers of celestial fire became stronger, more brilliant. Wind picked up. Thunder rolled.

Rain-plastered horses scrabbled up a steep slope to the bridge. They struggled for purchase against the slickness of mud, hooves slipping with every step, riders fighting to stay aboard. They could hear the animals' heavy breathing even above the storm.

Finally, they gained the heights. Before them, stood a hulking, steel truss bridge. It stretched the length of a football field across a deep gash in the earth that now ran to overflowing with tormented water. Built around the turn of the century, then abandoned when the road leading to it fell into ruin, the government declared the bridge unsafe and impassable. A new road a few miles away replaced it and the old bridge now amounted to little more than a rusted mass of steel girders and rivets. It called to mind the metal rib cage of some sci fi robotic beast.

Jayro pointed.

"If we can get across here, we will not have far to go."

"I don't know," Jack said. "I don't like this lightning. *Muy peligroso.*"

"*Sí.* But if we take it at a run, we can be across in no time."

*Take it at a run? Take the bridge at a run? Is that what Jayro said?*

Jack opened his mouth to lodge a protest, to offer some rational alternative. But before he got the words out of his mouth, Jayro aimed his horse at the bridge and put spurs to the animal's sides. He called out, "V*ámanos.*"

At Jayro's command, the bay charged forth at a dead run. With hardly any warning, Jayro was doing exactly what he said he would do. Out of loyalty or duty or something as lacking in noble character as fear of being left behind, Jack took off in hard pursuit. No time for thought, no time for bravery or cowardice. Only time for action and reaction. Before the echo of Jayro's voice faded, the two men rode side by side on galloping steeds again. No wide open prairie beneath them this time. Instead, a craggy blacktop running down the gullet of an iron contraption. No brilliant noonday sun. This time, the dead of night. Save periodic flares of lightning, the world around them closed in, as black as the inside of a buried coffin.

Overhead, lightning forked across the sky. Low down, steel-shod hooves struck sparks at every step. The sound of metal banging against pavement. Two gallopers raised the clamor of a stampeding herd. A distance of no more than a hundred yards seemed like miles. Men rode hard, held their breath. In stormlight, fear and excitement showed on their faces.

By some miracle, they made it. Neither horse stumbled. Neither went down. Equestrian *compañeros* and their surefooted mounts broke into the clear.

At the ass end of the long stretch of rusty iron, Jayro and Jack raised no whoops or hollers as they did earlier in the day. They had no voices. Too tired. Too scared. No spit.

Later, the storm eased. By the light of the moon, riders and rain-darkened horses straggled home. Well past midnight, they reached the barn and unloaded. Heads sagging, jaded animals shuffled to their stalls on mud-caked legs. A long day of work for them, nearly eighteen hours of faithful service. Hard used and footsore, they would fill their bellies with grain, and rest in familiar quarters on clean straw. Their just desert.

Saddles racked, bridles hung, Jack and Jayro stood numb-footed outside the barn. They stomped the feeling back into their legs and gazed up at the sky. Not a cloud in sight now. No rain. No wind. High moon and an entourage of stars.

Saddle weary from topknot to toe tip, the men looked at each other in the silvering light and smiled. Jayro put out his hand and Jack shook it.

"Some day," Jayro said.

Jack nodded.

"Humdinger."

The men turned in. Jack dropped his aching backside to the cot and pulled off his sodden boots. He fell against the pillow, and plummeted into the sleep his body cried for before he could raise his legs. He would remain in that posture, exhausted extremities hanging over the edge, until morning.

This day's storm passed. Horses and riders made it through unscathed. But in the unseen distance, the sky already quaked with unease. A new storm was on the rise. A different kind of storm. This one wrought by the hand of man. And it would take more than a hard rain and a strong wind to clear it.

## CHAPTER 17 – GHOST OF THE MOUNTAINS

Summer wore on. Warm days. Cool nights. From time to time, a fall of fine evening rain. A faint stir of wind. An occasional flicker of lightning in the southwest, but nothing came of it. No gully washers. For weeks, no real trouble at all. The calm ended one fine day near the trailing edge of the season. Without warning, disaster struck smack in the middle of Hatchet Rock Pasture, a tract of good grassland named for an outcropping of gray Arizona granite planted in the ground like an iron blade. Around the standing rock, a skirting of mottled fragments lay in a jumble. Toll of time.

Jayro knelt on the platform of a galvanized steel windmill some thirty feet above ground, wrench in hand. The blaze of vertical sun warming his shoulders, he struggled to repair a worn-out pump rod on an eighty year old Kenwood.

170

Claire's grandfather bought it from Sears and Roebuck, mail order. He and a Mexican he called "Tequila" assembled it.

Earthbound, Jack Breen stood drinking from a blanket-covered canteen, leaning against a circular stock trough. The trough's flaking red sides rose to the height of a horse's jaw. No less than a dozen feet in diameter, it held cool fresh water pumped from a subterranean spring. Best water on the entire spread.

"*Bueno*," Jayro called out from his lofty perch. "*Lo tengo.*"

Jack glanced up.

"*Hecho?*"

"*Sí. Hecho.*"

Work done, Jayro eased his hunkers to the windmill's platform and rested against the steel frame, legs dangling. He breathed in deeply, took his hat off and let the wind cool his bronze face, now glistening with sweat. He looked out with stolid black eyes, raven hair matted against his forehead. Less than an arm's length above, the mill's rigid vane extended like the tail of a bird dog on point. Turbine blades thrummed, lulled the Mexican into a midday drowse.

Jayro jackknifed a leg to the platform and rested an outstretched arm on his raised knee. He set his gaze on the blank immensity of open range before him, smiled at the untracked vastness, the beauty. Unsullied blue face of afternoon sky above. Below, an ocean of golden short grass stretched to the rim of the sky.

"*Agua?*" Jack called out.

Jayro roused from his reverie, rubbed his face.

"*Bueno. Ven arriba.*"

Jack Breen stepped to the ladder, lifted his gaze. He took off his hat to shield his eyes from the sun.

"Come up," Jayro said.

Jack did not move.

"Why don't you come on down?"

"No. Come up. Have to see this. Bring water."

"Uhh . . . well . . . okay," he said. "Okay, I guess."

From where Jack stood, the windmill appeared to climb into the sky like the beanstalk of another Jack, the boy of folklore fabled for a heroic tangle with a giant. He hesitated.

"*Oye, amigo,*" Jayro called. "Got to see this. Come. Bring water."

"Up there?" Jack said. "You want me to come up there?"

"*Sí. Porqué no? Qué pasa?*"

"*Nada,*" Jack said without conviction.

He slipped the canteen strap over his shoulder. With trepidation, he put a foot on the lowest rung of the windmill ladder. Slapping the law of gravity right in the face, he began his ascent.

"Fee-fi-fo-fum," he mumbled to himself.

He paused after only a few steps. Knees wobbling, unruly eyes turned toward the ground. His heart raced.

"I don't know about this. Not too big on heights."

"Ahh. You be okay. Do not look down."

"Too late," Jack said. "I already looked down."

But he carried on. Half way up, despite Jayro's instructions, he dropped his eyes again. His foot slipped off the rung and he gasped. He caught himself, bearhugged the ladder. Felt like a man clinging to an ice wall on Mount Everest.

"I said do not look down," Jayro called.

"All right. All right."

Jack made it to the topmost rung and Jayro lifted him awkwardly onto the platform. Both men laughed out loud. Sitting side-by-side, gazing out across the vast expanse of Raven Ranch, a reverent silence fell over them.

From windmill heights, they commanded an impressive reach of back country. All around, an undulating blanket of golden prairie grass, ankle high, lush, stirring in the breeze. At the margins, thickets of piñon pine and juniper—green, bristly, pristine. Beyond the trees, low hills. Farther on, cool gray silhouettes of the mother mountains of Mexico, *Sierra Madre.*

Jack slipped the canteen from his shoulder, offered it to Jayro.

172

"*Agua?*"

"*Sí,*" Jayro said, smiling. He gestured thanks, symbolically toasting his friend's conquest of the summit before taking a long pull on the canteen's clear, cool contents. He took a shorter drink and passed the vessel back to his *compañero*.

"*Gracias,* amigo," Jack said.

"Your Español is pretty good, for a Gringo."

Jack chuckled at the left-handed compliment.

"*Gracias . . .* I think."

Jayro raised a finger.

"Try this. *Rapidos corren los carros del ferrocarril.* A Spanish tongue twister I learn from my mother."

Jayro repeated the words, faster this time, exaggerating the roll of every R.

"Now you."

"Wait. Wait," Jack said. "Let me hear that again."

Jayro repeated the alliterative words, this time with the deliberateness and syllabic pronunciation of a diction coach.

Jack tried it. At first he stumbled, then discovered he could roll his R's as efficiently as any true blood *Mexicano*. Always a quick study, Jack Breen. Adaptable.

"*Bueno,*" Jayro said, laughing. "*Bueno.* Soon you pass for a real Mexican."

Jack handed the canteen to his friend. The Mexican took another swig, then put out an arm. Holding it level to the ground, he swept it through the air.

"Headquarters *por alla.* That way, town. Over there, Clouds Hill. Beyond those hills, *México Lindo.* Home."

He raised his nose like a hound on a scent.

"I can almost smell tortillas," he said, smiling.

For a while, no one spoke.

"So quiet out here," Jack said. "Never get over it."

"*Sí. Mucho quieto.*"

"*Mucho quieto,*" Jack repeated.

A few more moments passed without words.

"Tell me about Clouds Hill," Jack said.

"A little chapel. *Nada mas.* I build it years ago. A place to talk to God, maybe hear him."

"Do you hear him?"

"Sometimes."

"Never have" Jack said. "At least, I don't think so."

"Have to listen. *Quieto.*"

Just then, a pickup broke the skyline, rattled the cattle guard. It approached on the dirt road that stretched like a brown ribbon across the sea of grass, threw up a rooster tail of dust. Claire at the wheel. Molly at her side. Between them, Ace.

"Yack," Jayro said, pronouncing the J as a Y. He rifled an arm in the direction of the truck.

"*Almuerzo.*"

Jack raised his eyebrows.

"Lunch."

The two men descended the ladder and ambled to Jayro's pickup. When Claire came to a stop, Molly leaped from the cab and ran to Jayro, extending her arms, long honey colored hair flowing in the wind. She gave Jack not so much as a glance.

"Did you bring us some lunch?" Jack said.

The child ignored him.

"You bring lunch?" Jayro said.

"*Sí.* But no lunch for you."

Jayro feigned outrage.

"*Nada para mí?*"

"Maria says you have to come home. She needs your help this afternoon. Says she'll make you a special lunch there."

Claire carried a picnic basket lined with a red and white checked cloth.

"Ahh," Jayro said. "If Mama say come home, I better come home."

"Here," Claire said, handing him the keys. "Take my truck. We'll be along directly."

174

Jayro got into the truck and headed home. Molly called to Ace with a clap of hands. Ever loyal, the canine sprang to his feet and scampered after his diminutive impresario.

"Watch out for stickers," Claire called. "Don't go far."

"I won't," Molly answered over her shoulder, not breaking stride, only half-hearing her mother's warning.

Claire set the picnic basket on the tailgate.

"My. My," Jack said. "What have we here?"

"A fine lunch made specially by Raven Ranch women."

Claire spread the cloth over the tailgate and began arranging the basket's treasures. She served up sandwiches and chips. Bottles of water.

Jack seated himself on the tailgate, legs swinging. Longingly, he watched Claire work. His rapt attention did not go unnoticed. Claire caught his gaze and its meaning. She lowered her chin.

"What are you looking at?"

"You. Is it that obvious?"

"Pretty obvious."

"Obvious what's on my mind?"

Claire nodded.

"I thought I was more subtle than that."

"Hardly."

Jack looked around, then over both shoulders, carefully heeding his surroundings.

"We could–"

"Not likely."

"Didn't think so."

"Here," Claire said, handing him a sandwich. "Eat your lunch and behave yourself."

*****

Nearby, in a den of slate gray tumbledown granite blocks shadowed by the hatchet monument, a killer lurked, *El Fantasma de las Montañas.* Large amber eyes peered out.

The tawny devil cat waited in silence, watched with a fixed stare, deathly still except for the rhythmic rise and fall of warm flanks. The animal would measure a full nine feet from outstretched forepaw to tip of tail. Weigh more than a grown man. Have many times his strength and cunning. He could rip flesh with razor-sharp claws, snap a neck like a candy stick with powerful jaws.

By any name – puma, cougar, catamount – this was an elemental creature, virtually untouched by evolution for millennia. A solitary beast, patient, reclusive, deliberate by nature, a killer. Perfect in his dedication to his own preservation.

Jack eased himself down from the tailgate and took Claire in his arms. He drew her toward him, put his lips to hers. She accepted his kiss, but did not return it. Her mother's instincts set her on edge. She tore herself away and turned searching eyes in every cardinal direction. She saw nothing.

Unsuspecting, Molly frolicked with Ace. Girl and dog laughed and ran, rolled together on the grass. Little by little, they worked their way around a cape of buckbrush that jutted out from a nubbin of hill, just enough to cause them to be lost from sight.

"It's all right," Jack said. "She's right over there with Ace."

Not true.

Lithe and agile, the ghost of the mountains rose. Head low, tail straight and stiff, a kind of amoral grace in every murderous step, the beast padded toward his prey. Eyes in a set stare, ears peaked, muscles hard, he crouched in a stalking pose. Ace dropped his belly to the ground. Then, in a sign of sudden animal alertness, he sprang to his feet and froze. Hackles stood straight up along his spine. He gazed with hard focus into the dark jumble of rocks, not seeing, only sensing danger. He growled.

"Hear something?" Claire said, stiffening.

"I don't know."

176

Ace barked at the top of his domestic canine lungs. And then a spine-chilling, feline shriek shattered the tranquility of day with the force of a china plate thrown to a tile floor. A primal scream, wild and uncivilized. A sound neither Jack nor Claire had heard before. They jerked around with flaring terror.

"My God," Claire cried out. "Molly."

In a burst of panic, they raced toward the horrific sound. Rising yelps and cries, noise of animal combat growing louder with every step. When they rounded the point of the cape, they saw blood. With his claws, the mountain lion laid open Ace's shoulder. The force of the blow shattered bones, sent the dog tumbling, but he managed to get to his feet.

Firmly in control, *el gato* taunted Ace with superior strength, savored a moment of dominion before making an end to the ruckus. Ace barked and bellowed, ignoring or not knowing the seriousness of his wound, the hopelessness of battle. Molly stood rooted to a spot not a stone's throw from the melee.

The cat turned its attention to the child. He advanced on sinewed legs. But Ace limpingly intervened, placing himself in the beast's path. A noble act, but ineffective. With only the slightest effort, the cat swatted the wounded pup off his feet, flicked him away like a gnat on a sleeve. He took a swipe at Molly, lacerated her arm to the bone. The force of the blow spun her around, put her on the ground. Again, Ace went after the attacker, selflessly hurling his body at him. The lion buried his claws in Ace's back, ripped through hide and fascia, all the way to vertebrae. Ace let out a high-pitched squeal. The cat leaped onto the dog, clamped his jaws down hard on his neck, and with a sharp two-count movement, snapped it. He flung the dog aside like a rag doll.

Claire raced to Molly and gathered her limp body in her arms while the cat toyed with Ace's carcass. Jack ran, stumbling like a drunk, to the truck and grappled behind the seat for Jayro's Winchester. Coming out with it, he wheeled about and made for the field of battle.

Jowls dripping with blood, the lion trained his eyes on mother and child, shrieked again. He crouched, collecting himself, gathering strength to pounce.

Jack held the rifle before him, studied it a moment. He jacked a round into the chamber with a sharp pull of the lever and put the stock to his shoulder. He sighted down the barrel and squeezed the trigger. The instant before leaving his feet, a bullet ripped through the cat. The impact halted the attack, threw the beast back. He rolled, let out a hellish scream. But he had more fight in him. He struggled to his feet. Jack chambered another round and fired a second time. This time the bullet went wide of its mark, threw a handful of dirt into the air. Not a kill shot. Far from it. But enough to send the cat limping away.

Jack ran to Claire and Molly. On her knees, Claire cradled the unconscious child in her arms. Crazed with fear, Claire shook uncontrollably. Tears gushed from eyes held wide by shock and disbelief. She could not speak.

"Quick," Jack said. "Get in the truck."

Claire did not respond. Jack took her by the shoulders and yanked her to her feet.

"Let's go. Let's go."

He guided her to the truck and put her in. Claire held Molly in her lap. Jack sped down the dirt road toward town.

"God, God," Claire pleaded. "Don't let her die. Please, God, don't let her die."

Claire repeated the same desperate plea over and over.

"She's okay," Jack said. "She's okay. Just unconscious."

He did not know the truth. But he had to believe. Had to convince Claire.

Claire tried to staunch the bleeding with her hands. Jack loosed a blue cotton bandana from his neck and handed it to her.

"Here. Use this. Don't get it too tight."

With the bandana, Claire formed a tourniquet around Molly's arm above the gaping wound.

"She'll be all right," Jack said. "She's gonna be all right."

178

"God. God. Please," Claire repeated. "Molly. Molly. Baby."

The child lay limp in her mother's arms, did not move. Made no sound.

Jack drove to beat sixty, tore down country roads, fishtailed around corners, spraying dirt and gravel. A mile short of town, he blew through a roadside stand of switch cane, nearly dropping down into the bar ditch. Closer in, he laid on the horn, weaving in and out of traffic, burning tires, dodging slow moving cars and trucks. At the hospital, after a screeching halt, Jack and Claire, both slaked with blood, leaped from the truck. Jack took Molly in his arms and burst through the automatic doors to the emergency room.

"Help," he cried. "We need help. We need help."

A doctor and a nurse in green surgical scrubs met them and took the unresponsive child from Jack's arms, placed her on a gurney. Wheeling Molly down the hall, they shouted questions, demanded quick answers, issued orders. Jack and Claire followed, describing the attack, reporting that Molly had been thrown to the ground and may have hit her head.

Reaching for tubes and needles, the doctor and his team worked at fevered pitch. Helpless, Jack and Claire backed away and watched. And then Head Nurse Pig Campbell, dressed in white, put a meaty arm around Claire's trembling body. She walked her to the door.

"Come on," she said. "Let's wait out here. I'm sure Molly will be fine."

*****

A time of waiting followed. Desperate waiting. An hour, then two.

Claire sat in a blue vinyl chair, leaning against a gray wall, arms girded around her body, eyes closed, lips murmuring prayers. Jack leaned forward, elbows on knees, hands balled under his chin. He stared blankly at the floor.

"She'll be all right," Claire said, feigning calm. "She'll need some stitches in that arm. But she'll be okay."

"Yeah," Jack said. "Yeah. She'll be fine."

"Thanks, Jack. That was a good shot."

"More than that. A miracle. Haven't fired a gun in twenty years. Jayro's rifle."

Claire smiled faintly. Jack shrugged.

"Did you kill it?"

"Don't think so. Limping off, the last time I saw it."

And then the man in scrubs appeared, white mask on his face turned down, strings dangling. He smiled, guardedly. Jack and Claire rose. The doctor put out his hands and Claire took them.

"She's lost a lot of blood," the doctor said. "But I think she'll be okay."

Claire sighed, let her eyes close. More tears spilled. She put trembling fingers to her mouth.

"Thank God. Thank God."

But the doctor had more to say.

"She has a long, hard road ahead. Blood poisoning is the risk in this kind of thing. I've seen it before. It can be deadly. Best to transfer her to Children's Hospital in Tucson."

Jack put his arm around Claire to steady her.

"She's awake," the doctor said. "You can see her."

Claire hurried to the side of her stricken child. On trembling legs, she took the first steps on that long, hard road the doctor talked about. A road that would be fraught with peril. A road that would be longer and harder than she knew. God help her.

# CHAPTER 18 – EVERY STAR IN HEAVEN

Two weeks in the hospital and still not out of the woods. Touch and go for Molly. One step forward, two back. Sometimes, it seemed the devil had a hand.

Through long, feverish days and terror-filled nights, Claire never left her baby's side. No rest. No sleep. Eyes propped open with sticks of worry. Infection unleashed by filthy leonine claws threatened to snatch the life right out of little Molly. "Sepsis," the doctor named the enemy. "Blood poisoning. Hard hitting, fast moving. Deadly." It would take more than a bullet to turn back this assault.

Claire sat in a chair at Molly's side watching her sleep. The girl's face had the pallor of candle wax. Sweat beaded her forehead, matted her yellow hair. Claire clinched her eyelids, rubbed them with the heels of her hands to clear the fog from her vision and the cobwebs from her head. She raised her body, heavy with despair and fatigue. While Molly slept, she slipped into the hall to get Jack on the phone. She reached him at Jaime Passamonte's office.

"It's some antibiotic," Claire said. "The name . . . I don't know. They say it may not work."

"It'll work."

"The doctor said he didn't know."

"It'll work."

"So you're the optimist now?"

"Yes, I am. It will work."

"They're worried about side effects," Claire said. "They say that's a big concern in this kind of thing."

"It'll work. Give it time."

Claire raised her eyes to the ceiling, only the wall behind her to keep her upright. Eyes, red and moist, brimming with tears.

"What if it doesn't? God, what if it doesn't?"

Moments of silence passed. What to do? What to say?

"It'll work," Jack repeated. "Give it time."

Claire could not subdue her anger.

"Time," she snapped. "I've given it time. It's not like she's got a cold and we just have to wait for it to pass. This is my daughter we're talking about, not yours. Spare me the words of wisdom. She can't stand the sight or sound of you. You know that."

Claire raised a trembling hand to her face, covered her mouth. She turned, bowed her head against the wall. Began to cry. More than mere shedding of tears. Weeping. Silent wailing of a woman suffering an inextinguishable pain. She was losing her grip. Felt her body growing weak. She could hardly stay on her feet.

Jack remained mute.

After a while Claire collected herself. She snuffled and wiped tears from her face, steeling herself again. She tightened her muscles and forced her back to straighten.

"I'm sorry. I didn't mean that. Just tired, I guess."

182

"I know. It's all right."

"I have to go now," Claire said.

The line went dead, and Jack hung up the phone. He stood motionless and silent, staring at the floor.

"Bad news?" Jaime Passamonte said, law book in hand.

"Not good. Get back to work. She's gonna win her fight, and we're gonna win ours. By God, we will win it."

\*\*\*\*\*

While Molly slept, Claire stole away to see her father. Hope of comfort and counsel drew her. Perhaps, desire for absolution.

She found the old man in the courtyard of the Victoria Old Folks Home. Dressed in pale blue pajamas beneath a Black Watch robe, he sat in a wheel chair without moving, lost in an endless reverie. Hands rested in his lap, fingers joined. Eyes stared unfocused, dark corridors leading to empty rooms.

Despite his stillness, Jim Gaynor looked almost fit and well. Snowy hair neat and well kept. Clean shaven cheeks with a robust pink tint. Bushy eyebrows as white as his crown. His appearance gave the impression he might rise up at any moment, shake his head to clear it, begin shouting orders. A pleasant fantasy for the daughter, who loved and needed him.

Claire spotted the silent patriarch from a distance. The nurse at her side pointed.

"There. He won't know you, of course."

Claire nodded. She walked to her father, watching, imagining he might raise his arms to greet her. She stood before him and managed a feeble smile. The way he held his head with a slight inclination suggested deepness in thought, contemplation of the price of beef, perhaps remembering. But his blank stare held constant.

"Hi, Dad. It's me . . . Claire."

The adoring daughter knelt, folding her legs beneath her. She studied her father's countenance without speaking.

Experience showed in every line and crease. A small scar over the left eye bore witness to an encounter with a juniper branch during the fall gather in '57. Crow's feet at the corners of his eyes attested to years of squinting against the brightness of Arizona sun. A shallow notch in his right cheek where a fence barb nicked him one winter. He got that when a horse bolted with him. "Rank as hell," he said. "Gut twister." She smiled when she remembered her father saying, "That snuffy son of a bitch like to sent me to church."

The old man connected Claire to her history. A century of tradition came down to her through him. All her life, he stood as a tower of strength. He could do anything. Allay all fears, ease all worries. This was the man who carried her in his arms and tucked her into bed, the man to whom she ran when she was afraid. He made things right. And now, here he sat, an effigy of himself, mired in some grotesque pantomime of life.

Claire's eyes went to her father's hands. Powerful once, used for forceful gestures. In better days, they bore callouses, proof of how accustomed they were to hard labor. Hands that held leather reins and steel hammers, splintery two-by-fours. They lived and worked in wind and sun, rain and snow. But all of that occupied the past. Over time, the callouses disappeared. Heat tint of sun faded. Sear of wind healed. Now these liver-spotted appendages lay quiet and still, useless.

Claire covered her father's hands with her own. The old man's skin felt warm. *Strange*, she thought. *How strange. Life in some mysterious, incomplete form remains here.*

"Dad, can you hear me?" she said. "Any chance you can hear me?"

No response. Claire looked away. After a few moments of silence, she spoke again.

"We haven't talked for a while. I've been . . . busy. Things are going along at the ranch. Uncle Fountain, still whittling, still spitting."

The thought of the old codger with his pocket knife raised a momentary lightness of spirit. But then her face tightened. With the edge of a finger, she wiped tears from the corners of her eyes. She sighed and collected herself, prattled on.

"Jayro and Maria . . . they're fine. Don't know what I'd do without them. They keep things running."

More tears. Claire wiped them and looked away again. Lapsed into mournful silence. For a while she felt caught up in her father's oblivion, drawn into his place of stillness.

But then she roused.

"Jayro and Maria . . . No . . . I . . . I said that already."

Claire shook her head. She closed her eyes, rubbed them. Clutched her forehead.

"And there's Jack. Jack Breen. He's here now. You'd probably tell me to be cautious. Once burned, shame on you. Twice burned, shame on me. I know. But he's a good man. I love him. I've always loved him. You know that." She spoke the truth, but she was not about to surrender her wariness of men.

Claire searched her father's face for some sign of understanding, anything to bring hope. *Please hear me*, she thought. *Please talk to me. I need you. What else can I do? Where else can I go?* And then, she looked away again into that same far-off place that held her father's gaze. An empty place, a place without time, without life, a place of endless waiting. More tears came. When she subdued them, she moved closer and braced herself against the impact of distasteful words rising up within her. She lowered her head.

"I'm in trouble. I'm afraid I'm going to lose the ranch. What you'd call a long fight with a short stick. Looks like I'll be the one. After all these years, it's come down to me. And I'll be the one to lose it."

With the backs of her hands, Claire tried in vain to erase her tears. She closed her eyes and turned her face skyward. The heaviness of despair settled over her like a sagging, wet blanket.

Claire lifted herself to her knees and leaned forward. She brought her face into what should have been her father's line of sight, and pleaded in a thin, urgent whisper.

"Dad, I need help. I need you. Wake up. Please. Just for a minute."

No miracle.

Claire sank again and purged the last vapors of hope from her spirit with a deep sigh. She laid her head on her father's lap. She picked up his hand and stroked her own hair with it as he would do himself if he could. She held her father's hand on her head beneath her own and closed her eyes. She let go. Slipped away, descending into the shadowy mist of memory.

She saw her father as he was only a few short years before. Remembered when she was a little girl, no more than twelve, perhaps as young as ten. She and her dad sat before a camp fire. She leaned against his stout chest, muscular arms around her. He instructed her on their history, describing every branch of the family tree, every ring in its trunk. He told her the story of the ranch, how he'd met her mother and fallen in love. She hung on every word.

"Some day it will all be yours," he told her. "Yours and your brother's. Up to you to preserve it."

The little girl poked at coals with a stick, sent sparks rising like a swarm of fireflies. The glow lit up her father's face. She loved him, admired him. Wanted to be just like him. She had no doubt she would be worthy of her inheritance.

Claire remembered her brother, the day he died. Her mother. Seeing men lower her coffin into a grave on Clouds Hill. Saw it as clearly as if it were happening in the present, saw her father on that day, looking at her with red, moist eyes, saying, "Just you and me now. Just you and me."

And now, just Claire. Last in the line. Alone. She opened her eyes. A wave of acceptance and resignation washed over her. She lifted her head and wiped away tears.

"I'm sorry," she said with a hint of detachment in her voice. "I'm sure you'd get right up out of that chair if you

186

could. Well . . . it's all right, Dad. It's all right. No need to worry."

Claire composed her father's hands in his lap. She straightened herself and rose. Swept a strand of hair from her forehead. She smiled faintly, but only for a fraction of a second. She kissed her father's cheek, rested a hand on his shoulder.

"Good-bye, Dad. I love you. You rest now."

She turned and walked away. The moment before disappearing through an open door, she paused. Turned for one last look.

*****

Before leaving the nursing home, Claire checked in with Molly's nurse by phone. No change. Still sleeping. With that assurance, she decided to steal another hour and make a quick run to the ranch. She could use a shower and a change of clothes, check on things there before returning to the hospital for the night.

Dusk when she got there. Failing light. A time when nothing is what it seems.

Jayro met her. At first, the sight of him lifted her spirits, but then she realized he wore a look of panic. He waved his arms above his head. Jack came into view a moment later.

"Señora, come quick," Jayro shouted. "Sugar . . . she labors. Trouble, I think."

They hurried to the barn. Sugar lay in a clean stall prepared for foaling. Jayro described the day's events.

"Walking in a circle all morning. Stretching and biting at her side. Sweating. Lie down. Get up. Hold her tail out behind her."

"How long?" Claire said.

"Twelve hours, I think. Too long."

"Twelve hours? Why didn't you call me?"

Claire moved closer. No mistaking the throes of labor. Struggling and moaning, the mare pushed without effect. No sign of a foal, no front feet with nose following close behind. Jayro was right. Trouble. Big trouble.

"How long since her water broke?" Claire said.

"A while."

"How long, dammit? I have to know how long?"

"Long time. Hour."

"Too long. Too damn long."

Claire threw off her jacket and rolled up her sleeves. She readied herself for battle. All fear, all uncertainty departed. She saw only the task ahead. Wheeling toward Jack, she pointed to a bottle of dishwashing liquid on a bench outside the stall.

"Hand me that."

Jack did not move.

"Jack, quick."

Jack grabbed the bottle and handed it to Claire. She squirted the liquid on her hands and forearms.

"Jayro," she called out. "Water."

Jayro ran for the hose in the barn bay. He opened the valve and sprayed water over Claire's soapy arms. She rubbed her hands together and raised a lather. Jayro rinsed them, then squirted more liquid on Claire's right hand.

Claire pointed.

"Hold her head. Keep her still. I don't want to get kicked."

Jack and Jayro knelt at the mare's head. They stroked her neck and spoke to her.

"Easy, Sugar. Easy," Jack said.

"*Tranquila*," Jayro said. "*Tranquila.*"

Claire knelt at Sugar's rump.

"Don't let her kick."

She placed her left hand on the mare's fleshy hindquarters and took a deep breath. Grimacing, she eased her slick right hand into the mare, passing through the birth canal, exploring, searching, diagnosing. She felt the baby.

"There it is. Not in the right position. Head's hung up. Foot, too."

188

Claire struggled and strained. She breathed heavily. Face flushed. The mare groaned and struggled and writhed with contractions.

"Easy now," Jack said. "Steady."

"Shhhh . . . Shhhh . . ." said Jayro.

"This baby's got to come out," Claire said. "If it doesn't, the blood supply will be cut off. We'll lose it."

Claire struggled to move a foot into the proper position. She strained against the weight of equine muscles and organs, breathed open-mouthed. Her body became an inferno. The red of her face deepened. Sweat glazed her forehead.

"Come on," she said. "Come on."

Precious time was slipping away.

"If the umbilical cord is compressed, the foal's air will be cut off. It'll suffocate right in the womb. Can't breathe through its nose until we get the shoulder out."

There. She had the first forefoot in position. Searched for the second. Gripped it, carefully moved it. She felt the head and tried to rotate it. Not that way. Tried again.

"Got it. Come on, baby. Push. Push."

Jack and Jayro knelt at the mare's head, stroking, cajoling. The toiling mother groaned and strained. She raised her head, turned toward Claire. The mare's body trembled.

"Good," Claire said. "Stay with it, Sugar. Stay with it."

Claire now had a firm grip on the foal's front hooves. She had the nose down and the head tucked so it could pass through the birth canal. She coaxed and aligned. Pulled and pleaded.

"Come on. Come on. Come on."

She had it. Claire withdrew her hand from the mare. And then a hoof appeared. Another hoof. Gray nose. Head. Close to the end, so close. But the mare was exhausted. Powerful muscles that should push the foal out quickly at this stage of labor turned to jelly.

"Come on, Sugar. Almost there. Just one more push."

Claire took the foal by the head and heaved. She shifted her position, straddling the mare, placing one leg along her back, the other under the mare's legs. She heaved again. She groaned and breathed heavily, face wet with sweat, hair matted. The horse labored. Claire labored.

And then more of the foal emerged. Legs. Shoulders. Back. And then it broke free. Delivery. Birth.

Claire fell back when the foal burst forth. The baby landed in her lap. Wet and slick, pale gray in color, not sorrel like its dam and sire, not at all what she expected.

Claire eased out from under the foal and scrabbled to her knees. She lowered her face to the foal's and looked into its eyes. Cloudy. Glassy. Dead eyes.

Claire spread the newborn's lips with her fingers and looked into its mouth. Purple membranes.

"Dammit," Claire shouted.

On her knees, leaning over the lifeless infant, she ran a finger into its mouth and nostrils to clear the mucus. She cupped her hands over its nose and blew into it, forcing air from her own lungs into the foal's. With both hands, she pushed on the foal's side, trying to force it to breathe, insisting it live, demanding it.

"One. Two. Three. One. Two. Three."

Again she cupped her hands over the foal's nostrils, again she breathed in air. She pushed on the foal's side. Jack and Jayro stood over her, watching, saying nothing, not moving.

Claire continued. Sweating and breathing heavily. Eyes burning with determination. Not letting go, not giving up, not surrendering. *You will not die. I won't let you die. I'll make you live.*

"Breathe, dammit. Breathe."

The fight went on, but without effect. The foal lay on blood-stained straw, still as death itself. No sign of life. Not a gasp, not a flutter of an eyelid.

Sugar struggled to her feet and watched Claire's desperate attempt to save her baby's life. Jack moved to Claire's side. He put a comforting hand on her shoulder. She didn't even notice. Jack tightened his grip.

190

"Claire."

She ignored him, kept pushing on the foal's side.

"Breathe. Breathe. Breathe."

"Claire," Jack said in a soft voice. "It's too late. It's over."

Claire slung her arm and twisted free of Jack's grip. Still on her knees, she leaned over the foal and cupped her hands over its nose again. She blew. She put her hands on the foal's side and pushed.

"One. Two. Three. One. Two. Three."

"Claire," Jack said. "Let it go."

Claire continued. "One. Two. Three. One. Two. Three. One. Two."

Before reaching three again, she stopped. Sank back on her legs. She breathed heavily and rested her wet, bloody palms on her thighs. She looked into the foal's inanimate eyes. No light. No movement. *Nada.*

After a while, Claire rose, breathing hard, never shifting her eyes from the dead foal. Sugar nuzzled her baby. Sniffed it, licked it. But made no sound.

Claire sighed. Caught her breath. She shuddered, then became businesslike, in control of herself. She looked at Sugar.

"We'll have to make sure she expels all the placenta," she said. "She'll be nervous a while. Probably have to milk her three or four times a day. Have to be careful about mastitis."

"I take care of her," Jayro said. "Do not worry."

"Not a word to Molly," Claire said. "Not a word."

She shuddered again, then turned to leave. Jack and Jayro looked at each other. Jack followed Claire out.

Night had fallen. It brought unyielding darkness. Claire raised her eyes and faced the black sky, shotgunned with a million bright specks of light. Tears stained her face. Blood stained her hands. Jack stood at her side, but the woman was as distant as the full moon.

"If I could," Claire said in a voice purged of all feeling, "I'd trade them all. Every last one. Every star in heaven for Molly's life. For this ranch."

She turned toward Jack and looked into his eyes.

"I would, you know. I really would."

Claire took a deep breath and turned for the house.

"Come with me."

Inside, Claire took a whiskey bottle from a cabinet and poured a drink. She threw back the liquor.

"I thought that foal might bring enough money to pay off the mortgage. Get us out of this mess. That was Dad's plan. Not now."

Jack considered what she said.

"But why would you pay Porter if the mortgage is a forgery?"

Claire took a long time to answer. Poured another drink.

"Claire, why would you pay the mortgage if it's a forgery?"

Claire gave no answer. She walked to the desk, took an envelope from a drawer. Handed it to Jack.

"It's not a forgery."

Jack opened the envelope and read the letter inside. Jim Gaynor's *mea culpa*. His apology to his daughter for losing the ranch.

Claire drank again.

"Dad spent too much money. Always did. Then he got old and weak and foolish. Lucien Porter couldn't wait to tempt him with a handful of cash. He took advantage of him, suckered him. Offered him enough money to lose the ranch, not enough to save it. Pig in a poke."

She took another drink, set the glass on the cabinet. She nodded toward the letter.

"That's where Dad laid it all out. Said he took the money from Lucien. I guess that's what broke him."

Jack looked up. Claire's eyes bored into his.

192

"I'm not losing this place," Claire said. "I want you to do what you have to do to win. I don't care what it takes. That shouldn't be a problem for you."

"But, Claire. If the mortgage is authentic . . ."

She hardened.

"You'll think of something. I know I can count on you. I've always known it."

Jack studied her face.

"Why do you think you're here?" Claire said. "You think I'm just some lovesick school girl? Couldn't wait to give you a second chance? You think I just fell in love again the minute you showed up that day? Forgot what you did to me? You think I'm a fool?"

She took a step toward Jack.

"Think again. I knew you would do whatever it took. I'm not losing the ranch. So, do what you have to do."

Jack walked to the desk. Took a match from an ash tray and struck it alight. He put it to the letter and set the flaming paper in the tray. He looked up at Claire. He already had a plan.

"I know a handwriting expert. He owes me. The mortgage is a forgery. We can prove it."

Jack Breen set out to do what he did best. He was back on his turf, familiar ground. And he knew it better than anyone.

## CHAPTER 19 - JUDGMENT DAY

The bailiff's call to rise brought Jaime Passamonte to his feet. The entrance of Judge Billy McGrew braced him, sent tremors through his legs. The sight of the stern countenance of the man in a black robe ready to pour out hundred proof corruption sparked a surge of anger in him, ignited a fire in his belly.

Today, Jack Breen's hired gun expert, the one he "owned" would take the witness stand and swear under oath the Lucien Porter mortgage was a forgery. It would not be enough to carry the day. Breen knew it. He and Passamonte had no hope of winning the case outright. No chance McGrew would go their way. The plan was to build a record strong enough to support an appeal. Maybe, down the road, The Supremes in Phoenix would slap McGrew down. Breen and Passamonte took the long view.

"Well, gentlemen," the judge said, more than a hint of sarcasm and mockery in his tone. "We're gettin' down to the lick log here. What's this I hear about an expert witness?"

Jaime Passamonte spoke.

"Yes, sir. Dr. Harold C. Figg."

"Have you disclosed this witness to these other folks?"

"Yes, sir."

"So, they know what's comin'?"

"Yes, sir."

"All right then, what, pray tell, is Dr. Harold C. Figg gonna say?"

"The mortgage these folks are wavin' around is a forgery. That's the short of it."

The judge's eyebrows arched.

"Beg pardon."

"It's a forgery."

The judge sat back in his chair, looked askance at the notion.

"Ooohee. Let me get this straight. You are accusing these folks here of bein' scoundrels of the first order. Thieves. Way you see it, probably ought to do some prison time. Plain and simple, they're just lyin'."

"Like a rug," Passamonte said.

"Oughta be quite a show," the judge said. "Huckle-de-buck, as they say. He turned to his bailiff. Looks like we best fasten our seat belts, Sid."

The judge scanned the courtroom for reaction. The city lawyers showed none. Jack Breen straightened in his seat. Lucien Porter writhed and grimaced like a man suffering a case of hemorrhoids.

"Proceed, counsel. Call your witness."

Dr. Figg took the stand. Jaime Passamonte led the witness through a lengthy recitation of his credentials. A *bonafide* expert in questioned document examination, without a doubt. A dozen books to his credit. One by one, Passamonte stood them on the counsel table like a librarian ordering his stacks. Icing the cake, the witness talked about his military record, two Purple Hearts, a Bronze Star. Impressive, but somewhat incongruous with his untidy, sallow appearance. His hollow face dripped sweat. Hands trembled when he raised them to point to an exhibit.

But newly minted trial lawyer Jaime Passamonte hit his stride early on. Under the tutelage of Jack Breen, his friend and idol, a regular William Blackstone, the young barrister methodically made his case. He knew what to say, how to say it, knew the hand gestures to use, facial expressions. From time to time, he threw a glance at his mentor. Sensing the approbation he craved, his chest swelled beneath his corduroy jacket. He knew he had hold of something this day and it emboldened him. Moving about the courtroom, he displayed a hint of swagger. He could hold his own with the city lawyers. And he knew it. His eyes shone. He enjoyed the advantage of being underestimated.

The witness laid out the methodology he followed in scientific examination of a questioned document. He talked about writing forms and qualities, variations, individual characteristics. He explained the animation of the individual with pen in hand, how he starts, pauses, stops, pressure on the page, personal habits. The man knew his stuff. No doubt about it.

An hour into his direct examination, Passamonte reached the gut question. He had the city lawyers and their sorry ass clients by the short hairs and he was not about to let them up.

"So, Doctor Figg, do you have an opinion based upon a reasonable degree of scientific certainty or probability as to whether the signature of James Gaynor on the mortgage is genuine?"

"Yes, sir, I do."

"And that opinion is what, sir?"

The witness looked at Passamonte. He looked at the city lawyers and at Jack Breen. He sneaked a sidelong glance at the judge.

"Uhh . . . it's a forgery. Hotter than a two dollar pistol. Fake."

196

Lucien Porter squirmed in his seat. The judge knitted his brow. He raised his gavel and aimed it at the witness, spoke in a scalding tone.

"Dr. Figg, we can do without the hyperbole. Why don't you just stick to your opinion and the basis for it."

"So, just to wrap up, Doctor," Jaime Passamonte said. "Is there any way on God's green earth James Gaynor signed that mortgage?"

"No, sir. Not a chance."

Jaime Passamonte turned to Jack Breen and winked. He did a good job and he knew it. He turned to the judge.

"That's all, Judge. Pass the witness."

The city lawyer rose to cross-examine. He started with the man's credentials.

"Sir, you and I have never met before, have we?"

"Not to my knowledge."

"Your full name is Harold Charles Figg?"

"That is correct."

"And you are from Boston, Massachusetts?"

"Yes, sir."

"Harold Charles Figg. I have that right, don't I?"

"Yes, sir."

"And do I also have this right? Just about a year ago, you were found guilty by a Federal Court in Texas of a crime involving false statements and dishonesty, weren't you?"

A long silence ensued.

"I'm sorry, sir."

"Come on, Dr. Figg. It's a matter of public record. You were found guilty of falsely representing that you had been awarded military decorations and medals including the Bronze Star and Purple Heart."

Another long silence. Figg looked at Jaime Passamonte. He looked at Jack Breen. He tautened his face. Sweat dripped from it. He lowered his voice.

"Yes, sir. It's true."

"You never got a Bronze Star or a Purple Heart, did you?"

He dropped his gaze, shook his head.

"You lied, didn't you?"

"Yes. But."

"And you were convicted of a violation of the Stolen Valor Act, weren't you?"

"It was a misdemeanor."

"Whatever it was, you were convicted, weren't you, sir?"

"Yes."

"So, what it boils down to is this: You, sir, are a convicted liar, aren't you?"

The only response the witness could manage was a further drooping of the head.

In no more than a few minutes, everything Jaime Passamonte built fell apart. His expert witness, the man upon whom he and Jack and Claire pinned all hope, turned out to be a convicted liar. In the proverbial New York minute, the case went sideways, hopelessly and irretrievably.

But the hearing did not end there. Lucien Porter testified. He described how he talked to Jim Gaynor about his dire financial straits and about how a short term loan might save his bacon. He needed money for a stud fee. The old man had a grand vision of raising blooded horses. That was his plan for getting back on firm financial footing. Porter described how Gaynor signed the mortgage in his presence. With his own eyes, he saw him put pen to paper. The signature was good as gold.

Crestfallen, Jaime Passamonte did not ask Porter a single question. The apocryphal bravado the cub lawyer managed to gin up early in the day evaporated – like piss on a light bulb. Now, the kid grew taciturn, sullen. At Jack Breen's urging, he did muster enough gumption to beg the judge for more time. He admitted being completely blindsided by the expert's criminal record. But he stuck to his guns about the forgery. He said he could still prove it. He just needed more time.

198

Of course, the other lawyers objected. They had made short work of the hired gun and they were ready to put an end to the matter.

"Well, I'm not quite sure what to make of this," the judge said. "Sounds like somebody's tryin' to story to me. That gives me real heartburn."

But the judge knew that as long as the issue remained open, the value of the case, from his standpoint, went up. If he made the carpetbaggers sweat, he might squeeze a few more bucks out of them. He decided to take the matter under advisement. In a week or two he would announce his ruling. He might go ahead and decide the issue on the merits. He might hold another hearing. He had some head scratching to do, he said. With that, he left the courtroom.

Breen met the disgraced expert in the hall. He could hardly contain his anger.

"What the hell? Don't you think that would have been a nice little tidbit to pass on to me? A Federal Court conviction for lying? You son of a bitch."

The man opened his mouth to speak, but he could not manage even a squeak. He stared at the floor, then slunk away.

Breen turned to Passamonte.

"I didn't know. Lord's truth. I had no idea."

Passamonte said nothing. He looked at Breen dour faced. Jaw muscles rippled. Face and ears burned.

"I thought you were supposed to be some kind of big shot Boston lawyer. Make that ex-lawyer, disbarred lawyer. What kind of fool makes that kind of mistake?"

He could not say more. He just shook his head and stalked away. Breen followed after him.

On the steps outside the courthouse, Lucien Porter waited, seething with anger. So mad he could spit nails. He confronted Breen.

"I've had about a belly full of you, mister. Where do you get off accusing me of a crime? You're nothin' but a lyin' sack of shit. Only thief around here is you. We know all about you, Mr. Breen. Everything."

From a distance, Jaime Passamonte heard it all. Time was, he would have raced to Jack Breen's defense. Not now. Not any more.

# CHAPTER 20 – COMIN' UP A BAD CLOUD

Any time the weather threatened to turn bad, Uncle Fountain Hughes would look to the Southwest where storms make up and study the misanthropic sky. On the rising wind, he could smell trouble. He would spit and wipe his mouth with the back of a hand, hold his chin, strike a reflective pose. "Comin' up a bad cloud," he would say. "Yessir. Sure as God made little green apples. Comin' up a bad cloud." True to form, that's what he did the morning after the bloodletting in court. He had it right. A bad cloud was coming up. All through the day the sky grew increasingly malignant. By afternoon, it began weeping a fine, steady mist.

*****

Dispirited, Jaime Passamonte sat at his desk, swivel chair kicked back, legs crossed at the ankles, propped on a corner. He stared blankly at a sheaf of papers fanned out on his lap. Opposite, Jack Breen sat hunch-shouldered at a corner of the battered desk, studying a case on guardianship, underlining key passages with a red pen. No one spoke. Air thick with anger and tension hung like a coffin pall. If Jack Breen had looked at Jaime Passamonte the wrong way, the kid would have been at his throat.

After a while, a knock at the door roused Breen. He lifted his head.

"What was that?"

Jaime Passamonte did not answer.

"Someone come in?"

"How the hell would I know? Why don't you get your ass up and check."

Jack let the rudeness of his protégé pass without remark. He hoisted himself out of the chair, allowing his eyes to linger on the page he was reading. While in a state of preoccupation, he inserted the pen into the left front pocket of his shirt. Tip down, capless. The unthinking act scrawled a thin red streak across the white cotton over his heart.

The moment Jack darkened the door of the cramped reception area, he pulled up short. A chill rushed over him. What he saw robbed him of breath. Carolyn. Carolyn Ford Breen. His wife.

Carolyn stood before him, not two long strides away. Beautiful as ever. Jack half-thought to raise a hand to see if it might pass through her like an apparition. A muscle may even have twitched, but he could not move. The sight of the woman paralyzed him.

Jack's mind raced to make sense of what his eyes were taking in. He had not seen Carolyn in months, had scarcely thought of her. Encountering her in Arizona never crossed his mind. *Is this really her? Here? In this place? Now?*

Carolyn smiled. She swept a lock of damp hair from her forehead. She had the look of a lost waif, a child in need of help. When she spoke, an uncharacteristic innocence tinged her voice.

"The boy at the gas station said I might find you here. Looks like he was right."

Jack made no reply. His brain stumbled through a windstorm of confused images – Carolyn in Arizona, Carolyn in Jaime Passamonte's office, Carolyn wearing a silver and turquoise squash blossom around her neck. It all astonished him. White linen blouse, heavy with mist, clinging fast to her body. Sleeves rolled to the elbows, revealing silver bracelets at each delicate wrist. Hair golden blonde, cut short. Face deeply tanned. Finger nails and lips the same muted rose color. A little road-weary and forlorn, but packed tight into designer jeans. Nothing short of beautiful.

"I would have called," she said. "But I wasn't sure how to reach you. And, I didn't know. . ."

Her voice trailed off. A long silence followed. It carved out a dead space in time when no one spoke or breathed. Jack's face flashed an expression that may have suggested welcome. But then his countenance darkened. He looked Carolyn up and down with cautious deliberation. Finally, his eyes locked onto hers, but he still said nothing.

"You're making me nervous," Carolyn said. "Are you going to invite me in?"

The only response Breen could manage was a half-step back and a slight arcing of a hand, a move that resembled an invitation. With that encouragement, scant as it was, Carolyn stepped in and closed the door.

Jack finally unlimbered his voice.

"Why are you here?"

"I really didn't mean to shock you. I guess I did."

Carolyn took a few steps deeper into the office. She parted her lips and unleashed a smile with full force. Her face flushed. Jack's nostrils blazed with the familiar fragrance of her signature perfume. The seductive scent tickled his memory.

"Why are you here?" he said again.

"You. I came to see you."

"But why . . . after all this time?"

Carolyn shrugged, spoke with weary sincerity.

"I am your wife. Guess I just hated to see all we had go down the drain. Had to try. Frankly, I hoped for a warmer reception. I thought absence might have made the heart grow fonder."

Carolyn opened her purse and took out a cigarette. She put it to her rose colored lips and snapped the purse closed.

"Smoking?" Jack said.

Carolyn gave no answer. She lifted the cigarette, arched her eyebrows, waited expectantly for a light. Jack shook his head.

"No matches."

Carolyn opened the purse again and took out a gold, initialed lighter. She thumbed it twice but the effort produced no flame. Then, on Jack's right, a denim-sleeved, outstretched arm appeared. Jaime Passamonte held a burning match. When the cigarette was lit, he waved out the flame. Carolyn took a long drag, reclined her head, blew out a thin line of smoke. Passamonte stood dull-eyed, slack-jawed, staring at the beautiful smoking woman.

"And who might this be?" Carolyn said.

"Jaime Passamonte," the young man answered with rising intonation. It sounded more like a question than an answer.

Carolyn flicked a finger at the gold letters on the window.

"Attorney and counselor at law."

Passamonte nodded.

"That's the rumor."

Carolyn kept her eyes on the young Mexican lawyer and took another drag on the cigarette.

"Jack, aren't you going to introduce me?"

"This is Carolyn . . . my wife."

A look of disbelief smeared Jaime Passamonte's face. He turned toward Jack. It never occurred to him his mentor and erstwhile role model had a wife. In all the time they spent together he never once mentioned her. And Jaime Passamonte never asked.

204

Carolyn put the cigarette to her lips again and inhaled. She blew out smoke and looked around for an ashtray. Seeing none, she handed the smoldering butt to Jaime Passamonte.

"Mind disposing of this?"

Before he could answer, Passamonte had the cigarette between thumb and forefinger. He, too, searched for a place to dispose of it as if he were a stranger in his own office. Then, he hurried to the bathroom and tossed it into the toilet where it disappeared with a hiss.

During his absence, Carolyn put a hand on Jack's arm in urgent solicitation.

"Can we go somewhere and talk?"

At first, Jack did not respond.

"I've come a long way. We need to talk. Please."

Jack could not help being touched by the sincerity in her voice. He nodded.

"I'll be back," he said without moving his eyes from Carolyn.

He reached for his hat, but then drew his hand back and left the Stetson on the chair. He opened the door. When Carolyn was passing through it, Jaime Passamonte caught his eye and gave him a look of shock and confusion.

"What the hell?" he mouthed.

Without a word, Jack followed Carolyn outside.

After closing the door, Jaime Passamonte stepped to the window and peeked through a crack of curtain. He watched the backs of the curious, estranged spouses on their sashay down the sidewalk, following them with his eyes until they were lost to view. Then, he turned and slumped against the wall, gazed at the ceiling. He sighed.

"That tears it," he said in a low voice. "I should have known better than to trust you."

*****

The mist abated. Carolyn and Jack strolled down the sidewalk along Main Street, the town's busiest thoroughfare. Passed Roy Cobb's barber shop. Passed Bishop's Dry Goods. At the edge of the central business district of Victoria, they drifted into a small, green park. Under the shelter of a grove of cottonwood trees, Carolyn leaned against a gray stone picnic table. She gracefully eased her shapely haunches onto it, rested sandal clad feet on the bench.

Before she could reveal what was on her mind, an unexpected sight distracted her.

"Oh, Jack," she gasped and pointed to a blood red stain on his shirt.

"Are you bleeding?"

Jack looked down and raised a hand to his left chest.

"My pen," he said. And then he withdrew the leaking writing instrument from his pocket. He studied its moist tip a moment, then set it on the table.

"Careless of me," he said. "Foolish. I should be careful."

He put a boot on the bench next to Carolyn's foot and leaned against his knee. He looked into the woman's eyes and regarded her with curiosity.

"I don't get it. Never thought I'd see you here."

"You're not pleased, are you?"

"Just can't imagine why you're here."

"Why?" Carolyn said, a little hurt. "I am your wife, you know."

"Yeah. You said that."

Jack knew now to be cautious. The last time he saw Carolyn she was storming out the door of their Beacon Hill house, climbing into another man's car. She could not wait to be rid of him. She was then as she always had been, certain, decisive, supremely committed to herself. He saw no reason to expect a change. But then again, for some time now, change had been the order of the day.

"I thought you were anxious to be divorced," Jack said. "I thought you were going to marry Peter Farrell and live
206

happily ever after. A man your father, the real estate baron, could love and admire."

"I was. I admit I was. But then I thought I should take it slow. We share a long history, you and I."

"I would have thought your father would be happy to see us divorced. Never any love lost between the two of us."

"No. But he loathes divorce," Carolyn said. "Says marriage is the fabric of our society. A deal's a deal. Sounds funny coming from him, doesn't it? Anyway, I decided to be slow about it."

Jack mulled over what she said.

"How'd you find me?"

"Wasn't hard. Got some documents in the mail after you sold the car in Oklahoma. Put two and two together, figured out where you went. I remembered Arizona. Seemed like a place you might go. I just decided to head west and find you."

Jack shook his head.

"And I thought I was lost to the world."

"Not really. No one ever is. Eventually the world finds you."

"So it seems."

Carolyn fished another smoke from her purse. She located the lighter. Jack took it in hand. This time it worked.

"I thought you gave that up," Jack said. "Long ago."

Carolyn shrugged. She drew in the smoke and blew it out.

"What have you been doing out here?" she said.

"Working."

"With that young lawyer?"

Jack nodded, taking care to offer no unnecessary details.

"Is he the new Bert Zorn?"

Jack could not help but smile at the thought of his old friend. It disarmed him and put him at ease. He seated himself on the table next to Carolyn and leaned forward, resting elbows on knees. Talk of Bert Zorn pleased him.

"How is Bert?" he said.

"Fine. A little lost without you. I saw him not long ago. He thinks you can get your license reinstated early. He's looking forward to having you back. So am I."

Jack said nothing. Carolyn sidled up to him, put a hand on his knee.

"I've moved home, Jack. The place looks the way it did the day you left. Couldn't bring myself to sell it. Maybe –"

Jack raised a hand and cut her off. He lowered his eyes and studied the toes of his boots.

"Carolyn, I'm not the same man I was. I live here now."

"Jack, look. Neither of us has been perfect. God knows. But I think we can still make a go of it. Come home. Come home with me. Please. I love you. There, I said it. Told myself I wouldn't, but there it is."

Jack remained resolute. At that moment he meant to get up and walk away. He meant to tell Carolyn to leave and go back to Boston, to declare emphatically that he would stay in Arizona the rest of his life. He fully intended to tell her to go to her rental car, get in it, and drive away, leave right now, never come back. He meant to, but he didn't.

Carolyn moved closer. Her scent rose. She reached for Jack's forehead and ordered errant locks of hair with her fingers. She rested her palm against his cheek and let it fall away slowly.

"I like the new look," she said. "Never known you to wear your hair so long."

Jack did not answer.

Carolyn rose from the table and stood before him. She leaned forward and kissed him, once, lightly on the lips. Jack did not move, neither accepted nor rejected her overture, neither participated in the kiss, nor resisted it. She kissed him again, this time with greater commitment, this time searching out his tongue with her own. She smiled and sighed alluringly. She started to move close again, but Jack put his hands to her shoulders. He held them there, distancing himself from the siren. He shook his head.

"Carolyn, go home. You shouldn't have come. I'm not going back to Boston."

Carolyn wilted. The pain of lost love showed in her eyes. She shuddered, then turned away. She took a step and folded her arms, kept her back to her husband.

"Not ever?" she said wistfully. "You're not ever coming home?"

"This is my home now."

A moment passed, then she turned to face him. Her eyes glistened with tears. Jack did not know what to make of the unexpected display of feeling.

"All right then," she said. "All right. But I'm not sorry I tried. It was worth it."

Carolyn turned, took a step.

"Can you at least help me find a room for the night?"

"Sure."

Carolyn glanced over her shoulder.

"Maybe we could get something to eat. Is there a place to get some dinner?"

Jack pointed.

"Busy Bee Café."

"Sounds lovely."

"On second thought, you may want to head to Tucson. You can get a nice room for the night there. Find a restaurant."

"Ride with me," Carolyn entreated him. "We can at least have dinner. No harm in that. Tomorrow I'll be on my way."

Jack hesitated, but then agreed. He made up his mind to take Carolyn to Tucson. He could get her settled in a hotel, maybe one of the fine resorts. He could go by the hospital and visit Claire and Molly and ride back to the ranch later with Jayro if he was there. If not, he could stay at the hospital until morning. Taking Carolyn to Tucson made perfect sense. He would be careful to restrict the conversation to benign subjects, the weather, the terrain, history of the area, Bert Zorn. No problem. He owed Carolyn that much.

*****

An hour later, Jack followed Carolyn into the lobby of the Ventana Canyon Resort in Tucson. He carried a Luis Vuitton bag in each hand. While Carolyn stood at the registration desk checking in, he waited a few feet away and studied his surroundings. Luxurious. Four star. Large squares of Mexican tile covered the floor. Walls of salmon-colored stucco. Rustic bronze lamps and accents. Tall potted palms in great clay pots in the corners. Indian flute music in the air. Scent of piñon pine. Jack had not beheld such opulence since he left Boston. Truth be told, he felt pangs of hunger.

Carolyn turned and approached him.

"All set. Mind helping me to my room?"

Before Jack could answer, Carolyn wheeled about and headed for the elevator. Jack took the bags in hand and followed her as if he were the bellman.

Carolyn inserted the key card into the slot, pushed the door open. She entered the room without turning on the light. Jack propped the door open with a bag.

"Very nice," Carolyn said. "Every bit as elegant as the lobby."

She threw back the drapes. Outside, violet-hued mountains and saguaro cactus stood silhouetted against the magenta glow of evening sky.

"Remarkable stillness in the desert," she said. "Beautiful. Just beautiful. I'm coming to like this desolate mosaic. Frank Lloyd Wright called it *The Abstract Land*, you know."

Carolyn turned and faced him.

"Well," Jack said. "I –"

Carolyn cut him off.

"One drink before you go? Just one? Get that door, will you?"

Allowing no time for refusal of her invitation, Carolyn seated herself on the edge of the bed and lowered a hand to her foot.

"First, let me slip these off. They're killing me."

Jack moved the bag, let the door swing closed.

In the dim light of evening, desert images flooding in through the naked window, Carolyn unbuckled a thin leather strap. With the gracefulness of a ballerina and with full assurance Jack was watching every move, she raised a leg and slipped the sandal from her foot. Then she removed the other sandal, exposing delicately sculpted ankles in the process. Deeply tanned, smooth as silk. Familiar, enticing. Jack knew well what rose above those ankles just out of sight, barely hidden by fine denim fabric. Legs. Incredible honey legs.

Barefoot, Carolyn knelt before the mini-bar and searched it for a suitable bottle of wine. She made her selection and, with Jack still watching in silence, she read the label. She ran her tongue across her lips and her fingers along the bottle's long, hard neck. Satisfied with her choice, she handed it to Jack. He pulled the cork and handed the bottle back to Carolyn. She poured two glasses.

"I see why you like this place," Carolyn said. "I like it, too. I really do. It's ...," She paused to search for the right word – "romantic."

She handed Jack a glass of the crimson nectar known for its powers of persuasion. He eyed it a moment like a fish studying a baited hook, then he took it. His eyes met Carolyn's and his gaze disappeared in hers. She moved her glass close to his until they touched with the high-pitched tone of crystal striking crystal. They each raised a glass, took in the sweet blood of Bacchus.

Carolyn sighed, closed her eyes.

"Hmm," she said. "I needed that."

Her eyes settled on Jack's again. They invaded them. The look on her face, the dim light, the womanly form beneath the white linen blouse, sweet fragrance of perfume, they all raised their voices in sensual harmony. Beckoned, tempted.

After another sip of vino, Carolyn took the glass from Jack's hand and set it next to hers on the table by the bed. She ran her hand over the fine, cream-colored damask spread. She turned. After a moment of silence, in a slow deliberate motion, without taking her eyes from his, Carolyn unfastened the top button of her blouse. She lifted the tail from her jeans, moving hips enticingly from side to side. Coming closer, she took Jack's face in her hands and kissed him. He did not resist. She kissed him again, then took his hand and raised it to her breast. She sighed and closed her eyes and writhed beneath his touch. She composed his arms around her waist and pressed her body against his.

"This really is a beautiful place," she said in a breathy bedroom voice. "I see why you like it. We could build a winter home here. I understand there are plans for a spectacular development."

For Carolyn, it was an unfortunate choice of words. The moment Jack heard them, it dawned on him why she was there.

When Carolyn raised her hand to the next button and began to unfasten it, Jack reached for her wrists. He gripped them tightly.

"Jack, what is it?"

"Who sent you?" he said, voice and countenance stern. "What do you know about development plans?"

"No one sent me. What do you mean? I just heard some people talking."

"Where? Where did you hear that talk?"

"In my father's office. They were looking at some plans."

"Did he send you out here?"

"No, of course not. He encouraged me. Said I should come find you and bring you home. He hoped we could get back together. So did I."

212

Carolyn twisted her arms free and stepped back. Jack's manner became harsh.

"I'm not going back to Boston."

He turned to go. At the door, he stopped and shot a scolding look.

"Go home. Just go home."

Tears reddened Carolyn's eyes. The rebuke left her stunned and speechless.

When Jack was gone, she sat on the bed and started to cry. The weight of sorrow and loss. She had no mind to betray her husband. She loved him. Always had. She spoke the truth with him, every word.

*****

In the lobby, Jack called Jaime Passamonte from a pay phone. Wrought up and angry, the kid answered before the first ring ended.

"Where the hell you been, man? I been looking all over for you. Figgered you were half way to Boston by now."

"Hardly. Just got a little sidetracked."

"Yeah. I'll lay odds what that looked like."

"Oh, yeah? You'd lose. Is anything going on?"

"Nothing that would interest you."

"Knock off the bullshit. What's happening?"

"Not too much. Just a little call from Blind Dan."

"What? What did he say?"

"Nothing much."

"What did he say?"

"He overheard McGrew shooting his mouth off. Guess the big boys got tired of waiting. They upped the ante. Deal's goin' down tonight."

"Where?"

"Old drive-in. The Rio. And it ain't no movie."

"What time?"

"Midnight. Twelve o'clock sharp. Nice touch, don't you think?"

"Okay," Jack said. "I'll meet you at the office. Wait for me. Do not do anything or go out there without me. You hear?"

Passamonte humphed.

"Oh, yes, sir. Anything you say. You're gonna take care of everything, right? Ride to the rescue. I've seen how you take care of things."

"I'll be there as soon as I can. Wait for me. Do not go out there alone. Those sonsabitches would as soon shoot you as not."

"Why don't you mind your own business, Mr. Breen," Jaime Passamonte said. "Go back to Boston where you belong, with your wife."

Jaime Passamonte slammed down the phone. Breen's stern admonition to take no solo action served only to heighten his defiance and anger.

Jack Breen raced from the resort and jumped into a taxi. A few anxious minutes later he arrived at the hospital. He hurried to Molly's room, and stood outside peeking in through the partially open door. Claire sat in a chair at Molly's side, elbows on the wooden arms, hands joined at her chin. When Claire saw him, she rose and came into the hall.

"How is she?" Jack said.

"Better. I think the fever has broken."

Jack took Claire in his arms.

"You can see her if you want to. She asked about you."

"She asked about me?"

Claire nodded, smiled.

Jack sat in a chair at Molly's bedside. The little girl cracked her eyes and reached for his hand. She smiled. The first time, the very first time.

Jack took something from his shirt pocket and placed it in the child's tiny palm, the ancient pottery shard Pink Floyd gave him in the New Mexico ruins. Ash gray surface. Rough fracture edges. Black stripes.

214

"It's over a thousand years old," Jack said. "An old friend gave it to me once, said it meant *siempre*, forever. Now, I'm giving it to you."

He closed the little girl's fingers around it.

"*Siempre*," he said.

"*Siempre*," Molly answered, thinly.

Molly closed her eyes and slept. Jack got up to leave. Claire followed him into the hall.

"I've said some awful things, I know. I –"

Jack interrupted.

"No. No. Is Jayro here?"

"Was. Already gone home. Took my truck to do some work on it. Left his."

Jack's jaws tightened. He stepped back and put out a hand.

"I need the truck."

Claire reached into the pocket of her sweater and produced the keys.

"What's wrong?" she said. "How'd you get here?"

"I need to go now. Sorry. I'll be here in the morning."

"Jack, what's wrong?"

"Nothing. Just got something I need to do."

Jack kissed Claire on the lips again and turned to go.

The drive to Victoria took forever. Jack watched the clock incessantly. With each passing mile, he plotted and planned. He talked to himself and worried. He chastised himself for every sin in the book, real and imagined. But he pressed on, dogged by the fear that he would be too late, that this would be his chance to nail McGrew and he would miss it.

# CHAPTER 21 - THE STAND

Shame and anger pulled Jaime Passamonte tight as a bowstring. Making a fool of himself in court did not sit well with him. No matter the fault, he came up shy of the mark he set for himself that day, and it pained him deeply. He would be a long time getting over it. *Bonehead. Loser. Two cents worth of dog meat.* The kid assailed himself with all manner of harsh accusations. The city lawyers whipped him like a rented mule, and he could not suffer the humiliation without response. He had to find a way to save face. Had to do something spectacular if he hoped to come out on the far side of this mess looking like anything other than an idiot. He owed it to himself. Owed it to Claire. Be damned to the gainsayers. Be damned to Jack Breen.

Passamonte sat at his desk in the dark, brooding. Outside, the street light hued to its monotonous tricolor regimen. Green, yellow, red. Green, yellow, red. Over and over, the kid mumbled to himself the words of his hero Che Guevara, "Better to die on your feet than live on your knees."

He looked at his watch. Loath to admit it, he still expected Jack Breen to show up, secretly hoped for it. Or, Breen might call. He'd have a plan. Sure, he would. A good one. They might yet be in the fight together.

He stared at the phone. He could swear he heard it ring. He reached, then reconsidered. Reached again, picked up the receiver, returned it to its cradle. He rose, walked to the front window, stared into the darkness, searched in vain for headlights. He looked at his watch again, repeated the Che Guevara creed.

"Shit."

Passamonte imagined a conversation with Jack Breen. Imagined unloading on him. *Your wife shows up here? Your wife? You have a wife? Are you kidding me, man? A fucking wife?* Now, he figured Jack might be selling out, heading back to Boston. No more counting on the big shot lawyer from back East. Those days were over. For Jaime Passamonte, it all came down to this: he was on his own. He'd have to carry the day himself.

Eleven thirty. Time was running out. Anger became desperation.

*****

Jack Breen approached the north edge of town following Highway 83. No traffic this time of night. He glanced at the speedometer. Sixty-five. *Keep it there. Don't let up.* A few more miles and he'd be at Jaime Passamonte's office. A tight fit, but he was going to make it.

He held his foot on the gas, ignored the yellow warning sign with the squiggly line announcing the approach to Four Mile Curve, a dogleg named for its distance from the city limits. The day's persistent mist left the two-lane blacktop wet and treacherous. Radiant shafts thrown by the truck's headlamps ricocheted off the mixture of water and road oil like chaotic laser fire. Light played sadistically on shallow pools standing at the road's edges and in center low places, rendering blinding

217

refractions. Jack squinted against their assault and against the glare of random flares, flickers, and flashes glancing off his own rain-streaked windshield. He held the steering wheel with the grip of a man dangling at the end of a rope.

The moment he entered Four Mile Curve Jack knew he was in trouble. The truck fishtailed, careened, skidded out of control. First, to the right. Then it entered a counterclockwise yaw. He steered into the slide in a desperate attempt to regain control. Too little, too late. The pickup skidded bed-first into the bar ditch and slammed to a stop. Jack sat for a moment, stunned and confused. When fear and shock passed, anger set in. He hammered the steering wheel with his fist.

"Dammit. Son of a bitch."

The pickup sat catawampus on the incline, listing to the passenger side. Jack stepped on the gas. Tires spun. The truck throbbed and rocked, but did not gain an inch. He gave it more gas. Tires buzzed, threw sludge into the air, straining for purchase. Again they failed.

In a fit of rage, Jack beat the steering wheel with his fist again. He threw back his head, let it fall limp against the headrest. He closed his eyes, racking his brain for a solution. In a moment, he straightened himself and reached for the glove box. He came out with a flashlight. Checked it. A narrow column of light shot out through the lens.

He stumbled out of the truck and slammed the door. Circling the stranded vehicle, he assessed his predicament. *There's your trouble. Right rear tire buried a good twelve inches in the mud.*

Jack looked at his watch, 11:40.

"Shit."

He got into the truck, laid the flashlight on the seat, and started the engine. He stepped on the gas. Tires spun again. They hissed and groaned, but the right rear only buried itself deeper. He was going nowhere. He'd never just drive out of the ditch.

Jack thought a moment. He grabbed the flashlight and jumped out of the truck again. He climbed into the bed and

218

searched for the jack. He found it and tossed it in pieces over the side near the truck's right rear corner – base plate, mast, tire tool. He followed after them. Lowered the base plate into the mud, fastened the mast to it. He connected the mast to the truck's bumper, inserted the tire tool into the mast.

He started to jack. One. Two. Three. The load on the base plate grew and the square piece of black steel descended into the mud, all but disappearing in it. Despite that, it looked like it might hold. One. Two. Three. The base plate strained under the weight of the truck, sank deeper into the mud. One. Two. Three. Then the plan exploded. The base shifted. The mast flew out of the plate and nailed Jack right in the knee. A radiating pain shot through his leg all the way to his hip and put him down. He lay on his side and drew up his leg, clutching his knee with both hands. He rolled to his back, pinched his eyes closed, let out a squeal.

"Shit. Shit. Shit."

When the pain receded to a manageable level, he struggled to his feet to try again. Standing like a newborn colt on wobbly limbs, he repositioned the base plate and connected the mast to the bumper. Again, he set to jacking, this time taking care to avoid the likely path of steel shrapnel if it flew out.

One. Two. Three. He paused, then carried on. One. Two. Three.

The jack strained under its load and with uncertain footing.

One. Two. Three.

With each movement of his arm another second of precious time ticked away.

*****

In town, Jaime Passamonte stood at his office window studying an approaching pair of headlights. The vehicle slowed.

"It's about time," he said.

He stomped to the front door and threw it open. But the vehicle passed without stopping. Not Jack Breen. The kid tightened his lips. He exhaled loudly, making the sound of a relief valve taking the strain off a pressure vessel. He turned his face to the ceiling and shook his head in frustration.

"Oh, man. Oh, man. That's it. That is it."

He stepped quickly to an oak file cabinet in the corner of the office. He grabbed the brass pull and opened the top drawer, looked in. He turned his head toward the front door. Paused a moment, then made up his mind.

*No more. No more waiting. Better to die on your feet than live on your knees.*

From the drawer, he lifted Jack's photographic equipment, a thirty-five millimeter Nikon camera, night vision spotting scope with infrared front lens system, camera adapter.

With a broad sweep of an arm, he cleared the top of the desk, sending papers, pens, cups, books crashing to the floor. He laid the components of the camera system out on the battered surface, tried to line them up and arrange them as he would the pieces of a jigsaw puzzle.

He hurriedly read the instructions on the side of the spotting scope, "Amplifies light thirty-five thousand times."

"Cool. Really cool."

In no time, he figured it out. He had the spotting scope attached to the camera. He had the power on and he was ready to go. At the office window, he switched off the light for a trial run. In the darkness, he raised the spotting scope to his eye and aimed it into the obscurity of the park at the end of the street. The image in the view finder showed as bright as day, high resolution. A mongrel dog trotted by, stopped and pissed on the curb. He could see it clearly, every square inch of it. Amazing.

"Oh, man," Jaime Passamonte said. "Oh, man."

He switched on the office light and loaded the camera with infrared film. Sitting at the desk, he stuffed the components into a duffle bag and checked his watch again, 11:50. To make it to The Rio by midnight, he had to leave

220

now. Right now. Jack wasn't going to make it. If he waited for him, he'd miss his chance to nail McGrew. Deaf to Breen's admonition not to go alone, Jaime Passamonte set his mind. He sprang to his feet and slung the camera bag over his shoulder. "*Viva la revolución,*" he said. "Fuck it."

He stormed through the door. Sallied into the night, alone. Exactly what Jack Breen knew would be a big mistake.

*****

With the flashlight planted in the mud, Jack struggled with the tire tool, cranking for all he was worth. He watched the steel base plate strain and tremble in the mud. Close, but not quite. One more crank should do it, just one more. He had it. The tire cleared the mud. But the right rear of the truck perched on the jack like a plate on a knife point. If he could get enough traction from the other tires, he could drive right off the jack and climb out of the bar ditch. It had to work. Had to. Far from a sure thing, but his only chance.

Jack took the tire tool from the mast, gently lowered it into the truck bed. He walked to the driver's side and climbed in without slamming the door, avoiding any jostling of the pickup. He started the engine. Turned on the headlights. Accelerated.

Tires turned in the mud, slowly at first, then faster. They struggled to take hold. Finally, they did. Barely. Just enough. The pickup surged forward off the jack and sent it flying. The truck labored out of the muddy ditch, onto the narrow shoulder, then onto the pavement. Jack stepped on the foot feed. He sped away toward town, toward Jaime Passamonte's office, toward Lucien Porter and Billy McGrew.

A few anxious minutes later Jack arrived at Jaime Passamonte's office. He slid to a stop on the moist pavement, striking the curb with the front tires. Heart racing, he leaped from the truck and burst into the office, hailed the kid from the door.

"Jaime. Jaime, where are you?"

No answer. He searched the office looking for the young lawyer, leaving muddy footprints with every step. No sign of the kid. Nothing. Not even a note. He stepped to the oak cabinet. The drawer that held the camera equipment stood open. He looked in. Empty. He shook his head.

"I told you to wait," he said. "I told you to wait."

Jack slammed the drawer shut and looked at his watch. Eleven fifty-five. He headed for the door, for a crucible in the night.

## CHAPTER 22 - SHOWDOWN

A quarter of a mile from the Rio, Jaime Passamonte killed the headlights of the Jeep and steered onto the muddy shoulder. He pulled into the trees as far as he could. He waited quietly in darkness a few moments, then checked his watch. Midnight, straight up. High noon of the dark hours.

He gathered up the bag of camera equipment and stepped out, carefully closing the door. He looked up and down the road. Nothing. No cars. Not a sound. Dead calm. He shouldered the camera bag and took off on foot. He crawled over a fence and stealthily crossed a muddy pasture, staying low, keeping a sharp eye.

In a few minutes he stood across the road from the entrance of the Rio. He crouched in the brush at the fence line and studied the rusting theater hulk. Relic of a bygone era. As a kid, Jaime Passamonte came here with his parents to see movies like "Jaws" and "The Godfather." His mother would make sandwiches. Jaime and his kid brother would eat and play on the seesaw and swings. Later, they'd slip into their pajamas and fall asleep in the back seat. Better times. Long gone.

The sign, originally lighted in neon, had fallen to ruin. Faded and stained. Terraces, where rows of cars once parked, bristled with leaning speaker posts. Knee-high weeds shot up through sparsely scattered gravel. At the front, a peeling, dirty screen with a rusted frame towered over the place. At the rear, stood a low rectangular projection booth and concession stand constructed of whitewashed concrete blocks. Glass in the windows was broken out. Jagged fragments jutted from the frame like cat's teeth.

Jaime Passamonte advanced in the style of heroes he once watched on the Rio's big screen. Keeping his eyes peeled, he cautiously worked his way to the projection booth and concession stand. He crouched in the darkness at a corner. Inside the lightless building, tiny four-legged creatures stirred.

From his watchpost, Passamonte could barely make out the dim form of a single parked car. It faced the concession stand as if it had been lost in time along with the drive-in itself, as if the driver intended to watch a movie in his rearview mirror.

Jaime Passamonte looked up at the sky. Low clouds. No stars. No moon. But if the night vision device worked, he wouldn't need light. He would capture the action on film without it. He'd have what he needed to even the score, if it worked.

He looked at his watch, 12:05. Just then, another vehicle appeared at the Rio's entrance. It stopped at the box office near the road and waited. Jaime Passamonte eased around the corner of the building, concealing himself in blackness.

For the longest time, the first car did not move. Out of sight, hidden in the vehicle's murky interior, the driver, ever cautious and patient, studied the dilapidated drive-in grounds. Jaime Passamonte held his breath. Heart pounded.

The car at the box office started to move again. It came forward slowly until in the illumination of headlights he could see Billy McGrew at the wheel of the parked car. Stunned like a frightened rodent, McGrew did not move. He sat wide-eyed, perfectly motionless. Jaime Passamonte took the camera with

224

the attached night vision spotting scope from the bag and raised it to his eye. He framed McGrew's face. Focused, shot. Click. Had him. Pride and fear welled within the kid.

The headlights of the moving car went cold. The vehicle crept toward McGrew, making the familiar drive-in sound of tires on gravel. Soon, Jaime Passamonte's eyes adjusted to the darkness and he could see the vehicle clearly. A Suburban, a new silver one with running boards and tinted windows. The driver stopped the vehicle next to McGrew, driver's side to driver's side, cars facing in opposite directions.

Jaime Passamonte was laying for them. He slithered around the corner of the concrete block building again in order to avoid being seen. He raised the camera to his eye and waited.

A tall, lizardlike man got out of the Suburban. Jaime Passamonte zeroed in on him with the night vision scope. Lucien Porter. Blind Dan nailed it. The deal was going down tonight. Right now. This very moment. Incredible. Click. Got him.

Porter glanced around for unwanted, unwelcome eyes. Seeing nothing, he moved closer to the profusely sweating, highly agitated William D. McGrew. Through the camera lens and the night vision scope, the two men became pale ghostly figures, indistinctly formed but recognizable and shaded a sickly green. Now, Passamonte had both men in the same frame. Click. Got them.

The two men spoke. Jaime Passamonte focused hard and strained to hear.

"Evenin', Judge," Porter said.

McGrew looked up at him, smirked.

"Don't much care for this cloak and dagger stuff."

Porter hiked up his jeans, pulling on his belt at his sides with both hands. He snorted, hawked. He spat. Flashed what he would call when he saw it on others, a shit eating grin.

"Now that's a damn shame," he said. "Bet you like what I got for you."

Jaime Passamonte took in the goings on through the camera lens. Viewed with the night vision spotting scope, the images were other-worldly, unnatural. Nothing short of weird. Click. He snapped another picture. In the still night, the closing and opening of the shutter sounded like the slamming of a jail cell door.

Porter took a large manilla envelope from his hip pocket. Bloated and bulging like a tick on a dog's ear. He stood, worrying with a rubber band that held the overleaf down. Then he handed the envelope through the open car window to McGrew. Click. Jaime Passamonte got the shot.

"Oh, man," he muttered to himself. "Good stuff. *Viva la revolución.*"

He moved forward for a better shot. His early success made him bold and confident, eager for more. But it also made him careless. He tripped over his own feet, twisted an ankle. He dropped to hands and knees, sliding to a stop on loose rock fragments. The camera bag tumbled off his shoulder. The clumsy episode set up a terrible racket.

The hair on Porter's neck stood up. He turned wrathful eyes toward the noise. McGrew switched on his headlights. A hundred feet away, sprawled out on the ground, lay Jaime Passamonte, looking up wide-eyed and terrified. Porter charged after him. Passamonte jumped to his feet and tried to flee, limping on a bum ankle. He ducked around the corner of the concession building and stashed the camera and night scope in the weeds. Then he started hobbling across the open stretches of the drive-in toward the road.

Porter followed hard on his heels and easily ran him down. He tackled him, slamming him to the ground. He climbed onto his chest and sat straddling him at the waist. When he saw the face of the man under him, he smiled. Almost lighthearted, he spoke in a voice garnished with sarcasm.

"Why, howdy-do, counselor. You just full of mischief, ain't you."

Passamonte arched his back with all his might and threw his captor off. He rolled over, rose to his hands and knees,

226

pawed his way forward. He struggled to his feet, tried to run. But again Porter overtook him. This time he wheeled him around and sent a fist crashing into his face. Jaime Passamonte fell back, went down hard.

McGrew peeled out on the drive-in gravel, tires throwing up dirt and rocks, raising a ghastly dust cloud that hung in the air like a swarm of vaporous spirits. He drove at top speed, bouncing across terraces, taking out three speaker posts along the way. Whop. Whop. Whop. He ran like the coward he was. Piss and vinegar gone out of him, no longer the bully. Now a scared little man. Only one response came to him, run, run away. Get the hell out.

Jaime Passamonte struggled to his feet and stood spraddlelegged. He could not run, not with a mangled ankle, not with his head spinning from the collision with Porter's fist, not with his vision blurred by a concussion.

Porter sauntered up to him slowly, confidently, viciously. Froth of anger and disgust at the corners of his mouth.

"Just how in the hell did you know we was comin' out here?"

Jaime Passamonte said nothing. Porter struck him again, this time in the belly. The young man doubled over and Porter kneed him in the face, sending him to the ground again.

"You made a big mistake, kid. We'll see if we cain't do somethin' about that."

Jaime Passamonte tried to recover his wits and get to his feet. *Get up*, he told himself. *Don't stay down. Don't give up.* He could barely make out Porter's figure through the warm blood streaming down his face and the swelling of his eyes that threatened to reduce them to thin cracks. He finally managed to stand, but he could barely hold himself up. He hung his head and hugged his pain-racked belly with both arms, rocked his body. Blood and saliva oozed from his mouth in long, viscous strands. He breathed heavily.

Porter had complete control now. He could take his time. The kid could not run away or fight back. Porter reached into his pocket and took out a knife, a switchblade he picked up in Nogales after a visit to a whorehouse on the Mexican side. The knife had a dark wood handle and brass fixtures polished to a high gloss. He pressed the button on the side with a thumb and the shiny steel blade snapped into place.

Eyes cold as a marble floor, Porter stepped forward and without saying a word he thrust the knife into the soft tissue of the young man's mid-section. He stabbed him again and again in a series of quick blows, then ripped the blade across his belly with all his might. Jaime Passamonte gasped open-mouthed, unable to scream or cry out. He buckled at the knees, crumbled to the ground. He lay on his side at first, then rolled over onto his back, legs awkwardly tangled beneath him.

Porter stood looking at his victim a moment, catching his breath, then he leaned down and wiped the blood from the knife blade on Jaime Passamonte's jeans. He looked around. The night became still and quiet again. Seeing no one, he calmly straightened himself and folded the knife blade into the handle. He walked to his car and got in and drove away.

Jaime Passamonte lay on the ground in a pathetic heap, clutching his belly with his hands, drenched in blood. An owl called.

*****

Minutes later, Jack Breen appeared. He knelt at the kid's side.

"Oh, God. What happened? Oh, God."

The kid cracked his eyes, forced a trembly smile.

"Kind of in a bad way. I put my hand down there."

He started to cry.

"I'm here," Jack said. "You'll be okay."

The kid eased up.

"Got McGrew," he whispered. "Got him. Camera's in the bushes by the building."

228

He pointed with a bloody finger.

"It's okay," Jack said. "It's okay. Don't worry about that now."

"Got 'em both. Porter and McGrew. *Viva* –"

The boy groaned when Jack started to move him as if he could stand him up, make him walk, or pick him up and carry him, as if he could do something to save him, as if by dint of his own will he could set things right.

"Come on," Jack said. "Gotta get you to the hospital."

"No. No. I can't."

Jack lowered the kid to the ground.

"I'm sorry, Jack, but I had to."

"I know. It's all right. Don't worry."

"Did I do good?"

"Yeah. You did good. You did very good."

The kid smiled.

"Are you proud of me?"

Jack's eyes filled with tears. He wiped blood and matted strands of hair from the kid's face.

"Yes, I'm very proud of you."

The kid shivered.

"Jack, I'm cold. I'm scared."

Jack took off his jacket and covered him. He leaned over him and held the boy's shoulders in his arms, trying to warm him with his own body. Jaime whispered in his ear.

"Where were you, man? Where were you?"

Jack shook his head. Tears streamed down his face.

"I . . . I tried. I tried."

Jaime Passamonte's eyes clouded. His body went limp. An owl called again, for the last time.

Jack Breen hung his head and wept.

*****

Two hours later Jack stood outside Carolyn's door at Ventana Canyon. He knocked three times, then knocked three times again. Carolyn dragged herself out of bed and looked bleary-eyed through the peep hole. When she saw Jack, rising spirits showed on her face. She released the chain lock and started to let him in. Jack blasted the door open with both hands. He burst into the room and grabbed Carolyn by the shoulders. He backed her up and forced her down on the edge of the bed. He loomed over her, glowering. Carolyn hugged herself in fear.

"Jack, what is it? What's wrong?"

Jack's eyes burned with rage. Boots muddy, hands blood-stained.

"Who sent you?" he said in a loud, angry voice. "Why are you here?"

"Jack, I told you. What? What's happened?"

She saw blood on Jack's shirt and on the sleeves of his jacket.

"Jack, are you hurt? What's wrong?"

Jack straightened himself. He paced. He clutched his forehead. He spoke rapidly, barely under control. His tone did not change.

"You know that kid, that kid you met this afternoon? He's dead. Murdered."

He held out his arms and showed the blood stains.

"See that? Do you see that? That's his blood. His blood, Carolyn. He's dead. *Muerto.*"

Carolyn gasped, raised her hands to her mouth, eyes round as saucers. She trembled.

Jack collapsed into the chair near the bed and leaned forward. He buried his face in his hands a moment, then looked up.

"Today, I put it all together. Finally, added two and two and came up with four. One of your father's goons killed him. He's been hooked up with your father's people from day one. I should have known it."

"Jack . . . I . . . I . . ."

Jack raised a hand in a peremptory gesture. He shook his head.

230

"Don't bother. Don't bother telling me how sorry you are. How you didn't know a damn thing about it."

Jack pointed at her with a finger as rigid as a knife blade. He gritted his teeth, squinted. Moved toward her.

"I want to know why you're here."

His voice trembled with rage.

"I want to know what you know about real estate developments. I want to know everything and I want to know it right now."

"I don't know anything," Carolyn said. "All I know is my father said this might be a way for you to get back on your feet, make a new start. I swear it."

Jack eased up. He turned and thought a moment.

"And I wanted a new start," Carolyn said. "I thought we might make it. Hoped we might."

Jack shook his head. He rubbed his face with his hands. He sat down in the chair.

"God. God Almighty."

Carolyn rose and went to him, fell to her knees before him.

"Jack, I had no idea anything like this would happen. You have to believe me. I didn't know. I know my father's been talking to some Arizona people about a real estate deal. That's all."

Jack raised his eyes. A look of complete revulsion contorted his face. Carolyn tacked on a footnote.

"And, he said one more thing. He said the other shoe was about to drop. More trouble for you. You know . . . the Cavanaugh money."

Jack looked up sharply.

"Yeah . . . the Cavanaugh money. He knew about that, huh? Of course, he knew about it. Just a matter of time, I guess. Had to come out. Gotta pay the piper."

"I don't know what that's about, Jack. But my father said with the money you could make on the Arizona deal you could buy your peace. Get a fresh start."

Jack shook his head. Anger boiled over. He stood and headed for the door. Turned.

"He used you. Used you to get to me. He didn't care anything about me, our marriage. He wanted me out of the way, out of Arizona. That's all."

Carolyn rose and took a step toward him.

"I didn't know, Jack. I didn't know. You have to believe me. I'm so sorry about that boy."

"Sorry's not enough," he said.

"I love you, Jack. For God's sake, I love you. I'd never hurt you. Never hurt that boy. You know that."

Jack put a hand on her cheek.

"Go home, Carolyn. Just go home."

With that, Jack Breen left and closed another door. He shut it tight and walked out into a raging fire.

# CHAPTER 23 - HELL WITH THE LAW

At nine a.m. Jack dozed in the truck outside the one hour photo development shop. He was holding a film canister, rolling it between thumb and forefinger, studying his own vague reflection in the dead blackness of the plastic. Jaime Passamonte gave his life for the images captured on the cellulose. Value of gold, power of dynamite.

When the technician in the ill-fitting red baseball cap and vest bearing the company logo unlocked and opened the door, Jack stepped out of the truck. He meant to be the first customer of the day, and he was. He reached across the counter, handed the film to the pimply-faced kid. In return, he got a form and a pen.

"Fill this out," the kid said. "Tomorrow okay?"

"No. One hour. Like the sign says."

The young man rolled his eyes and gestured toward trays of film canisters and prints and order forms stacked at various locations on the premises. He started to speak again, but Jack raised a hand and shook his head.

"I need these pictures right away. One hour like the sign says. Please."

233

The kid shrugged.

"Okay. One hour. No more. No less."

Jack nodded and seated himself in a chrome chair by the door. The kid looked at him with surprise.

"You just gonna wait?"

Jack did not answer. He sank down onto the chair and stretched out his legs. He folded his arms over his chest, raked his hat for shade, let his head fall rearward against the wall. He closed his eyes and descended into sleep. Soon, a feverish dream overtook him.

Jaime Passamonte. Pink Floyd in the ruins, sitting at a council fire with his ancestors. The woman from the bombing memorial in Oklahoma, arm-in-arm with her husband. His own mother and father. Images in the rippling surface of Lago Esperanza. Then, they were all together, laughing, smiling, talking as if they were sharing a secret only they knew and could know. And walking. In time they disappeared over a grassy hill. Clouds Hill. Jack and Claire stood in the distance watching, longing, wondering. But not moving, not following. Somehow, they couldn't.

Then, with a harsh awakening, the dream ended.

"Mister. Hey, Mister."

Jack woke with a start, opened his eyes. He raised his head and hoisted himself up. The kid in the red cap stood behind the counter holding a package, calling out to him.

Jack dragged himself from the chair and stood. Rubbed his eyes, cleared his head. He stomped the tingle from his feet. The kid set the envelope of prints on the counter and pushed them forward.

"Man, those are some weird pictures," the kid said. "Looks like green snow."

Jack said nothing. He opened the envelope and thumbed through the prints. The kid was right. Weird as hell. A nightmarish landscape of nuclear winter. What was light in reality looked dark in the picture. Dark was light. Black sky. Overgrown drive-in grass, white as an old hermit's whiskers.

234

The pictures may have been coarse-grained, but the figures in them were plain and recognizable. Billy McGrew at the wheel of his car looking like a wide-eyed varmint. Lucien Porter standing outside, handing a bloated manilla envelope through the window. Only a few pictures, but good ones all. Jaime Passamonte nailed them.

"Good stuff, Kid," Jack said. "You did good. *Viva la revolución.*"

Jack paid the boy behind the counter and left. The fight was not over. Time to make an end to it.

*****

Jack's first stop was the Post Office. There, he mailed the negatives to Bert Zorn. Later, at Jaime Passamonte's office, he sat at the desk and labored over the computer keyboard with thick, hurried fingers. He pounded out an order for the signature of Judge Billy McGrew, an order he hoped would be the last one McGrew would ever sign. The order granted Claire's application as guardian of her father's estate for leave to donate the development rights of Raven Ranch to the Ranchers Association. What Jack had in mind, he did not learn at Harvard Law School. It might not hold up on appeal, but he'd worry about that later. For now, he would get McGrew's signature on the order, even if he had to do it at gunpoint.

Jack composed and corrected, composed and corrected, until he finally had it. He studied the words on the screen, then nodded and hit "Print." In a matter of seconds, the document appeared. He plucked it from the printer and studied it. Perfect. Just what he wanted.

Armed with the order and the photographs, he headed for McGrew, to confront him, to look him directly in the eyes, to mince no words, pull no punches, to drive a stake into his heart and be done with him. He wasn't fool enough to think it would be easy, but by God, he would avenge Jaime

Passamonte's blood, whatever it took. The judge had no notion of the wrath that was about to set down on him.

*****

Jack halted the truck on the quiet, country road in front of McGrew's house. He watched and waited. Saw nothing. No movement. He turned off the road, onto the driveway. He waited some minutes more, then slowly followed the long stretch of blacktop to its end. He parked in front of the house, facing the door. A grand two story structure. White Corinthian columns, wide porch. Cottonwoods all around. The home place McGrew inherited from his parents.

For a while, Jack maintained the quiet vigil of a sentry. He sat like a coiled spring, watching, waiting. He saw no sign of life. All quiet. He looked down at the floorboard of the truck on the passenger side. There lay Jayro's Winchester where it remained since the day he used it to shoot the mountain lion. Ready at hand. On the seat beside him lay the photographs of McGrew and Porter and the order prepared for the judge's signature.

Finally, Jack detected a ripple in the drapes hanging over the wide living room window, but McGrew did not show himself. Jack tensed. He glanced once more at the gun, that most favored tool in the trade of homicide. He almost reached for it, but he didn't. Drapes rippled again, then parted, just enough to reveal a sallow hemisphere of McGrew's face.

Jack got out of the truck, taking with him the small stack of explosive photographs and the order. He stepped away from the vehicle, leaving the door ajar, glancing once more at the rifle.

Jack stepped to the front of the pickup and leaned against it, displaying an artificially casual manner. He folded his arms, still holding the photographs and the order. In that posture, he waited. He watched the house without speaking or making a sound.

236

Before long, the front door opened, but only slightly, a crack. McGrew's full face appeared in the opening. The two men watched each other in silence, each weighing the risks of their encounter, calculating, thinking, sweating.

Finally, McGrew widened the opening of the door and showed himself. For an instant, Jack thought about throwing down on him with the rifle. He could just blow his head off and be done with him. He didn't do it, but he could have. And he might do it yet.

At first, McGrew tried to act tough.

"I know all about you, Mr. Breen. If you think I'm gonna stand here and bandy words with some disbarred Boston lawyer, you got another thing comin'. Way I hear it, a ton of bricks is about to fall on you back East. You got more trouble comin'. 'Fore long you'll be behind bars. Get the hell off my place."

But the show of bravado did not last. McGrew had no stomach for this kind of fight. He started trembling, shrank in size. Looked like some cornered, slobbering critter, too afraid to fight or run. Breen had him buffaloed and he knew it. Fearing his life was forfeit, the judge changed his tune.

"You here to do for me?" he said in a puny voice through the door opening.

Jack remained silent. He did not move.

"I didn't mean for anything to happen to that boy," McGrew squeaked. "I swear it. But he shouldn't have been out there. His own damn fault."

Jack's blood boiled. He stiffened. At that moment he could have put a bullet through the son of a bitch. It would have been easy, so easy. But he refrained, kept his cool. More than anything, he wanted McGrew's signature on the order. That meant more than seeing the man dead.

When Jack finally spoke, it was with a deliberate, controlled voice.

"I brought you something, Billy. You don't mind if I call you Billy, do you? I'm gonna bring it up on the porch now. You wait right there. I'm not gonna hurt you."

Jack climbed the steps. McGrew shielded himself with the door, peeking around the edge.

"Want you to see something," Jack said.

Jack handed him a stack of Jaime Passamonte's photographs. McGrew reached around the edge of the door and took them. When he laid eyes on them, he turned white as a sheet. Thunderstruck, his face slickened with sweat. He had trouble breathing. For a minute, Jack thought the judge might drop dead. Or puke.

"Pretty good stuff," Jack said. "They'll make nice prosecution exhibits. Don't you think?"

McGrew could not talk. Jack smirked, spoke again.

"All this talk about going to prison. Reminds me of a guy I represented on a parole revocation one time. Said he spent most of his life behind bars. Big guy. About six three, two fifty. Said he really didn't mind prison much. He liked the sex. You know what else he said? Said, 'I don't turn any of it down. Except old men. I turn them face down.' You're going face down, Billy."

McGrew quailed before his accuser. His cur nature. Blood drained from his face. He trembled. Sweat flooded from every pore of his body. He breathed heavily. Leaned against the door and closed his eyes.

"Don't pass out on me," Jack said. "Not yet. I brought you an order. You need to sign it. Maybe you can stay out of prison if you do."

Jack handed him the order. McGrew took it with a shaky hand. He studied it a minute. His eyes jumped from line to line, raced from page to page. The paper fluttered in his grasp. He needed both hands to steady it.

"I can't sign this," he said. "If I do, there's no telling what they'll do. They might even kill me."

Jack lunged forward and flung the door open. He grabbed McGrew by the throat and yanked him onto the porch.

238

His glasses and the photographs and the order went flying. Jack forced him onto a wicker chair and slammed his head back against the wall.

"Listen to me, you son of a bitch. If you don't sign this order and sign it right now, you won't have to worry about them. You won't live out the next thirty seconds."

Jack pushed McGrew's head against the wall once more for good measure. He picked up the order from the porch and handed it to him. Then he handed him a pen.

"Sign it."

McGrew hesitated.

"I wish I had more time."

"You don't. Sign it."

McGrew scribbled his name. Jack took the order and heaved a sigh of relief tinged with disgust and loathing. He gestured toward the photographs lying scattered on the porch.

"These are for your scrapbook. I've got another set. In fact, I've got several sets. You need to look into retirement, judge. Need to look into it today. If you don't, those pictures will find their way to the FBI. I promise you. Court's adjourned. Permanently."

Jack turned to go. He took one step and stopped cold. That's when he saw him. Lucien Porter. He was sitting behind the wheel of his Suburban, blocking the way to the road. Porter had Jack cut off and penned in.

Showing no sign of panic, Jack folded the order and stuck it in his shirt pocket. He glanced at the truck with the open door. Porter waited and watched like a calculating, bloodthirsty predator.

The Suburban came forward slowly, cautiously. Jack descended the porch steps and moved to his truck. He stood inside the open driver's door. Less than a car length away, Porter sat and waited. Studied Jack with an iniquitous stare.

Porter got out of the Suburban and moved toward Jack. He stopped a few steps away and sized him up, looked him up and down. Then he looked at McGrew.

"Judge, what are you and this pilgrim up to? Havin' a little meetin'?"

McGrew did not move. He couldn't. He opened his mouth as if to speak, as if to offer some benign explanation for Jack Breen's presence at his house. But no words emerged.

Porter sneered at the judge.

"You look like you 'bout to squirt. Take off runnin' like a turpentined cat. Makes me want to puke."

Jack stepped away from the truck. He and Porter squared off, facing each other. Each man aimed his eyes at the other man's eyes, held them steady, cold, squinted. No one flinched or blinked. Hearts pounded. Time stopped. The world became singular, quiet and still. Everything around the two men receded from what was happening on this small piece of troubled ground.

"You murdered Jaime Passamonte," Jack said.

Porter smiled.

"You mean that chile-eatin' greaser lawyer with the pony tail?"

Anger broke across Jack's face. He felt the skin burn.

"He needed killin'," Porter said. "So do you."

*This is it*, Jack thought. *No more talk. No more threats. No more looks.* It all came down to this. No lawsuit, no trial. Tough talk would count for nothing. To get out of here, to survive, he was going to have to go through Lucien Porter. No going around, no stepping wide of the trouble. One way or another, it would all end right here, right now.

Jack made his move. To bring the rifle into play, he threw himself headlong into the truck and lay sprawled across the front seat, arms extended, reaching for the gun. In an instant, Porter was on him, trying to drag him from the truck through the open door. Jack resisted, kicking and stretching, groping and struggling for a grip on the rifle. Porter clawed at his back. He fended off kicks and tried to subdue Jack's legs. He grappled. Reached. Strained. There. He had him. And Jack had the rifle, one hand on the wooden stock. All he needed.

240

Porter hauled him out of the truck and flung him to the ground. When he did, the rifle in Jack's hand went sliding and spinning down the driveway like a runaway compass needle. It came to a rest a good twenty feet from him. Jack went hard to the pavement and skidded to a stop on all fours. The coarse asphalt abraded the palms of his hands and his knees like tire rubber. He was breathing hard, trying to get his bearings.

For Jack Breen, the fracas had a bad start. Porter had him down. Cocky now, the ruffian meant to have his life, and he figured he could take his time.

"Been lookin' forward to this," he said. "Lookin' forward to this for a long time. I will piss on your grave."

Before Jack could get to his feet, Porter was on him again. When Jack tried to rise, he planted a boot heel in his chest, sent him tumbling. The blow knocked the wind out of him, left his chest muscles knotted in a painful spasm. Porter smiled. He stood over Jack, watching him gasp and struggle for air.

"We know all about you, Mr. Breen. Mr. Boston lawyer. You and your whore wife."

Jack heaved himself to his feet, hugging his chest with both hands. Before he got his wind, Porter laid his cheek open with a crashing blow from a fist. A glancing blow, but enough to spin Jack around and put him down again. The massive silver ring Porter wore left a three inch gash. Blood erupted from it.

Seconds later, Porter attacked again. From behind, he forced Jack's head back and tried to bury his fingers in his eyes. Finally Jack managed to fill his lungs with air. With newfound strength, he flexed his right arm and brought it back hard. His elbow caught Porter in the crotch. At last, he was in the fight. Not a great shot, not exactly on target, but a start. It had enough power to break Porter's hold and back him up. Good enough to take his breath away and double him over in pain. Bought him some time. Doing away with Jack Breen wasn't going to be as easy as Lucien Porter thought.

241

Jack struggled to his feet. He had plenty of air now and adrenalin flooded his body. While Porter remained breathless and wadded up in pain, Jack clenched a fist tightly and sent it thundering into his attacker's jaw. This time it connected. Porter spun and fell.

Jack clutched his wounded side and grimaced in pain. When he moved, he could hear the crunch of broken ribs. He was lightheaded and he felt sick. He turned and, with blurred vision, searched for the rifle. He rubbed his eyes and shook his head. *Come on. Come on. Clear up. Where's the gun? Where's the damn gun?* There. He spotted it.

Jack stumbled toward the rifle. He hadn't taken three steps before Porter tackled him. Porter wrapped up his legs with apelike arms and brought him down. Porter climbed on top of him and Jack rolled over to his back. Porter sat on his belly and pinned him to the pavement like a playground bully. But his advantage did not last. Jack heaved and arched his back. Both men went tumbling.

No thrusting and parrying in this fight. No strategy, no punching and counter-punching. Just flailing, swinging and grappling, groaning and grunting. The most primitive form of combat, the kind where you hear your opponent breathing, smell his body, sense his excitement and his fear, hand to hand, skin touching skin, sweat of one man blending with the sweat and blood of the other.

The two men broke free of each other. Porter lay on his back. Jack came to his feet and lunged for him. Porter raised a leg and caught him with the heel of a boot just above the right eye. The blow threw Jack rearward. He sat down hard, head spinning. The swelling of his eye almost closed it completely by the time he hit the ground.

Jack sat, stunned and disoriented. Face blood slaked. Gasping for air. Bleeding from the gash on his cheek. His body convulsed with pain. He could barely see. He thought he might lose consciousness. *No. No. Get up. Fight. Fight or die.*

Porter came to his feet and stumbled toward Jack. He was panting heavily like some primitive beast, bleeding from

242

nose and mouth. A bloody mess. He could barely stay on his feet at all. There would be no more smiling, no more taunting, no more talk. Time to finish this while he still could. He reached into his jeans and took out a knife, the same blade he used to cut Jaime Passamonte to pieces.

Jack looked around for the rifle. There. He saw it. He knew right where it was, but he couldn't get up. Heavy legs did not respond to command. He started crawling toward the gun. Porter followed him, pursuing him slowly but deliberately, looking down on him from above, glistening blade in hand.

On his side, moving like a dog struck by a car on a highway, Jack inched his way along the blacktop toward the rifle. He could hear the crunch of broken bones with every move. He could feel skin being stripped away by pavement.

He dragged himself to within an arm's length of the rifle. All he had to do was grab it. But Porter loomed over him. Knife in hand, he moved in for the kill.

And then Judge Billy McGrew cried out in a loud, shrill voice from the porch, "Luuucien."

Porter hesitated. He froze in a half-crouch wrought by pain and exhaustion. Then in the manner of a brittle old man, he turned sideways to McGrew and looked up at him, arms dangling limply at his sides. When he saw him, he straightened and faced him. He stood waiting.

The distraction gave Jack the chance he needed. He reached for the rifle. He leaned and propped himself up with the stock, took aim at Porter's back. He worked the lever with a trembling hand. An empty brass shell casing tumbled through the air. He laid his finger on the trigger. Porter wheeled around in his direction. A shot rang out. The thundering sound filled the air. Devoured all other sounds, stood in the place of everything.

Porter jerked. The look on his bloody face showed complete surprise and confusion, disbelief. His expression betrayed his desperation to understand and restrain the rampaging hot steel beast unleashed within him. The stricken man struggled to remain erect, but his legs grew weak. He tried to plug the hole with his hand, hold back the flood of blood pouring from his body. No use. His eyes rolled white in his head. He crumbled and fell at Jack's side. Gone to judgment.

Jack sat up and studied the rifle. He did not remember firing. Didn't remember pulling the trigger or feeling the recoil. He looked up and saw McGrew. He was standing on the porch, arm extended. In his hand he held a revolver, crooked ribbon of smoke rising from the barrel. Judge Billy McGrew had just put a bullet through the heart of Lucien Porter.

McGrew stood wide-eyed and open-mouthed, frozen like a scarecrow. In a haze of gunsmoke, he looked like a man dispossessed of himself, separated by disbelief from the reality of where he was and what he'd done.

Jack struggled to his feet and took the rifle in his hands. He held it at the ready, watching McGrew through purple eye slits. He spat blood, then spoke.

"What are you gonna do with that gun?"

At first, McGrew did not respond. He said and did nothing. He only looked at Jack, then his eyes fell to the weapon in his hand. He spread his fingers and let the hot-barreled piece fall to the porch.

Jack looked at Lucien Porter's lifeless body on the ground. He raised a heavy hand and pointed with a crooked finger.

"You gonna get rid of this?"

McGrew did not answer. He just stared. Jack spat blood again and winced at the pain. The swelling of his mouth and face slurred his words.

"Hey. Listen to me. You gonna get rid of this?"

McGrew nodded.

Jack levered the rifle's breach open and looked in. Empty. No bullets. Might have made a club, but nothing more.

He limped to the truck and laid the rifle on the seat. His own blood and the blood of Lucien Porter covered him. Wet, bloody hands slipped on the steering wheel when he collapsed onto the seat and closed the door. Backing out of the driveway,

244

he clipped the front end of Porter's Suburban with the rear of the truck. When he turned onto the road, he toppled McGrew's mailbox.

That morning, Jack filed the order signed by McGrew with the court. The guardianship issue died. Claire would be free to donate the development rights of Raven Ranch to the Ranchers Association. She won. Complete victory. But at what cost?

# CHAPTER 24 - CLOUDS HILL

A night of torment followed. Cruel and pitiless dark. It showed no quarter, throbbing along moment by tortured moment, hour by wearisome hour. Jack spent most of that time sitting up in a chair, trying not to move or breathe deeply. The slightest turning of the head, lifting of an arm, even the blinking of an eye, sent waves of pain through his entire body. He could find no relief from it, no peace.

Despite Jack's resistance, Maria Paz made a fuss over him. She cleaned and doctored his wounds, delicately dabbing at them with cotton balls saturated with harsh medicines that smelled to high heaven and burned with the intensity of an open flame. With tweezers, she plucked fragments of asphalt and paving aggregate from his knees and the palms of his hands. She held an ice pack to his eye and applied a series of butterfly bandages to the gash across his cheek. A grave expression clung to her face while she went about the grim business. At every touch, she winced with sympathetic misery.

"*No te mueves,*" she said in a gentle but earnest voice. "*Por favor.* Do not move."

246

But Jack had to move. He could not be still. Haunted by memories of the brawl, the face of Lucien Porter, din of combat, grunts, groans. Acrid smell of gunsmoke singeing his nostrils. Foul odor of death. His spirit, like his body, ached and bled. Soul laid bare, like the palms of his hands, down to thready nerves. Only time would bring healing and peace, if it came at all. Time. A lot of time.

"You should go to the hospital," Maria told him again and again. "You should see a doctor."

But Jack refused. His pain and his scars, his suffering would be his penance for a host of sins, real and apocryphal. With each refusal, Maria blessed herself and repeated prayers in Spanish. A night to survive. And not the last of them.

*****

Day following, when the sun rose high, they buried Jaime Passamonte on Clouds Hill. Claire, Jack, Molly. Jayro and Maria, Uncle Fountain, Pig Campbell, everyone, who knew and loved the boy, gathered to lay him to his final rest. Only a handful of mourners. But the orphan kid traveled light in the world, had small purchase on it. Few would note his passing. But the few would feel it to the depths of their hearts.

A fine day on Clouds Hill. Warm. Sky of delicate blue. Gentle breeze. Prairie grasses, still nicely greened, cloaked the facing slope. Cloud shadows darkened the back slope. A sprinkling of scarlet wild flowers brightened the flanks of the incline. Claire and Maria wore black.

Inside a low wrought iron fence, a garden of headstones called the role of Gaynor generations, Claire's grandparents, great grandparents, her mother, brother. A double headstone bore on one side a carving of her mother's name, the day life began, the day it ended. Next to it, her father's name, only the date of birth. For him, eternity would have to wait. But not for long.

Simple obsequies took little time. A prayer. A scripture reading about eternal life. A few kind words of remembrance. A woman from the church sang *Goin' Home*. A fiddler accompanied. He bowed a mournful tune, rhythm and counterpoint taken from the largo theme of Dvorak's New World symphony. Words from an old spiritual:

> *I'm goin' home; quiet-like some still day*
> *I'm just goin' home*
> *It's not far, just close by, through an open door*
> *Work all done, care laid by, goin' to fear no more*
> *Mother's there expecting me, father's waitin' too*
> *Lots of folk are gathered there, all the friends I knew*
> *Home, home, I'm goin' home*

Jayro and three other stout men bore the pine casket, palled with a Navajo blanket. Geometric patterns of red and black. With his chest busted up, Jack could only watch. Uncle Fountain was too old to lend a hand.

Bearers lowered the casket into the bosom of the earth. They went about the undertaking in the way of ranchers of centuries past, with ropes and muscle and loving care. Then, taking up shovels, men covered the roughhewn box with good earth of the San Rafael. Ashes to ashes. Dust to dust.

Jayro fashioned a small cross from cottonwood branches bleached white by sun and time. He lashed the branches together with a leather thong and stood the crude monument in the ground at the head of Jaime Passamonte's grave. After the funeral, he lingered in that place, holding his hat in front of him. At his side, Maria wept, hand to her mouth, tears streaming down her face, bathing her fingers. Nearby, Jack looked on. He could barely hold himself upright.

Jayro gestured toward the cross.

"Just temporary," he said. "But God knows who lies here."

248

Jack lowered himself awkwardly to a knee before the mound of freshly turned earth. He put a hand on the cottonwood.

"*Viva la revolución, amigo*," he said. He could not say more.

Jack rose slowly and turned. Uncle Fountain waited behind him, hat in hand.

"Just cain't reckon it out," the old man said. "Cain't figger why God would let me live so long and take this young one. I declare."

The old man lifted a red bandana from a hip pocket and wiped his tired eyes. Then he turned and walked away. After a couple of steps, he halted and raised his face to the sky, took the scent of the wind. He breathed in and threw his shoulders back.

"Be fall soon. I can feel it. World just keep on turnin'."

Uncle Fountain put on his hat and ambled down the hill. Claire and Jack remained at the cemetery until the others peeled off one by one, leaving them alone. The weight of sorrow took Claire's eyes to the sacred ground.

"This is my family," she said tearfully, sweeping a hand. "Jaime's family now. Dad will be here soon. Uncle Fountain, and the rest."

With that, she turned and made her way down the hill. Jack watched her drift away.

*****

That night, Jack stood on the porch of Claire's house, coffee cup in hand. Clear sky, bright with a full moon, a wonderment of stars. Wind lay calm. Crisp air bore a hint of piñon smoke. Claire eased the screen door open and stepped out onto the porch. Still wearing her black funeral dress, she folded her arms around her body and stood at Jack's side.

"Did we do the right thing?"

"We did what we had to do."

249

"And now we have to live with it."

Jack gave a slow nod.

"You've been good to us, Jack. You came at a time we needed you. And I thank you for it."

"What now?" Jack said.

Claire looked away. Moments of silence.

"I have some business I have to take care of," Jack said. "In Boston. A few unreckoned sins. I'll be leaving tomorrow."

Claire nodded. She faced about and walked to the door. She opened it. Jack made a half-turn in her direction.

"Claire," he said.

She paused and turned toward him. Light spilling into the night from within the house wreathed her silhouette the way it did when Jack saw her there the first time. In that light, she resembled the sun at a total eclipse, brilliant at the edges, dark at the center, obscured features. Light years away.

"I love you," Jack said. "You know that."

Claire nodded.

Without a word, she went inside and closed the door. Jack stood on the porch alone. He slung coffee dregs into the yard. He set the empty cup on the rail, and walked away into the darkness.

## CHAPTER 25 - REQUIEM

Daybreak, Jack stood at his cot in the Bunk House stuffing clothes into a duffle bag. He didn't have much, just the basics, a few shirts, a few pairs of jeans, the pair of old boots he was wearing. His hat hung from a wall peg.

Behind him, the outer door of the trailer squeaked open. Jayro. Jack glimpsed him over a shoulder and smiled.

"*Buenos Días.*"

"Not so good, *amigo.*"

"Come in. Just packing."

Jayro climbed the two steel steps and entered. Inside, he stood awkwardly, watching, holding his hat before him in both hands. Jack continued packing.

"Do you have to do this?" Jayro said.

Jack smiled, but did not look up.

"Afraid so."

"When will you be coming back?"

"*No sé.* I have some things I have to do. Could take a while."

Jack stuffed another pair of jeans into the bag and zipped it up. He turned to his friend.

"That's it. Traveling light."

"*Sí*," Jayro said. "The best way. Easy to come back."

Jack put out his injured hand. Jayro took it and gripped it gently. The two men donned their hats. They looked at each other and nodded, but did not speak. Jack slung the bag over his good shoulder and winced in pain. Chuckled at himself.

"*Adiós*," he said.

Jayro put a hand on his arm.

"No. *Hasta luego*. There will always be a place for you here."

Outside, Maria stood waiting. Jack smiled when he saw her. She held both hands in front of her apron and gripped them together tightly. Eyes red rimmed. A look of sorrow and disbelief veiled her face.

"Another sad day for us," she said.

Jack set the duffle bag on the ground and removed his hat.

"*Gracias*," he said. "*Gracias para todo*."

He leaned forward. Maria raised her arms and put them around him. Jack kissed her on the cheek. Maria gently held his injured face in her hands.

"*Vaya con Dios*," she said.

"*Y tu*."

"Will you say good-bye to Claire and Molly?"

Jack looked around but did not see them. He sighed.

"Where are they?"

"Clouds Hill."

Jack shook his head.

"I don't think so. Claire and I said good-bye last night. And, Molly . . . well . . ."

Uncle Fountain waited behind Maria. When Jack looked at him, the old man doffed his hat and held it before him. Jack stepped forward, and the old man spoke.

"You a good man, Jack Breen. You took a stand, for all of us. And we are all much obliged."

252

Uncle Fountain extended his hand and Jack took it.

"Don't forget where home is," Uncle Fountain said. "You just follow the settin' sun. Keep your face in the wind, put one foot in front of the other. You can always find it. Hear?"

Jack nodded. His eyes became red and moist. He walked to his pickup and tossed the duffle bag into the bed. He glanced once more in the direction of Clouds Hill. Then at Jayro and Maria and Uncle Fountain. He thought to say something wise, or grateful, profound. But he could not do it. Without another word and without looking at his friends again, he climbed into the truck and started the engine. He put the truck in gear and drove away.

And so, Jack Breen took his leave of the San Rafael Valley. He slowly made his way along the ranch road to the highway. When he got there, he paused a moment and offered a sort of unspoken benediction. In an instant he remembered every sight, every smell, every sound. He thanked God, then turned onto the long, lonely road that would take him east.

Time to face the music.

## CHAPTER 26 - FULL CIRCLE

Autumn in Boston, October, the month poets say is steeped in melancholy. Chill air. Leaves burning red and gold, seething and hissing in windy swirls. Time of change.

Jack Breen stood at his office window, gazing out over the square below. Still a hint of purple above his right eye. Faint scar across the opposite cheek. He raised a hand to his face, ran a finger along the vague, fleshy track. He dropped his eyes to his hands. Skin soft, paling. Callouses on the wane. City hands.

Next instant, Bert Zorn burst in. He was sporting a new look these days. A toupee of thick, black hair. A pair of brass wire rim glasses. A thin moustache, neatly trimmed. Charcoal gray suit, freshly pressed. His new associate, a buxom woman with long, blonde hair, bright lips and cheeks, kept to his side. Decked out in a short skirt and tight-fitting blouse, her attire left little to the imagination about every key aspect of her anatomy. In high heels, the woman towered a good six inches over her boss. Her muscular, athletic form allowed no doubt she could make short work of him mano-a-mano.

Bert was smiling broadly and waving a handful of papers. A hint of foam lurked in the corners of his mouth. He could barely contain his excitement.

"It's done," he said. "The Cavanaugh settlement is done. D. U. N. Stick a fork in it. It's done."

Laughing at his own humor, Bert plucked a check from the stack of papers and held it aloft between thumb and forefinger. Fluttered it ceremoniously.

"Here's what's left. Legal tender. Sweet. Tidy sum for you. Tidy sum for me."

He raised it to his face and kissed it.

"Back in business. Back on course. We are rolling, my friend."

Jack turned toward him, smiled *pro forma,* but said nothing. Then he stared out the window again.

"One more thing," Bert said. "Thought you might like to know. Carolyn came up with the cash to put the quietus on the, shall we say less tidy aspect of the case. Said she owed it to you. Called it your *bon voyage* gift."

Jack smiled.

"Well, I'll be damned."

"Like all of us, you should be. But you're not. She loves you, you know. Why, I do not know, but she does."

Jack did not move. He kept his aimless vigil at the window. For Bert Zorn, the puzzle pieces began falling into place. He was getting the picture. He motioned his associate out of the office with a joggle of his head and a wink of an eye. Glanced at her ass when she turned. After the woman took her leave, he stepped toward Jack. He furrowed his brow, spoke in a cautious voice.

"I don't like that look," he said. "I've seen it before. At that very window, doing exactly what you're doing right now. Didn't like it then. Don't like it now."

Jack said nothing.

"Getting a bad feeling here. What's that expression you use? 'Comin' up a bad cloud.'"

He spat out the B.

Slowly, Jack snugged his collar. Tightened the knot of his tie, buttoned his vest, tugged at the bottom of it.

"Jack, what's going on? What are you doing?"

Bert Zorn spoke slowly, knowingly. He took another step.

"You stop right there. Just stop and tell me what you're doing."

Jack still did not speak. He took his suit coat from the back of the chair where it hung and put it on. He looked down at his feet. He was wearing the same rough-out boots he wore every day he spent in the San Rafael. Fire to the ice of everything else he wore and everything around him.

"You don't need me, Bert."

Bert started to protest, but thought better of it. He shrugged and shook his head. His voice became soft.

"Maybe I don't need you. But I kinda like having you around. We made a pretty good team. Note the past tense."

Jack looked at Bert and smiled.

"Yes, sir. A pretty good team"

Jack put out his hand. Bert took it.

"Where are you going?" he said. "As if I didn't know."

Jack broadened his smile. He moved to the door and opened it. Knob in hand, he turned toward his trusted friend.

"West. I'm going west."

Bert nodded. He folded his arms.

"Well, what are you waitin' for? You want me to kiss you? Go on. Get out of here."

Jack Breen took one last look at his old friend. And then he stepped through the door and closed it. For the last time.

# CHAPTER 27 - THE RETURN

Jayro Paz cradled a horse's foreleg between his knees, calming his inquisitive equine charge with reassuring words. He was smoothing out the rough edge of a hoof with a steel rasp. The horse, the one called Dodger, a veteran of the late night ride across the iron bridge in a thunderstorm, brought his ears erect and nickered. He was the first to take note of Jack Breen's arrival.

Jayro stopped mid-stroke. He looked up. At the sight of the returned prodigal, a welcoming smile spread across his face. Jayro lowered the hoof, put a fist at the small of his back and straightened. He stretched.

"Guess I am getting a little old for this. Could use a helping hand."

He patted the horse on its muscular neck, dropped the rasp into a bucket of tools. Peeling the glove from his right hand, he approached his old *amigo,* extended his arm.

Jack eagerly took the offered hand. Jayro held him in a momentary embrace.

"*Bienvenidos. Bienvenidos a tu casa.*"

"*Gracias.*"

Jayro snaked a bandana from a hip pocket and mopped the sweat from his face.

"When I get up this morning, I tell to Maria I think this will be a good day. I do not know why. Now I do."

"How's Claire?" Jack said. "Molly."

"*Bien.* Both well. They miss you."

Jayro slipped off the stained leather chinks he was wearing and hung them on a high peg.

"Where is she?" Jack said.

"Clouds Hill, I think. She goes there a lot. Putting flowers on the grave of Jaime Passamonte. He had no family but us."

"Do you think –"

But Jack did not go on.

Jayro took a step forward. He put a hand on his friend's arm.

"*Cada cosa en su momento.*"

Jack looked away.

"My Spanish is a little rusty."

"Everything in its moment," Jayro said. "Everything in its own good time."

Jack accepted the wise counsel. Without another word, he set off for Clouds Hill. Jayro followed him into the yard, then stopped and, forked his hands on his hips. Maria appeared and stood at his side. Together, they looked toward the lofty place with the little stone chapel.

Maria put an arm through her husband's and brought him near.

"Has he come back to us for good?" she said.

"Who can say?"

"I shall pray that he has."

"May God hear you."

\*\*\*\*\*

Jack made a deliberate ascent up the gentle rise of Clouds Hill. Knee-high stalks of grass swayed in the wind, clutching at him like adoring arms. At the landmark peak, the gate to the fenced graveyard stood open. He passed through the wrought iron portal, and removed his hat. Before the newest grave, the one marked with crossed cottonwood branches, he went to his knees. A quiet tempest of emotions broke out within him. Memories, sweet and beautiful, painful, almost unbearably sad, streaked through the storm like branched lightning.

"*Siempre*," he whispered. "*Siempre*."

Sensing he was not alone, he rose and turned. There, stood Claire. She smiled.

"I knew you'd come back. I knew it. Jayro says, 'Everything in its moment. Everything in its own good time.' Do you think that's true?"

"I do."

"Is this the time?"

"I think so."

"So do I. Let's find out."

Claire put her hand in Jack's. Side by side, they took their first tentative steps into the uncertain future. Overhead, a raven soared.

## THE END

formation can be obtained at www.ICGtesting.com
the USA
1856101212

ILV00008B/1292/P

CPSIA i
Printed i
LVOW04
31096